P9-CRG-141

"You," a distinctly female voice said.

Matt's mouth nearly dropped open at the sound of that voice. Courtney Wallace stood three steps from the top of the staircase with a couple of grocery sacks in her arms and her hair piled on top of her head in a messy knot. Sweat-dampened tendrils fell around her ears, and her breasts swelled above the neckline of her skimpy striped T-shirt. She was delicious, and he was suddenly very, very hungry.

Matt gave her a slow smile. "Me," he responded.

"This is a joke, right?"

He shook his head. "Nope."

"Did you choose this apartment because you knew I lived here?"

He leaned against the doorframe and crossed his arms over his chest. "I didn't know you lived here. But now that I do, I can't say I'm disappointed."

"But you walked me home once, remember? Back in September?"

"Vaguely," he lied.

She pressed her lips together, obviously annoyed. "Welcome to the building."

Praise for Hope Ramsay

Here Comes the Bride

"Getting hitched was never funnier."
—FreshFiction.com

"A satisfying tale about finding love by finding yourself. This is a well-paced, expertly characterized, and fun story."
—*Publishers Weekly*

A Small-Town Bride

"My favorite read of April 2017 is the sparkling gem *A Small-Town Bride* by Hope Ramsay. How Amy makes it on her own AND finds the man of her dreams is a fast-paced, occasionally poignant, always enjoyable story."
—HeroesandHeartbreakers.com

"Ramsay charms in her second Chapel of Love contemporary...[and] wins readers' hearts with likable characters, an engaging plot (and a hilarious subplot), and a well-deserved happy ending."
—*Publishers Weekly*

A Christmas Bride

"Happiness is a new Hope Ramsay series."
—**FreshFiction.com**

"I'm so glad that *A Christmas Bride* is the first of Ramsay's Chapel of Love series because there are more stories to be told—and I'll be reading them."
—**HeroesandHeartbreakers.com**

Last Chance Hero

"Fans will enjoy another visit to Last Chance, the quintessential Southern small town. The characters in this town are priceless...Readers can expect to have a whole lot of fun."
—*RT Book Reviews*

"I love visiting Last Chance and getting to revisit old friends, funny situations, the magic and the mystery that always seems to find their way into these wonderful stories."
—**HarlequinJunkie.com**

Last Chance Family

"4 stars! Ramsay uses a light-toned plot and sweet characters to illustrate some important truths in this entry in the series."
—*RT Book Reviews*

"[This book] has the humor and heartwarming quality that have characterized the series…Mike and Charlene are appealing characters—unconsciously funny, vulnerable, and genuinely likable—and Rainbow will touch readers' hearts."

—TheRomanceDish.com

Inn at Last Chance

"5 stars! I really enjoyed this book. I love a little mystery with my romance, and that is exactly what I got with *Inn at Last Chance*."

—HarlequinJunkie.com

"5 stars! The suspense and mystery behind it all kept me on the edge of my seat. I just could not put this book down."

—LongandShortReviews.com

Last Chance Knit and Stitch

"Hope Ramsay is going on my auto-read list for sure. *Last Chance Knit & Stitch* may be my first Last Chance book, but it won't be my last."

—HeroesandHeartbreakers.com

"Ramsay writes with heart and humor. Truly a book to be treasured and [a] heartwarming foray into a great series."

—NightOwlReviews.com

Last Chance Book Club

"The ladies of the Last Chance Book Club keep the gossip flowing in this story graced with abundant Southern charm and quirky, caring people. Another welcome chapter to Ramsay's engaging, funny, hope-filled series."

—*Library Journal*

"Last Chance is a place we've come to know as well as we know our own hometowns. It's become real, filled with people who could be our aunts, uncles, cousins, friends, or the crazy cat lady down the street. It's familiar, comfortable, welcoming."

—RubySlipperedSisterhood.com

Last Chance Christmas

"Amazing...This story spoke to me on so many levels about faith, strength, courage, and choices. If you're looking for a good Christmas story with a few angels, then *Last Chance Christmas* is a must-read."

—TheSeasonforRomance.com

"Visiting Last Chance is always a joy, but Hope Ramsay has outdone herself this time. She took a difficult hero, a wounded heroine, familiar characters, added a little Christmas magic, and—voilà!—gave us a story sure to touch the Scroogiest of hearts."

—RubySlipperedSisterhood.com

Last Chance Beauty Queen

"4½ stars! Enchantingly funny and heartwarmingly charming." **—RT Book Reviews**

"A little Bridget Jones meets *Sweet Home Alabama*." **—GrafWV.com**

Home at Last Chance

"An enjoyable ride that will capture interest and hold it to the very end." **—RomRevToday.blogspot.com**

"Full of small-town charm and Southern hospitality... You will want to grab a copy." **—TopRomanceNovels.com**

Welcome to Last Chance

"Ramsay's delicious contemporary debut introduces the town of Last Chance, SC, and its warmhearted inhabitants...[she] strikes an excellent balance between tension and humor as she spins a fine yarn." **—*Publishers Weekly* (starred review)**

"[A] charming series, featuring quirky characters you won't soon forget." **—Barbara Freethy, *New York Times* bestselling author of *At Hidden Falls***

THE BRIDE NEXT DOOR

THE BRIDE
NEXT DOOR

Hope Ramsay

FOREVER

NEW YORK BOSTON

This book is a work of fiction. Names, characters, places, and incidents are the product of the author's imagination or are used fictitiously. Any resemblance to actual events, locales, or persons, living or dead, is coincidental.

Copyright © 2018 by Robin Lanier
Excerpt from *Here Comes the Bride* © 2017 by Robin Lanier
Cover illustration and design by Elizabeth Turner Stokes. Cover copyright © 2018 by Hachette Book Group, Inc.

Hachette Book Group supports the right to free expression and the value of copyright. The purpose of copyright is to encourage writers and artists to produce the creative works that enrich our culture.

The scanning, uploading, and distribution of this book without permission is a theft of the author's intellectual property. If you would like permission to use material from the book (other than for review purposes), please contact permissions@hbgusa.com. Thank you for your support of the author's rights.

Forever
Hachette Book Group
1290 Avenue of the Americas, New York, NY 10104
forever-romance.com
twitter.com/foreverromance

First Edition: April 2018

Forever is an imprint of Grand Central Publishing. The Forever name and logo are trademarks of Hachette Book Group, Inc.

The publisher is not responsible for websites (or their content) that are not owned by the publisher.

The Hachette Speakers Bureau provides a wide range of authors for speaking events. To find out more, go to www.hachettespeakersbureau.com or call (866) 376-6591.

ISBNs: 978-1-5387-1286-3 (mass market); 978-1-5387-1287-0 (ebook)

Printed in the United States of America
OPM
10 9 8 7 6 5 4 3 2 1

ATTENTION CORPORATIONS AND ORGANIZATIONS:
Most Hachette Book Group books are available at quantity discounts with bulk purchase for educational, business, or sales promotional use. For information, please call or write:
Special Markets Department, Hachette Book Group
1290 Avenue of the Americas, New York, NY 10104
Telephone: 1-800-222-6747 Fax: 1-800-477-5925

For Carla

Acknowledgments

First and foremost I'd like to thank my friend Caroline Bradley for helping me flesh out Courtney's list of "man types." Caroline and I had great fun coming up with this list. Even though we may have descended into a tiny bit of man-bashing, it was for a good cause. I always intended to redeem both Courtney and Matt. I'd also like to acknowledge the authors in the Ruby Slippered Sisterhood's chat room, who kept me accountable during the three months of almost non-stop writing that was necessary in order to meet this book's deadline. In particular, I want to thank AJ, Janet, Cynthia, Lenee, and Debbie. You guys rock as cheerleaders. As always, I would be nowhere in my career without my agent, Elaine English, my wonderful editor of many years, Alex Logan, and the fabulous team at Forever Romance, who continue to support me through the ups and downs of this business. Thank you all very much.

Chapter One ─────────────

Courtney Wallace hated the month of June.

The sixth month of the year brought heat, humidity, and a mother lode of brides. Why everyone wanted to get married in June was a mystery. In Courtney's opinion, September and October were the best months to get married.

But for some reason, September and October were slow months at Eagle Hill Manor, where Courtney was the main wedding and event planner. And June was nothing short of a madhouse. It was still a week shy of Memorial Day, and already the inn's lineup of June brides had stressed her out. Today she'd had to deal with no less than three June-bride meltdowns.

So drinks at the Jaybird Café and Music Hall sounded like a great way to unwind, especially since it was Wednesday—open mic night—and Courtney's friend Arwen Jacobs was planning to perform. Arwen, who was painfully shy about singing in public, needed all the support she could get. Her songs were wonderful, complicated, and insightful, which meant people tended to talk over them.

Courtney and Arwen sat at their favorite table, toward the back of the room, away from the stage. As usual, Arwen looked like an accountant in a blue suit and a white silk T-shirt. She'd pulled her brown hair into a side part with a tortoiseshell clip in a no-nonsense style that made her look about nineteen. The freckles across her nose added to the impression. Unlike the other musicians and wannabes who showed up on Wednesday nights, Arwen didn't believe in pretending to be someone she wasn't. Most of the other performers sat close to the stage, and their hair color ran the gamut from natural to bright purple.

"You'll be fine," Courtney said.

"If I can get my fingers to stop shaking." Arwen took a long swig of her Diet Coke. She never drank on open mic nights.

Courtney rolled her head to loosen her tight neck muscles and drew in a deep breath filled with the scent of the bacon and cheese potato skins sitting on the table between them. She loved this place with its scarred tables and exposed-brick walls. The music hall was anything but pretentious. To Courtney, it was like her home away from home.

She took a swig of her Manhattan. "Ah, this drink is exactly what I need tonight. Have I mentioned how much I hate June brides?" she said.

Arwen nodded and then suddenly stilled, like a fawn caught in the headlights.

Courtney followed her friend's gaze to the front door, where Matthew Lyndon had just strolled into the Jaybird looking precisely like Casanova, or maybe Don Juan.

Whichever. It didn't matter. He was pure sex in motion, all wide shoulders and slim hips and a sinewy way of moving, like an athlete, or a dancer, or a dangerous, predatory cat. Courtney didn't know very much about him, except that he was a member of the Lyndon family, which around these parts made him local royalty. That, and the fact that he was a Hook-up Artist and a jerk.

Courtney had developed a list of male loser types that any woman should avoid at all costs. The list included the Man Baby, the Nice Guy Not, the Space Invader, the Too Selfless to Be True, and the Emotionally Unavailable. But the Hook-up Artist was number one on her list of losers. A Hook-up Artist was the kind of player any wise woman would stay away from.

Courtney was about to look away from the loser when Brandon Kopp strolled in right behind him.

"Oh my God, the Lyndons and the Kopps have arrived," Arwen said. "Damn. I hate it when people from work show up on Wednesdays. Maybe I'll take my name off the list." Arwen curled into herself, trying to become as inconspicuous as possible.

Courtney continued to watch the two men as they moved toward the bar at the side of the dining room. Matthew and Brandon were a pair—the Hook-up Artist and the Nice Guy Not, who had dumped his fiancée at the altar. A Nice Guy Not looked like a perfect mate until you realized that he expected adoration for common courtesies like saying please and thank you.

The men settled on a pair of barstools right next to Ryan Pierce, the epitome of the Emotionally Unavailable Man—a man type that needed no real explanation. It was sort of like a rogue's gallery of guys on Courtney's list.

"Has Brandon left his job on Capitol Hill?" Courtney asked, turning back toward Arwen. Last autumn, Brandon Kopp was supposed to have joined his father's law firm, Lyndon, Lyndon & Kopp, but instead he'd dumped his bride at the altar and taken a job in DC.

Arwen shook her head. "Not Brandon, Matt. He joined the firm. Today. They made Andrew Lyndon a partner and then brought Matt in as an associate. So now Lyndon, Lyndon, and Kopp is more like Lyndon, Lyndon, Lyndon, Lyndon, and Kopp. At least they're all easy on the eye."

Arwen's day job as a paralegal at LL&K was in every respect more important to her than the songs she wrote and performed as a hobby. She worked on all the firm's pro bono cases and tried to right the world's wrongs.

Courtney leaned forward. "Arwen, promise me you will stay as far away from Matt Lyndon as you can. The guy's a Hook-up Artist."

"No worries. Even if he wasn't a player, I'd have to be careful. It's just not a good idea to hook up with anyone you work with, especially in a law firm. And besides, I don't think a guy like Matt Lyndon would look at me twice." She paused a moment, her gaze riding over the men at the bar. "But he's sure looking at you."

"No, he's not," Courtney insisted even as Matt Lyndon's three-hundred-watt gaze rode over her body, stirring up awareness. What was it about that man? He gave off heat like an industrial furnace.

"Yes, he is," Arwen said. "And to be honest, Ryan's throwing shade at you too."

Courtney turned her head a little for a quick glimpse of Ryan. Oh boy, he was giving her *the look*. There was nothing sexy about this. The ex-marine with the giant biceps and the military buzz cut was a member of the Shenandoah Falls Police Force. In addition to being emotionally unavailable, he masqueraded as Dudley Do-Right.

Ryan had potential, but whoever unlocked him would have to be ready to deal with his emotional baggage, whatever it was. That made Ryan ten times more dangerous than Matt in some ways. Ryan could fool a girl into thinking he cared. And even worse, a girl could delude herself into thinking she could change him, or heal him, or whatever. Not a good risk all the way around.

"Oh my God, he's coming over here."

"Who? Matt?" A three-alarm fire ignited in Courtney's core.

Arwen shook her head just as Ryan appeared at Courtney's elbow.

"May I?" His voice came from the depths of his chest. He could probably do a great Barry White imitation if he wanted to.

He didn't wait for a formal invitation. He simply slipped into a seat and said, "Hey," in that monosyllabic way that proved without question that he was emotionally unavailable.

Arwen helped herself to another loaded potato skin and sat back in her chair, watching Courtney as if she was making mental notes for her next song. Arwen had captured quite a few of Courtney's romantic mistakes and turned them into imaginative hook lines like "he broke my heart and I broke his car."

"I saw you looking at Brandon Kopp," Ryan said.

Oh, the dear man was so wrong; she hadn't spared one minute looking at that loser. But she didn't disabuse Ryan of his mistake. "So? It's a free country."

"His Camaro is out in the parking lot, and if you do anything to it—I mean anything—I'll take you in for destruction of property. Is that clear? This vendetta has got to stop."

"Anything?" she asked, giving him a wide-eyed

innocent stare. "What if I put a bumper sticker on his fender that says 'Humanitarian Onboard' or something like that?"

Ryan scowled. "No bumper stickers. Not even nice ones. And do not unscrew his license plates again, please."

"You're no fun, you know that?" She let go of a long sigh. Harassing Brandon by sabotaging his car was fair game in her book, even though Brandon had gotten his comeuppance when Laurie Wilson dumped him for Brandon's best friend. But she just couldn't let it go. Any guy who dumped his fiancée at the altar deserved to have his life disrupted in small but annoying ways.

"It's not my job to be fun, Courtney. It's my job to keep the peace."

And he took that so seriously, didn't he? "All right. I guess that's fair. I mean Laurie is marrying Andrew in a couple of weeks."

Ryan nodded and took a sip of his Coke. "Good. And I don't want you raiding the cradle either." He managed a crooked smile.

"Whatever does that mean?" she asked, even though she had a good idea what he was trying to say.

"Courtney, you were just ogling Matt Lyndon like he's a pint of Ben and Jerry's Karamel Sutra ice cream."

"And this is your business because?"

"Because I actually care about you. Because Matt Lyndon is too young for you. Because we both know he's a player. But mostly because I just overheard Brandon Kopp express the opinion that you are an ice queen, and Matt countered that he could seduce you in less than two dates." Ryan grinned like the Cheshire cat.

"No way. He didn't," Arwen said, suddenly coming out of her shell. Oh brother. Courtney could almost see the musical wheels turning in Arwen's mind.

"Oh yes. He did," Ryan said with a sober look in his blue eyes. "And then Brandon bet him a hundred dollars that he couldn't."

"No," Arwen and Courtney said in unison.

Ryan nodded. "And Matt took the bet."

Matt tucked Brandon's business card into the inside pocket of his suit jacket. Of course he didn't need Brandon's contact information, but the card served as Brandon's marker. One hundred dollars if he wrangled the ice queen into bed.

"You sure you don't want to put a time frame on that?" he asked. "Because having an indefinite period of time to pursue her gives me the advantage, you know."

Brandon snorted a laugh. "You're delusional."

"Why do you say that?" Matt turned on his barstool and studied his friend. Brandon was a couple of years older, but that didn't mean he had any experience. Not when it came to women. Brandon had spent the last ten years in a serious, committed relationship with Laurie Wilson. Last August, he'd halted the wedding with a heartfelt speech about needing to date other people. The drama had been hard on Laurie, and Matt truly felt for her.

But he'd also understood Brandon's fear. Matt had done everything in his power to help Brandon learn how to play the field, but the guy just wasn't a player. And he'd been a jerk to think that he could dump his girlfriend at the altar and then somehow win her back.

"Courtney Wallace is a little psycho if you ask me," Brandon said. "I'm really tired of her messing with my car. Someone needs to teach her a lesson."

"Whoa, wait a sec. I'm happy to have a little fun with her, but I'm not into teaching her a lesson."

"A little fun? Bro, I want you to break her heart. Honestly, I'd throw another C note into it if you could assure me of that."

Matt straightened on the barstool. "I can't take that bet."

"Why not?"

"Because I never lead a woman on. It's one of my rules. I'm not into breaking hearts, Brandon. I'm into enjoying women."

"Well, rule or not, I'd like to see that woman suffer. Do you have any idea how hard it is to get the smell of spoiled milk out of a car's carpets?"

"No. And I truly feel your pain," Matt said.

"So you're not taking the bet?"

"Oh, I'm taking the bet, all right. I've had my eye on her for quite some time." He stood up.

"You're making a move now? But she's sitting with Ryan Pierce."

Matt shrugged nonchalantly. "I'm not worried about the competition." He snagged his beer and strolled across the bar's dining room.

Brandon didn't understand how this game worked. A guy looking for action needed to be ready at all times. The world was filled with hot women, and Courtney Wallace was the definition of hot. She had curves, lots of them, and a sweet little rack that was mouthwatering. Combine that with that wide-open, blue-eyed stare of hers. If you didn't know better, you might think Courtney Wallace was sweet and naive.

But Courtney fell into the category of wise beyond her years. And that made her a special challenge.

Not that Matt usually wasted his time with women like Courtney when there were so many ready to tumble into his bed. Why waste his time on someone who'd built walls around herself and made it clear she wasn't interested?

He had two reasons. First, he needed to show Brandon that any woman was fair game. It was a matter of attitude. Matt had once been where Brandon was now. Kind of dorky when it came to women. The guy needed inspiration.

And his second reason was entirely personal. If he was going to be stuck here in Shenandoah Falls, working for his father, he needed something adventurous to fill his time. This wasn't Washington, DC, where the number of single, willing females was plentiful. This was little Shenandoah Falls. And Courtney Wallace probably ranked right up there as the hottest single girl in town.

And she just happened to be sitting with Ryan Pierce. Pierce knew a hot woman when he saw one. So taking a full-frontal approach wasn't going to work. Besides, he had some history with Courtney. She'd shut him down a couple of times already.

Instead he headed straight for Arwen Jacobs because he had something in common with her. They both worked at LL&K, and that gave him a hook. A reason to approach, something to say, and the appearance of spontaneity. All of which were crucial.

"Arwen, I see you're signed up for the open mic tonight. I didn't know you had musical talent."

She blushed, probably because she was embarrassed that someone from work was here to see her perform. He took a seat next to her, gave Courtney a quick glance, and then asked, "What kind of music do you do?"

"She's a singer-songwriter," Courtney said. "And you probably should be careful because anything you say or do is likely to end up in one of her songs. She's got a talent for capturing the ups and downs of life as a single woman."

Score. Courtney just couldn't help herself. He turned toward her with a smile. "I guess I'll have to be careful, then."

Courtney leaned forward, cocked her head, and tossed her hair back. Bingo. That little hair toss was a giveaway. She was interested. But then, he already knew that. He'd danced this dance with Courtney a couple of times already.

And that was the thing about Courtney Wallace that he couldn't quite figure out. Matt was exceptionally good at reading body language. He could tell when a woman was interested in a casual hook-up. And for quite some time now, Courtney had been sending casual hook-up signals loud and clear.

But he'd never been able to close the deal. He'd tried for a while, right after Brandon had broken up with Laurie, but the wedding planner wanted Mr. Right even though she knew he didn't exist. Normally, a woman looking for Mr. Right wasn't looking for casual hook-ups. Courtney Wallace was an enigma and a challenge. She was also a beautiful woman. More than that really, Courtney was a babe.

"Arwen tells me you've moved back to Shenandoah Falls." Courtney gave him the tiniest of smiles, just a curl at the corner of her sweet mouth. By the spark in her eyes, Matt knew she was up to something.

"I'm working at my father's law firm for the moment while I reassess my career choices."

Her smile deepened. "I hope that means you don't plan to hit on Arwen."

She was so predictable. Standing there trying to protect her friends from the big, bad wolf. "Okay," he said with a smile. "But what are you doing on Saturday?"

"Saturday? Are you kidding? It's Memorial Day weekend. I've got three weddings on Saturday and another three on Sunday. And excuse me, but did you just ask me out?"

What a stupid blunder. He needed to remember that Courtney's busiest workdays were Saturday and Sunday. So no long walks up to the falls or anything like that. "How about dinner in Winchester on Tuesday?"

She drummed her fingers on the top of the table, a nervous tic that suggested she wasn't all that into him. And yet she'd cocked her head in a way that was most definitely a come-on. What else was new? Courtney was a master at sending mixed signals. A wiser man would cut his losses and move on. But for some reason, Matt didn't want to. Courtney intrigued him.

After a very long moment, she said, "Sure. I'll have dinner with you on Tuesday."

The moment Courtney agreed, Ryan Pierce sat up straight. "But—"

Courtney interrupted whatever Ryan was about to say with the gesture. "It's okay, Ryan. I know what I'm doing." She gave Matt a big smile. "I'd love to have dinner with you in Winchester."

Matt paused for a moment, his gaze flicking between Ryan and Courtney. Was she trying to make Ryan jealous? Maybe. In some ways, she was a player too, and she definitely had an agenda. He'd need to proceed with caution.

But then again, it might be fun to discover exactly what game she was playing. He nodded and smiled. "How about the Union Jack, at six thirty?" he said.

Ten minutes later, Arwen excused herself from the sparring match between Courtney and Matt. She headed to the café's ready room, a large, concrete-floored area edged in metal storage shelves stuffed with paper products, giant-sized bottles of ketchup, and cans of tomato sauce. The room, which always smelled of French fries, doubled as a spot for musicians to relax and tune their instruments before they performed. A couple of beat-up sofas and a half dozen folding chairs occupied the space.

On open mic nights, the room got pretty crowded with a mix of serious musicians, wannabees, and amateurs, and it wasn't all that unusual for Kent Henderson, who had an ego the size of Alaska, to initiate a jam session just to impress everyone by playing Doc Watson's bluegrass version of "Tennessee Stud." He always played it too fast and too loud.

But for some inexplicable reason, his rendition of "Tennessee Stud" made Kent the most popular performer with the Jaybird's regulars. People listened to Kent even though he played the same songs week after week.

Arwen would be following Kent this evening, so of course, he was already in the back room playing his guitar so loud that no one else could possibly hear themselves, much less tune their guitars. Not that anyone else cared, since everyone, except Arwen, used electronic tuners.

Arwen had no problems with electronic tuners, but she used a variety of nonstandard, open tunings for her songs, which required frequent readjustments, so she'd honed the ability to tune her guitar by ear and to change the tunings on the fly. For that she needed to be able to hear herself.

She took her guitar out of its case and headed through the back door into the alleyway behind the Jaybird. A single streetlight dispelled the night like a spotlight. She stepped into it and adjusted the strap around her neck and shoulders. She tuned the guitar to open G and began practicing her new song—an ode to the rocking chair that used to sit on her grandmother's porch. This new song had nothing to do with love or relationships. It told a sentimental story about a chair found by the side of the road, restored and repaired and handed down. It was sweet and not remotely commercial, but it pleased Arwen because it made her feel warm inside when she sang it. She'd loved her grandmother, who had passed away in February.

She finished the last chord and was startled by the sound of a single pair of hands clapping. "That was sweet, lass."

She turned to find the Jaybird's main bartender, Rory Ahearn, sitting on the back stoop. The night cast dark shadows across his deep-set blue eyes and accentuated the dimple in his chin. The rolled-up sleeves of his Henley tee exposed a pair of matching tattoos in a Celtic knot pattern, which wound around his arms like a pair of snakes.

He took a long drag on his cigarette, holding the smoke inside and then exhaling. No, wait, not a cigarette. The breeze blew the pungent scent of weed in Arwen's direction.

"Want some?" he asked, holding the joint out in her direction.

She shook her head, her heart thundering in her chest. Was it some deep-seated need for adventure that had her second-guessing her response? Rory had been tending bar at the Jaybird for at least two years. He had a gift when it came to margaritas and a sexy-as-hell accent. He also listened when she played on open mic nights. She'd watch him going through the motions behind the bar, but she knew he paid attention when she sang. Which made him the only person, besides her friends.

And for that reason, she lived for the moment when Rory would look up and nod his head in approval. Still, she could count on the fingers of one hand the number of times she'd actually spoken to him, beyond ordering a drink.

They came from different worlds. She was a nice Jewish girl from the Washington, DC, suburbs who had never ever in her life broken any rules. And Rory gave every appearance of being a bad boy from across the ocean who truly didn't give a damn. He had a dark Irish look that was at once both unsettling and deeply poetic.

Arwen had a weakness for poetry.

"You should give that up," she said, nodding toward the joint.

That earned her a dark bark of a laugh. "Love, the occasional joint is the only thing that gets me through the day." He leaned forward into the light, which sparked in the dark, endless blue of his eyes. "Just like the occasional margarita helps you over the day-to-day heartbreak of life as a single girl."

That was the thing about bartenders. They knew everything. And of course, he actually listened to her songs. Which meant he knew all her fears and insecurities because she poured them into her lyrics.

She took a step in his direction. "I guess you're right about me and margaritas. But the thing is, margaritas are legal in the Commonwealth of Virginia."

"Aye, true enough. But I like to live on the wild side." His half smile grew into a full grin. He was incredibly handsome with that scruffy black hair hanging down over the collar of his shirt and the shadow of stubble across his cheeks. She ought to write a song about him, but she wasn't sure yet what it would be about.

"The wild side can get you in trouble," she said, as much to herself as to him.

He nodded. "That's a fact, lass." He hauled in a big breath, stubbed the joint out on the brick step, and stood up. "Looking forward to hearing you sing tonight," he said with a little wink.

And then he turned and slipped back into the café, leaving Arwen to wonder if Rory Ahearn had followed her out here to flirt, give her encouragement, or just to take his pot break.

Maybe it was wishful thinking, but she didn't believe her encounter with him was entirely accidental.

Chapter Two————————————

Losing his job in DC had completely blindsided Matt. One day he'd been a member of the Heartland Industries government affairs team, and the next he'd been out on his ass. The big manufacturer of tractors and other earth-moving equipment had decided to close its DC office to save money, and headquarters hadn't invited anyone, least of all an entry-level legislative representative like Matt, to move back to the company's Kansas City headquarters.

Not that Matt would have moved to Kansas City, but still.

In a family where everyone valued success, being fired made Matt feel like a complete failure. Even worse, Matt's inability to find another government affairs job rankled. Despite the fact that his uncle was a US senator and his cousin a member of Congress, despite his politically connected last name, despite his Ivy League education and his two years of government affairs experience, he'd failed. Six weeks of searching and dozens of interviews had netted him exactly zero offers—a turn of events that shook him to his core.

He could have fallen back on the trust fund Grandpa Artzen had set up for him, but Matt had promised Dad he wouldn't touch that money unless it was for something important. And after the way Danny had gone through his inheritance, Matt was determined to save that legacy for a rainy day. The money was safely in the care of his financial adviser, tied up in investments that weren't particularly liquid.

So he needed a job. Besides, he wasn't about to waste his assets on Washington, DC, rent. That would be foolish. So he'd done the one thing he'd been trying to avoid for most of his life. He'd accepted an associate's position in his father's law firm. It had always been Dad's hope that one of his sons would join him in practice. Matt had never seen himself as that son, and to be brutally honest, neither had Dad.

Jason was the one Dad really wanted. But Jason had other ideas, which involved the criminal justice system. He had taken a job with the FBI. So Matt, middle child extraordinaire, was left holding the bag.

Yesterday—his first day on the job—Matt had filled out employment forms and endured a two-hour lunch with Dad at the Red Fern Inn. It had been the longest lunch of his life. Dad had pontificated about the firm, talked about his hopes for Matt making partner, and stressed the necessity of hard work and good service.

On his second day at the firm, Matt strolled into the tiny cubicle of an office that Dad had given him in order to send a message that even though Matt was the son of the firm's founding partner he'd get no special perks. In fact, knowing Dad, Matt expected to get absolutely no special privileges. He sat down at a standard-issue, boxy brown desk and stared at the framed photograph of the Shenandoah Mountains that hung on the opposite wall. No doubt the print was there as a stand-in for a window.

He desperately missed his K Street office with the big windows and its view of Farragut Square. Despite his low pay grade, there had been a few perks with his last job. He leaned back into his chair and stared at the photograph, waiting for the rest of his life to begin.

He didn't have to wait long. Arwen Jacobs popped her head into his doorway and said, "Meeting in the small conference room. Five minutes," and then disappeared down the hall.

He opened the drawers of his desk looking for a legal pad, but Cousin Andrew—the previous occupant of this office—had evidently cleaned up after himself. No surprise there. Andrew had a reputation for being clean and organized.

Matt's desk drawers were completely empty. He

didn't even have a pen. And when he showed up for the meeting without an attorney's basic tools, he'd be ridiculed. He wandered out into the hallway, carpeted in a deep-pile off-white that muffled his footsteps. He looked left and right, trying to remember where the small conference room was located. He had no idea where the supply closet was. He mentally flipped a coin and turned left, which took him on a roundabout tour of the office. Gillian, David's assistant, finally pointed him in the right direction and told him not to worry about legal pads or pens.

When he arrived at his destination, a small conference room with basic dark brown furniture, he understood. A pile of legal pads sat in the middle of the table along with a leather cup holding a collection of pens.

He should have known this. Practicing lawyers, even lowly associates, didn't have to know where to find legal pads. They would eventually find him.

Arwen was already seated, dressed in a man-tailored navy-blue suit jacket with a pencil skirt and a white silk blouse. She looked competent and professional, and like a woman who was trying to hide her femininity.

Matt hated man-tailored suits on women. In his view, women shouldn't try to become men. And they shouldn't feel as if they had to hide their beauty behind lapels in order to be taken seriously. His boss at Heartland Industries had been an extremely smart and capable woman who had taught him many things about government affairs. But she dressed in pantsuits and long tunics, as if she was ashamed of her curves.

On some level, Matt understood why professional women felt the need to do that. But it irked him. He liked and appreciated women for all that they were and could be. He despised men who took advantage of women or behaved badly in the workplace, especially when they blamed their brutish behavior on the woman's clothing. He had no use for any work colleague who believed that women were intellectually inferior too. Guys like that were idiots.

"Welcome to the firm," Arwen said. She seemed nervous, her shoulders tense. Probably because he'd used her as an approach for Courtney Wallace at the Jaybird last night. He needed to set her at ease.

"Thanks. I enjoyed your performance at the open mic last night. Your songs are very insightful."

Pink crawled up her cheeks, and she looked away. Interesting. Her quiet performance had been the musical highlight last night, but she didn't seem to know it. Her songs would probably never top any pop music charts, but they spoke to the heart; they had poetry. And Matt loved poetry. He had Grandma to thank for that.

Just then, David strolled into the room, ending further conversation. Matt's cousin was twelve years older and had always intimidated him. For many years, David was the family's fair-haired child, the one everyone thought would run for Congress, become a senator like his father and grandfather before him, and eventually make a bid for the White House. But those plans had changed after his first wife died.

David had walked away from politics to focus on being a small-town lawyer. Two years ago, he'd married Willow Petersen, the owner of Eagle Hill Manor, the bed-and-breakfast that had become one of the most successful businesses in Shenandoah Falls.

He carried a fat brown manila expansion folder, which he dropped on the conference table right in front of Matt before taking a seat at the head of the table. "In that folder, you'll find several new cases from the Blue Ridge Legal Services Corporation. Mostly landlord-tenant disputes. Study them; get up to speed on them. You will be the main attorney on all of them."

"Landlord-tenant disputes?" Matt's voice cracked adolescently. He knew nothing about resolving disputes. That was Andrew's thing.

"Yeah, and just because these cases are part of our pro bono commitment doesn't mean we don't care about them. These tenants are dealing with absentee landlords, landlords who have no business owning buildings, and potential safety violations. We'll solve most of these cases through arbitration. But some of them, like the dispute at Dogwood Estates, are headed for court."

"Court?" His heart jumped in his chest. He'd only argued cases in moot court competitions, and he'd sucked at it.

"Yeah, court." David's eyebrows lowered into a scowl that looked surprisingly like the frightening expression on William Lyndon's portrait, which hung over the mantel at Charlotte's Grove, Uncle Mark's three-hundred-year-old home.

"Don't worry," Arwen said. "I've been working with the Blue Ridge Legal Services Corporation for years, and I've been involved in dozens of landlord-tenant suits. You'll get the hang of it."

She gave him a shy smile. Oh yeah, she'd seen right through him. But he was grateful for her kindness, especially since David continued to glower.

"I want to make this clear," David said. "Maybe in DC paralegals are treated the same as secretaries or personal assistants, but out here in the country, people like Arwen are assets. You may have a law degree, Matt, but you're as green as an unripe apple. You listen to Arwen. She'll teach you everything you need to know about how to be a compassionate attorney."

Matt nodded, but deep down he resented his cousin's words even if the part about him being green was accurate. He was green. But he hated the way David assumed he would treat Arwen badly. Or that he'd try to take the easy way out.

That attitude came from Dad. His father seemed to think he was lazy. Or stupid. Or incompetent. Or something. No matter what he did, Dad always found a way to criticize. He would have to work his balls off in order to get anything close to a pat on the back.

The Union Jack Pub and Restaurant sat in the middle of Winchester's historic old town promenade. Matt arrived fifteen minutes late, on purpose, because he never arrived precisely on time for any date.

But Courtney had outfoxed him once again. She wasn't waiting for him, and since Matt refused to stand around in the entrance foyer, he asked the hostess to seat him at one of the outside café tables. The car-free historic area was a perfect venue for people-watching, especially on a warm May evening when the entire female population of Winchester, Virginia, had busted out their sundresses.

He enjoyed the view as the sun sank low and he sipped a local beer with a hoppy, thirst-quenching taste. He made a point of ignoring his watch. He had nowhere to be, no schedule to worry about. He could kick back and enjoy.

Courtney eventually arrived, wearing a turquoise sundress of almost the same color blue as her eyes. The scooped neck displayed a sweet, soft cleavage that jiggled a tiny bit with every step she took on her high-heeled sandals as she came down the promenade. Her dark, unbound hair feathered back from her face as she walked with the confident, hips-forward stride of a runway model.

She was built like a brick outhouse, and Matt wanted to explore every inch of that incredible body. But getting her naked was going to be a challenge.

She'd had so much experience fending off guys that she knew every trick in the male book of seduction. It was one of those ironies that a woman built for sex had chosen to become an ice maiden.

She sat down at the table and gave him a coy, knowing smile, as if she expected him to say something predictable. He was too smart for that. He needed to surprise her or he'd never make any headway.

So he decided not to play her at all. He'd simply be honest with her. And in that vein, he said, "You look gorgeous tonight. Did you pick that dress because it's the same color as your eyes?"

She cocked her head and gave him a look. This was not the look of a woman who was buying what he was selling. "Do you always use that line?" she asked.

"It wasn't a line. I'm trying to be honest and sincere with you."

That earned him a laugh that lit a couple of tiny blue flames in her eyes. "Are you capable of being honest and sincere?"

"I'm always honest."

"Really?"

He leaned forward, making extended eye contact. "I'm not here to break your heart. I'm here to buy you dinner, have a few laughs, get to know you better, and hook up with you if you're interested. If you're not interested, that's okay too."

She blinked. Score one for his side.

She recovered quickly and shot him a killer smile

complete with adorable dimples. "I'm not hooking up with you. But dinner sounds good."

She picked up the menu and studied it with an air of nonchalance that was about as phony as a three-dollar bill. He didn't call her on it though. He simply sat back, took a sip of his beer, and enjoyed the view.

A moment later, the waitress came by. He fully expected Courtney to order a Manhattan, but she surprised him by asking for a beer and a cheeseburger.

He liked that. He couldn't remember the last time he'd gone out with a woman who'd ordered a cheeseburger. It was a shame the way so many women obsessed about their diets and their hips sizes. Courtney wasn't a skinny little thing. She had round hips and a tiny waist and that rack, which was enough to distract any straight guy. In fact, Courtney's cleavage had been scoring looks right and left, which she completely ignored. He wondered if she even realized that she was the object of anyone's admiration.

When the waitress took away her menu, he leaned in again. "So, how does someone become a wedding planner? I mean, did you study that in college, or did you get one of those useless degrees like a BA in English?"

She gave him another quelling look, which he richly deserved. But then he'd asked the obnoxious question precisely to elicit that response. She was beautiful when she glared like that. And he was a lot like the boy in the back row who couldn't resist pulling the pigtails of the girl sitting in front of him.

He found both joy and a weird kind of excitement in teasing Courtney.

"I've got a master's of science in nursing. I'm a registered nurse."

"No way? How did you go from nursing to wedding planning?"

"I burned out on nursing two years ago at about the same time Willow bought Eagle Hill Manor. I helped Willow plan Jeff and Melissa Talbert's wedding and discovered I had a knack. When she offered me a job, I jumped at it. It can be stressful, and there are bittersweet moments, like that day Brandon left Laurie at the altar, but on balance, there are more good days than bad, and that's more than I can say about working at the hospital.

"How about you? Did you want to study law, or was it one of those things you had to do in order to get your Lyndon family man card?"

He laughed. "Lyndon family man card?"

She shrugged, dimpling again. "As near as I can tell, the only male Lyndon without a law degree is your brother Daniel. And didn't he go to law school for a couple of years too?"

"Yeah, he did. But you're not counting Jeff. He doesn't have a law degree, and I don't think he ever went to law school."

"Yes, but Jeff has refused to take the Lyndon last name, so he doesn't count. He doesn't need a Lyndon man card."

"Okay, I can see your point."

"So lawyering is your dream job, huh?" Courtney asked.

Wow, she wasn't going to let this go. Should he change the subject? He wanted to, but he jettisoned the idea. She'd call him on it if he tried to deflect. So he continued being honest. "Funny you should ask that," he said.

"Funny why?" she asked.

"Look, if you really want to know, I'm the one with the useless degree—a BA in political science. And when I expressed the desire to go into public policy or government affairs, my dad and my uncle Mark convinced me that I needed a law degree. So off I went to the University of Virginia, where I managed, barely, to get through the experience. When I graduated, Dad wanted me to join the family firm, but I decided that practicing law wasn't for me. So I got a job working for Heartland Industries as a legislative representative."

"What the hell is that?"

"It's what they call an entry-level lobbyist. I became an expert in international trade policy because Heartland exports a shit-ton of tractors and other large farm implements. It was a fun job but it didn't pay all that well, if you really want to know. I lived in a house with five roommates, all of whom were slobs."

"Ah, so you've grown up and decided that lawyers make more money, huh?"

He shrugged. "No. Heartland closed its DC office

and I lost my job. So I came back here and joined the family business, so to speak. I'm doing pro bono work for the moment."

"Pro bono work? Really? You must be working with Arwen, then."

He nodded.

"So tell me about some of your cases."

She seemed genuinely interested, which sort of blew his mind. Usually his dates were interested in talking about stupid YouTube videos or whatever was trending on Twitter or Facebook. Courtney didn't strike him as the kind of woman who wasted time on stupid social media. She was interesting. And interested in him. And beautiful to look at too.

Maybe he should thank Brandon for the bet. Whether he got her into bed or not, this evening was turning out better than expected.

Courtney glanced at her watch, surprised to discover that dinner with Matt had lasted more than an hour and a half. The warm, late-May sun had slipped behind the building, casting Winchester's old town into twilight shadow, where trees permanently wrapped in white Christmas lights provided a festive, midsummer atmosphere.

Matt's choice of the Union Jack had surprised Courtney because it wasn't a very romantic restaurant. There were no white tablecloths here, no fancy sauces or high-priced menu items, although you could get bangers and mash if you were so inclined.

Hook-up Artists like Matt Lyndon operated under a set of rules that almost never varied. A Hook-up Artist would make a move on a woman, and once he confirmed her interest, he'd go for the dinner invitation. If she said yes, he would always interpret that as a prelude to sex. He'd pick the most expensive restaurant he could afford and then proceed to spend way more money than was absolutely necessary in order to make his date think he valued her.

Then he would mess with his date's mind. He'd pick the one thing she felt most insecure about and compliment it. He might sneak in a few pet names like "darling" or "sweetheart" or "baby." He'd ask questions and give all the appearance of being genuinely interested, but the next morning, after he'd left her bed, she'd suddenly come to her senses and realize that none of his questions had been about her. Not really. They'd been about surface stuff like her favorite color or recording artist.

Matt Lyndon had done none of those things. He'd invited her out to a moderately priced burger joint, had not used one term of endearment, and had spent a lot of time exposing his own insecurities with a great deal of good humor.

Right at the moment, they were sharing a piece of apple pie, and he was regaling her with a story about his experience arguing in a moot court competition.

"So, after giving my less-than-articulate oral argument," Matt said with an adorable smile, "I returned to my seat while my co-counsel wrapped up our case.

Unfortunately, one of the casters on my chair had mysteriously come out of its slot, and when I leaned back, I was unceremoniously dumped on my ass."

He paused a moment to polish off the last bite of pie. "Needless to say, we didn't win that moot court competition, and I had to endure a lecture from Judge Chapman about decorum, which I'm sure my father heard about, since the moot court judge is a law school buddy of his." Matt sighed deeply and mournfully. "So you can imagine how I'm feeling at the moment about the prospect of having to argue anything before the Twenty-Sixth Judicial Circuit of Virginia, where Chapman is still a judge."

"You'll be fine," she said, and really meant it.

"Yeah, I hope. To tell you the truth, I only went out for moot court competition because I knew I would never make Law Review, unlike my dear cousins, David and Andrew, who preceded me at UVA."

He leaned forward, bracing his head on his fists. "Tell me, Courtney, did you ever take a pratfall in front of someone you wanted to impress?"

Damn. Matt Lyndon had game. He was pretending to be the Nice Guy Not, all interested in getting to know her insecurities while simultaneously telling her stories that showed him to be a humble guy with a sense of humor. She wasn't fooled. She made a note of the judge's name. She had a connection to that judge that Matt probably didn't even realize. As for his question, she sure wasn't going to expose any weaknesses that he could use against her at some future time.

Her most embarrassing moments had occurred in high school. And since she was probably ten years older than Matt and they'd gone to different high schools, she felt no need to expose her own stupidity for his enjoyment. Maybe if he were genuinely interested in her instead of trying to win a bet, she might reveal the nightmare of her teen years. But Matthew Lyndon didn't need to hear about the geek girl she'd once been.

And besides, although she truly had enjoyed this dinner, she could never forget the way Matt had encouraged Brandon to go out cruising for women after dumping Laurie at the altar. So Courtney refused to be fooled by that easy Lyndon charm or those dark espresso eyes that reflected the twinkle lights at her.

The waitress came by and asked if they wanted another round. Courtney shook her head. "No. I need to be going. Just a couple of checks. We're splitting the bill."

"Um, no—"

"We're splitting the check," Courtney said a little more emphatically. She may have given him Nana's evil eye at the same time just to punctuate the point. He squirmed for a moment, clearly outside of his comfort zone. A Hook-up Artist always paid the bill. It was his way of justifying the sex. As if a dinner was payment for access or something.

The waitress hurried away, and he leaned back in

his chair, his brown-eyed gaze running over her from waist to head and back again, pausing at her breasts. The look was hungry, and damned if it didn't unleash a torrent of hormones that made her nipples harden. She didn't dare look down to see if they showed through the fabric of her dress. She wouldn't give him that much satisfaction. Also, she had to continue the pretense that she had no interest when it came to his abilities in the bedroom.

Was he a Casanova or a Don Juan? Was he a man who loved making love or was he a complete libertine?

No, no, no. She didn't need to satisfy her curiosity. She had accepted his invitation only in order to lead him on a merry chase. How long would he pursue her? A hundred dollars didn't seem like enough of an inducement to make Matt work too hard. But then his bet with Brandon had to be about more than money. Brandon wanted revenge for the damage done to his Camaro, and Matt was one of Brandon's good friends.

She could do this. In fact, right this minute, she was thoroughly enjoying the surprised and uncomfortable look on Matt Lyndon's face. Confusing the crap out of him was going to be fun.

Chapter Three———

Allison Chapman, one of Courtney's brides, came in for a consultation on Thursday afternoon. They met in Eagle Hill Manor's dining room to sample hors d'oeuvres for the wedding's reception, which was scheduled for the third Saturday in June.

Every bride wanted a one-of-a-kind wedding, but some brides wanted more than that. Allison Chapman, the fiancée of a hedge fund manager and the daughter of a state circuit court judge, was one of those brides.

A Who's Who of Virginia's elite would be attending her reception, including Supreme Court justices, members of the state assembly, and a couple of US congressional representatives.

Money was no object because Erik, Allison's fiancé, had more money than God. But money alone wasn't enough because Allison wanted an assurance that her wedding would be absolutely perfect. But no wedding ever was. Something always happened at the last minute that required a workaround or a compromise. Given the inevitability of some small change in plans, Courtney fully expected Allison to have a gigantic meltdown on her wedding morning. Brides who obsessed over every small detail usually burned themselves out and never truly enjoyed their special day.

Courtney had given up trying to get brides like Allison to delegate some of the work. Instead she waited in the wings, providing advice and then swooping in to save the day when the inevitable meltdown occurred. "They also serve who only stand and wait" was one of Courtney's favorite mottoes.

Today, Allison was in her element, passing judgment on the canapés while Antonin, Eagle Hill Manor's chef, stood by surreptitiously rolling his eyes. Courtney made copious notes on her computer tablet—notes that Antonin would probably ignore on the day of the wedding.

"I think that will do it," Allison said, nodding at Antonin and giving him a surprisingly sweet smile.

Antonin returned to his kitchen, where no doubt, he'd drop a giant expletive bomb. But only in French because his sous chef was a devout Baptist who frowned on profanity. Sometimes Courtney wished she could curse in another language.

She turned off her tablet and plastered the sweetest smile on her face. "I was wondering if I could ask you a question that has nothing to do with the wedding."

Allison, an attorney at one of DC's many law firms, gave her a probing stare. "About what?"

Courtney dropped her voice into a semi-whisper. "Well, to tell you the truth, it's about this guy I know who told me he argued a case in moot court where your father was presiding. And I'm just trying to see if what he told me is true."

"Well, Daddy does preside over moot court competitions. Who is this guy? And why are you so curious?"

"He told me a funny story, and I didn't believe it. Something about him falling out of the chair and embarrassing himself."

Allison's jaw dropped, but not in a good way. Her expression was more horrified consternation than delighted surprise. "Oh my God, Matt Lyndon? You know him? Really?"

There was something snotty in Allison's response. As if Courtney wasn't important enough or pretty enough or something enough to actually know Matt Lyndon. Allison was a terrible snob, and Courtney truly disliked the woman.

"Yes, I know Matt. And you do too, apparently."

Allison nodded.

"And the story he told was true?"

"Yes. It was true. And he was a total ass about it."

"In what way?"

Allison picked up the glass of ice water on the table and took several long swallows, the pause clearly an attempt to calm herself. What was up with that? Had Matthew broken Allison's heart? Maybe.

"He accused Daddy of sabotaging his chair," Allison said in a slightly sneering tone.

"In court?" Moot court or not, Courtney didn't think accusing judges was a smart thing to do.

Allison shook her head. "No, afterward. Look, Courtney, you should know that Matt and I went to high school together. And we were both at UVA for a while, and…"

Allison looked away and drummed her fingers on the table for a moment. Courtney found it difficult to read the emotion on her face. Was it annoyance, anger, sadness? "Matt Lyndon and I hooked up briefly in college," she finally said in a hushed tone.

Oh. Yeah. Now Courtney understood. Allison was another one of Matt's victims. Courtney didn't like Allison much, but she felt a certain solidarity with her. She covered the bride-to-be's restless fingers with her hand and gave a squeeze. "I understand."

Allison pulled her hand away. "How could you understand?"

Courtney didn't know what to make of Allison's surprised tone. Maybe she just didn't want to revisit the past, which was understandable mere weeks before her wedding.

"Believe me, I do understand. And you don't have to worry about him anymore. I've got a plan for him."

"What? What kind of plan?" Allison seemed truly agitated.

"It's still evolving at the moment. But trust me, when I'm done with him he won't know what hit him."

Later that day, Courtney and her assistant, Amy, strolled into Willow's office on Eagle Hill Manor's third floor, where once a bevy of servants had lived, back when the house had been home to a wealthy family. The servants' quarters were spartan, so the office space was small and cramped. But Willow's office had a gorgeous antique desk, which her husband had given her as a gift on their wedding day. The desk gave Willow's office a certain kind of formality that was lacking in the space Amy and Courtney shared.

"What's up?" Courtney asked as she settled into one of the small side chairs. "If this is about Allison Chapman and the nasty things she said about Antonin's canapés, I can explain."

Willow chuckled and tucked a strand of blond hair behind her ear. "I heard all about it from Antonin, but I'm not worried. Allison is the worst bridezilla we've had in quite some time. And I know how emotional Antonin can get about his canapés."

"Okay. Glad to hear that Antonin's pride has not been mortally wounded."

Willow folded her hands in front of her, and for an instant, she looked the tiniest bit uncomfortable. This was strange because Willow never showed any weakness. She tended to square her shoulders and sit up straight in her chair when she was negotiating. And the woman had a take-no-crap attitude about a lot of things.

Something was up. Courtney's pulse went into overdrive. She'd be upset if Eagle Hill Manor closed, or if Willow sold it or something like that. She had no reason to believe anything was amiss with operations, but Courtney didn't know much about finances, except that even healthy-looking businesses could have balance-sheet issues.

Courtney leaned forward in her chair, bracing her elbows on the arms. "Okay, spit it out. We're about to get fired, right?"

Amy squirmed in her chair, and Willow cocked her head. A slow smile spread across her face. "Courtney, you are such a drama queen sometimes."

"Okay, so what's up?"

"How would you like to become the chief operating officer of Eagle Hill Manor?"

"What?" Courtney's mouth fell open.

"I need to back off a little bit," Willow said. "And you know more about this business than anyone else. I could hire someone from the outside, or I could promote from within. So, what do you say?"

Willow turned toward Amy. "If Courtney takes the job, that means you become the director of special events."

"What? No." Amy shook her head. "Um...Ah... Willow, I'm flattered, but I was about to come talk to you about resigning." Amy rolled her dark eyes in Courtney's direction, and Courtney's pulse redlined. What the hell was happening?

"You want to resign?" Willow's eyebrows arched.

"Um. Okay, I wasn't going to tell you this until I told Dad, so you're officially sworn to secrecy. But the thing is...I'm pregnant. And between Eagle Hill Manor and Dusty's new ecotourism business, it's like I'm working two jobs. I love working here, but Dusty needs me. Shenandoah River Guides will be opening in September. I'm only planning to work through August."

"Oh my God. Really? I'm pregnant too. When are you due? I'm due on November seventh."

"No. Really? I'm due October twenty-ninth."

"They'll be cousins. Isn't that wonderful?"

Amy and Willow jumped up and proceeded to happy dance around the small office while a toxic dose of envy spilled through Courtney's blood stream. When would it be her turn? All these years fending off Mr. Wrong while she waited for Mr. Right had left her with a biological clock ticking away like a time bomb.

She ought to be thrilled with this promotion, even if it meant she had to find another assistant. She ought to be thrilled for Willow, knowing that at thirty-six her biological clock was ticking too.

But instead, a hollow place opened in the middle

of her chest and a lump formed in her throat that she had to swallow down.

Maybe it was time to give up on the idea of Mr. Right. Maybe it was time to embrace spinsterhood and get a cat.

Dogwood Estates, a forty-unit walk-up apartment development five miles south of Shenandoah Falls, didn't have a single dogwood tree. In fact, its landscaping was nonexistent except for weeds edging the blacktop parking lot and the squat junipers that blocked the first-floor apartment windows. The red-brick building exemplified the worst of boxy, mid-century architecture, and now the signs of neglect were everywhere.

The dirty white shutters, rusting balcony railings, and unkempt trash Dumpster explained why the Dogwood Estates Tenants Association had been paying rent into a legal escrow account for the last two months.

"Leslie Heath's apartment is down here," Arwen said as she got out of Matt's Acura. The two of them had given up an evening in order to meet with their client about their dispute with Scott Anderson, the deadbeat who owned Dogwood Estates.

Arwen had briefed Matt on the tenants' grievances. The complex's roof had been leaking for months, setting off a mold issue for many of the tenants living on the third floor. The trash area was not secure and had drawn raccoons and other wildlife, including a black bear that had required a visit from Jefferson County Animal Control. One deep breath and Matt could confirm that the trash was in open containers. The place stank.

Dogwood Estates was a dump. Anyone with other options would have moved out a long time ago.

Matt ground his teeth and followed Arwen down the weed-choked sidewalk and up a rusty metal stairway to a second-floor apartment. As she knocked on the door, a familiar guilt unfurled inside Matt like a pennant in the wind.

But for the grace of God, he might have grown up in a place like this. An undeserved twist of fate had made him a member of one of America's oldest families. He didn't deserve to be so lucky. And the members of the tenants association deserved better than an inexperienced lawyer with an impressive family name.

Heaven help them.

Of course he wouldn't show any of his doubts. If he'd learned anything growing up as a Lyndon, it was never to show weakness. He would approach this meeting the way he approached women, with confidence and the sure knowledge that the best players strike out two-thirds of the time. But they deserved better.

The door opened to reveal a tall, sixtysomething woman with feathery white hair that framed a surprisingly youthful face. A pair of wide hazel eyes fringed with dark eyelashes studied Matt. A big smile widened her lipstick-bright mouth.

"Leslie, this is Matthew Lyndon. He's LL&K's new legal associate. He's taking over Andrew's cases." Arwen gestured toward Matt.

Leslie Heath, the president of the Dogwood Estates Tenants Association, didn't look poor or downtrodden or any other kind of stereotype that had been running through his mind a moment ago. In fact, her embroidered peasant shirt, big hoop earrings, and skinny jeans gave her a hip 1960s throwback look. She might be old enough to be a granny, but she was a beautiful woman.

"Y'all sure do have a lot of Lyndons in that law firm. Are you Andrew's brother?" Leslie's voice had the unmistakable twang of the West Virginia mountains in it.

"His cousin," Matt said.

"Would that make you David's brother?"

Matt shook his head. "No. David is also a cousin."

"He's Charles Lyndon's son," Arwen said. "So you guys are in good hands."

Holy crap. Arwen, who knew all his failings and all the gaps in his knowledge, was one hell of a good liar. It surprised the heck out of him. So far, Arwen hadn't failed to call him on his ignorance whenever he displayed it, which was often. Until that moment, Matt hadn't thought Arwen was capable of lying.

"I'm glad to hear that, y'all. Living in this dump is getting old."

"Well, I think we have some good news," Matt said.

"Hallelujah, honey. Because it's been nothing but bad news for months." Leslie's wide smile grew even wider as she stepped forward and took Matt by the crook of his arm and pulled him deeper into the apartment, which smelled of garlic and onions and other spices he couldn't quite name. "Come on in, now, and get some refreshments. Delia's made some of her *pain patate*, which in American is sweet potato and banana pudding. It tastes better than it sounds."

Leslie ushered him into an L-shaped living/dining room dominated by a heavily used, brown leather sectional and a couple of blue recliners. The sliding doors to the balcony stood open, but with more than two dozen people jammed into the small space, Matt started to sweat. Clearly, the air-conditioning wasn't working correctly.

Leslie half pushed, half dragged him into the dining room, where she sliced a wedge of some kind of bread and put it on a pink paper plate with an image of Minnie Mouse. She handed him a purple plastic fork and a blue cocktail napkin imprinted with the words *Baby Jessica, coming this fall*. "Honestly, honey, you have to try Delia's sweet potato pudding once in your life. It's supposed to be a traditional Haitian dish."

He suddenly felt like a candidate out on the campaign trail. Uncle Mark, a United States senator, had dozens of stories about the weird food he'd eaten during his campaigns. Matt gave Leslie one of his best smiles and cut a healthy chunk out of the bread. He popped it in his mouth.

He hated sweet potatoes. And the bread had a sweet potato taste that almost made him gag. But he swallowed it down. No sense in getting off on the wrong foot with these people. He wanted to succeed if for no other reason than to gain his father's approval. Thank God Arwen pressed a plastic cup of cola into his hands. He was able to wash down the sweet potato bread before he hurled it back up.

"So, why don't we call this meeting to order?" he asked, anxious to get the job over with.

Arwen gave him her patented Frown of Disapproval. "Don't you want to meet everyone?" she asked.

"Uh, yeah, I guess." Matt once again found himself tugged around the room by a female. The Dogwood Estates tenants included single mothers, recent immigrants, and old folks. In short, the type of people without the income necessary to rent one of the newer apartments springing up all over Jefferson County. These folks were retirees, farm laborers, retail store clerks, and maids. Precisely the sort of people the rich folks in Jefferson County depended on. Leslie, he soon learned, was a widow living on her husband's Social Security and supplementing that meager income with a part-time greeter's job at the Walmart in Winchester.

When the introductions were finished, the tenants

found places to sit or stand, and Matt stood facing them. "It's very nice to meet all of you," he said. "And I think I have good news to report. The complaint we lodged with the county has yielded some results. The building inspections office has fined Scott Anderson for the mold and garbage problems. I understand that the landlord was served notice on Monday of this week and a lien was placed on the property. So hopefully, this will light a fire under him."

Matt wasn't entirely sure what kind of reaction he was expecting, but certainly it wasn't the open-mouthed horror that greeted his announcement.

The old guy sitting on the couch spoke first. Matt didn't remember the man's name, but he did remember that his wife had passed away a year ago. He was a tall, rail-thin man with a fringe of brown hair and a pair of deep-set blue eyes. His nose meandered a little, as if it had been broken once or twice, and he had a square jaw and rows of laugh lines bracketing his mouth, as if he'd gone through life with a smile on his face. But he wasn't smiling now. "You think fining that bastard's going to fix anything?" he asked in a low, smooth voice.

"It's a start," Matt replied.

The old guy shook his head. "You're wet behind the ears, aren't you, son? What do ya think these fines will do? You think Anderson will decide to fix up this place?" He shook his head. "No. Ain't gonna happen. The landlord doesn't have enough money to make the repairs. Fining him more money won't change that."

"Maybe it will induce him to sell the apartments to some other manager."

Arwen's Frown of Disapproval made another appearance. Damn. What had he done wrong?

"You really are stupid, aren't you?" the old guy said. "If Scott Anderson sells this place to someone else, do you think the new developer's gonna let these places stand?"

Matt stood there for a long moment, shifting his gaze over the faces of the tenants. The old guy was right. Matt *was* wet behind the ears. But he wasn't stupid. He recognized the truth when someone shoved his nose in it.

"If the building inspector's office is using fines to force people to sell out, that's not right."

"Damn straight it's not," the old guy said, pounding his knee with his fist.

"Sid, don't get your blood pressure up," Leslie said, giving the old guy a dewy-eyed look.

Matt suddenly remembered the old guy's name. Sidney Miller. "Look, Mr. Miller, I hear what you're saying. Let me see what I can find out, okay?"

"Whatever. It don't matter; people like us get the shaft every time." The guy leaned back onto the couch, his complexion slightly gray.

Sid Miller wasn't well, and Matt had no intention of continuing their argument. Instead he straightened his shoulders and said, "Look, I promise you folks that I'll do everything I possibly can to get these apartments fixed and to make sure you don't lose your homes."

It wasn't until he finished his speech that he turned and noticed Arwen's Frown of Disapproval, again.

What the hell? Did she expect him to stand there and tell them they should start packing? He decided, right then, that he'd find a way to help these people no matter what.

Chapter Four

Seriously, I think the world needs more love songs," Arwen said as she piled crab dip onto a pita chip. She popped it into her mouth and closed her eyes for a moment, emitting a little groan of pleasure. It was Thursday-night happy hour at the Jaybird Café, and the drinks and appetizers were half-priced—a good thing because Courtney and Arwen needed self-medication.

"If the world needs more love songs, why do you write so many songs about heartbreak?" Courtney asked. Arwen had come directly from work and looked professional, preppy, and uptight in her J.Crew business suit.

"I'm just saying," Arwen said as she scooped another mound of dip onto a chip, "when every popular song is about getting it on, it leads to unrealistic expectations."

"Lyrics have nothing to do with it," Courtney replied. "Guys are guys. They're born with sex on the brain."

"I concede that point. And I'll concede that women like sex too. A lot. But our generation has taken a bad turn somewhere. We've substituted Netflix and chill for dinner and a movie. Where's the romance?" Arwen loaded up another chip and pointed it at Courtney like a weapon. "Has anyone ever sent you flowers?"

Courtney paused, her Manhattan halfway to her mouth. "Damn. You're right." She proceeded to take a big gulp of her drink. "You know, that's depressing. I mean, I'm freaking out because both my boss and my assistant are pregnant, and I haven't even gotten to the stage where a guy likes me enough to send flowers."

"That's my point. No one sends flowers anymore, except to their mothers on Mother's Day. Romance is dead in America."

Courtney pulled the cherry out of her Manhattan and popped it into her mouth. The intense sweetness burst onto her tongue like a vivid memory of younger days. Right after her mother passed away, Daddy had started a tradition of Friday-night dinner "dates." Friday became their special time together. She would never forget that night, a few weeks after Mom had died from leukemia, when he'd taken her to the Red

Fern and ordered her a Shirley Temple cocktail. The taste of maraschino cherries would always remind her of Mommy who had died so young.

Arwen was right. Guys like her dad, who used to send Mom flowers all the time, no longer existed. "I should stop waiting around for Mr. Right."

"Waiting around in what way?"

Arwen's question startled Courtney. "What's that supposed to mean?"

"I don't know. It's just that we say that all the time, and when you parse it out, what does it mean? Why are we waiting? Is real life going to start when some guy arrives? Shouldn't we concentrate on enjoying our lives now?" She helped herself to another pita chip smothered with crab dip and chewed with a thoughtful expression on her face.

Leave it to Arwen to get philosophical. Courtney leaned back in her chair, took another sip of her Manhattan, and cast her gaze over the usual Jaybird regulars: Juni Petersen, the Jaybird's owner, dressed in a long, flowing India-print dress; Rory Ahearn, chatting up the ladies and flashing them his Irish smile; and Ryan Pierce, sitting at the end of the bar nursing a Coke, all of them single, all of them damaged in some way.

Damn. Half the people in the bar were waiting for something.

"Maybe I should find some guy with great genes and ask him to donate some sperm," Courtney said, half in jest.

"Maybe you should get a cat." Arwen's eyebrows lowered in her signature look of disdain.

"I don't want a cat. Getting a cat would be like, I don't know, surrendering or something."

"But do you want to be a single mother?"

Courtney shook her head. "No. It's hard to believe, but I'd like to have the whole nine yards, you know: the doting husband, the three-bedroom house, the two kids. I suppose I could settle for somebody." She cast her gaze toward Ryan Pierce and wondered about his demons. Could she lead him to the altar?

Did she even want to was a better question.

"I see where you're looking." Arwen said. "Do not even think about going there. I know he's adorable, but he's not the guy you're looking for. I don't ever see him with 2.3 kids and a minivan."

"You're right. On the other hand, he might be just what I need in order to mess with Matthew Lyndon's head."

"In what way?"

"Well, it's only been a few days since Matt and I had dinner at the Union Jack. He's sent me the obligatory three texts, designed to let me know that he's still interested, but it's too early for him to call. I figure he'll reach out to me on Tuesday night, when he'll either ask me out for drinks or in for Netflix. So that means I need to be busy next Wednesday night."

"You know, Matt is a puzzle actually. I can't decide whether he's a jerk or just unsure of himself."

"Unsure of himself? You've got to be kidding me."

"Yeah, I know. But the thing is, he's got this way of BSing people when he doesn't know what else to do. He's good at winging it, sort of like a politician."

"Well, duh. He comes from a long line of politicians. It's probably in the Lyndon genome. And besides, all politicians lie."

"He surprised me last night though."

"You were out with him last night?" A shiver ran up Courtney's spine. Arwen was too smart to fall for Matt Lyndon, wasn't she?

"Yeah. We had a meeting with the Dogwood Estates Tenants Association, and your old buddy Sid Miller ripped him a new one. Justifiably so because Matt had missed something obvious. But once Sid made him see the truth, Matt got all passionate about seeing justice done."

"Sid is a good judge of character. If he ripped him a new one, then Matt deserved it." Sid Miller and Courtney's father had been lifelong friends. As boys, they'd fished together. As men, they'd worked at the same hardware store. They'd married two best friends, and until Mom had passed away, Sid and Barbara and Mom and Dad had played bridge together. After Mom died, Barbara had stepped in to help Dad raise Courtney. It had pained Courtney when Sid had sold his little house on Rice Street and moved into Dogwood Estates. That was a little more than a year ago, right after Barbara died. Her long battle with cancer had taken whatever small savings he'd put away.

"Yeah, you're right." Arwen leaned back in her chair, and her thoughtful expression morphed into one of pure delight. And then, for no apparent reason at all, a wicked gleam lit up her eyes. "I just had a devious thought."

"About Matt Lyndon? Do tell."

"I think you should get him in a dark corner, all revved up and ready to go, and then ask him if he'd be okay being your sperm donor." Arwen could hardly finish speaking before she started laughing uncontrollably, tears rolling down her cheeks. "Oh my God, what if he says yes?" she managed between giggles.

What if he says yes? The idea had a certain weird appeal, which was frightening. "Shut up," Courtney said. "I'm not going to ask Matt Lyndon to be a sperm donor. Can you imagine the scandal that would cause in this town?"

"You should do it just to blow his mind."

"No. That's too crazy." Courtney twisted in her seat. "But I do need to ask Ryan out for Wednesday night." She looked back at Arwen, over her shoulder. "Unless you're planning to do next Wednesday's open mic?"

Arwen shook her head. "No. My brother's going to be in DC that day. I'm meeting him for drinks in the city." She paused a moment. "How can you be so sure that Matt's going to ask you out for Wednesday?"

"Because he's a Hook-up Artist who's made a bet

with a Nice Guy Not. Trust me, there's a timeline for his seduction. And my guess is he'll ask me in for Netflix. I intend to be otherwise engaged." She pushed up from the table. "Give me a second. I'll be right back." She scooped up her half-finished Manhattan and headed toward Ryan and the bar.

Matt needed a beer. Thursday had been a difficult and depressing day at work. He'd started by taking the Dogwood Estates file apart, reading every single document in it. Then he'd pulled up the Jefferson County code and read through all the provisions regarding building health and safety. He also shamelessly used his last name, and like the lobbyist he had been, he made a few cold calls to various county government employees.

The picture his research painted was grim. That old guy, Sid Miller, had been right. A few days after the tenants had set up their legal escrow account, the Jefferson County building and fire inspectors had paid a visit to Dogwood Estates, after which they'd notified the landlord of the repairs needed. The landlord was given thirty days to bring the property up to code, but he'd done nothing.

Forty days later—last Monday, to be precise—the government had fined the landlord and placed a lien on his property.

It was clear that the landlord didn't have the money for the repairs or the fines. So it was only a matter of time before the county either condemned the building or the landlord sold out. Either way, the law would grind on, and eventually eviction notices would be issued. Given recent development in the area and escalating property values, those folks might have a hard time finding housing they could afford.

And the worst thing about it was that Matt couldn't stop it from happening. At the end of the day, LL&K may have provided adequate legal counsel to the tenants, but the firm certainly hadn't given them a just or fair resolution to their problems.

So, after work, he headed directly to the Jaybird Café, looking for a diversion. He found it in the person of Courtney Wallace, who was sitting at the bar with Ryan Pierce.

Of course it was too early to talk to Courtney. Only a few days had passed since their dinner at the Union Jack. He ought to wait a week before speaking with her again or run the risk of appearing too anxious. He knew from experience that women didn't like desperate men.

But he could hardly ignore her, could he? Especially when she looked so delicious this evening in a dark-blue dress that hugged every curve and plunged in the front to display enticing cleavage. She turned the moment he crossed the threshold, those incredible turquoise eyes blinking up at him from behind her bangs.

Instant awareness. Instant desire. Instant want.

Once, a long, long time ago, he would have been

stupid enough to act on this attraction. He would have rushed in and said something profoundly dumb that would hand her all the leverage in the encounter. He was smarter now.

Still, she was hard to resist.

And for some reason, it irked him that every time he ran into her at the Jaybird Café she was sitting with Ryan Pierce. Guys like Ryan, who'd served their country and who spent hours in the gym pumping up their biceps, intimidated the crap out of him. In normal pickup situations, he steered clear of any woman sitting next to a guy like Ryan Pierce.

But this was Courtney. And it had been a thoroughly lousy day at work. So he strolled right up to the empty stool beside her and took a seat.

She turned her back on him, pretending that she hadn't seen him walk into the room. Or maybe she was just being her normal contrary self. He had to admit that her contrariness was oddly attractive.

"Hey, Matt," Ryan Pierce said, leaning forward a little so he could peer around Courtney.

Courtney's shoulders stiffened, but she didn't turn in his direction.

"Hey. What's up?"

"Oh, nothing much. But if you're planning to ask Courtney out on a date for next Wednesday, she's busy," Ryan said.

The possessiveness in Ryan's voice irritated Matt for some reason. He squared his shoulders. "Well, that's a relief," he said, "because I was going to ask her out for Thursday night."

"Good," Ryan said in a tone that sounded almost amused. "We're not doing anything on Thursday. So she's free."

Courtney snatched up her Manhattan and drained it in a single gulp. She slammed the glass down, turned, pointed her finger at Matt, and then said, "Okay, where are you taking me this time?"

Her eyes focused on him like a pair of blue lasers. The question was a test. His usual approach, inviting a woman in for dinner and movies at his place, wasn't going to work. First of all, he was still living with his parents until he could find an apartment in town. But more important, Courtney knew he was going to ask her in for an evening of movies, and possibly some making out. The key to Courtney was surprise.

"How about dinner at the Red Fern Inn?"

Wow. That did it. Her gaze softened and her breath hitched visibly. She bit her lip. The surprised expression on her face was unbelievably sexy. Oh, man, did he have an itch. It took real restraint not to grab her by the shoulders and kiss her.

"Okay, Thursday night," she said in a soft voice barely above a whisper. "Now I've got to go back to my table." She pointed with her thumb over her shoulder to where Arwen Jacobs was sitting. As usual, Arwen was shooting him the Frown of Disapproval.

Matt didn't want her to go, but it would be a mistake to ask her to stay. So he let her slip away.

"I'd be careful with her if I were you."

He turned toward the voice and found Juni Petersen standing behind her bar with a sober expression on her face. It always amazed Matt that Juni and Willow were sisters. They didn't look at all alike, and their personalities were as different as night and day.

"Why do you say that?" he asked.

"Because she believes in romance."

"Courtney? Are you out of your mind?"

Juni shook her head. "She's only tough because she's been hurt so many times. If you're out to hurt her, then you should know that I have the right to kick your ass out of my bar. So don't hurt her." Juni paused for a moment as a smile unfolded on her face. "Now that we've come to an understanding, what can I get you to drink?"

Arwen watched from across the room as Courtney spoke with Matt. Holy hell, what was going on inside her head? She gazed up at Matt as if she wanted to devour him.

That was bad.

No, maybe it was good.

Crap. Like most things in life, the idea of Courtney hooking up with Matt tweaked Arwen's finely tuned sense of irony, or maybe her funny bone. Either way, the public display of lust proved Arwen's point about the world of modern relationships.

Courtship had gone the way of the dodo birds. It was extinct. Today's single girl had to be sexually liberated and possess an unbreakable heart and truly thick skin.

She finished her margarita just as Courtney returned to the table.

"So, how did he react when you told him you had a date with Ryan?"

"He didn't. Ryan threw me under the bus. And then Matt asked if I'd go out with him to the Red Fern and..." Courtney ended the sentence with a long sigh. "You know I have a thing about the Red Fern, right?"

Arwen knew, and Matt's invitation struck her as odd somehow. "So you said yes?"

Courtney refused to make eye contact. "You were the one who started the evening off talking about romance. When was the last time someone took you to a restaurant with white tablecloths?"

"Point taken. But you know he's a Hook-up Artist, right? They always take women to restaurants with white tablecloths."

Courtney propped her chin on her hand. "You're right. I'm an idiot." She drew circles on the table with her index finger. "Is he looking at me...? No wait, don't tell me. I'm not going to behave like a middle school kid."

Arwen leaned forward and stilled Courtney's hand. "Look, Court, earlier tonight you said you were tired of waiting for Mr. Right. So don't wait for him. Go out with Matt, have a good time, and keep your expectations low."

"I guess that would be better than breaking off the date, going to the shelter, and adopting a cat, huh?"

"I don't know if it's better or worse, to tell you the truth. It's just what it is. We are living in the twenty-first century, we have sexual freedom, and that requires a certain amount of sacrifice."

"That sounds like a hook line for a song."

Arwen smiled and nodded. "Yeah kind of."

"Look, I need to go. It's like I can feel him looking at me, you know? And I don't want to give him the satisfaction."

"It's okay. You go, and I'll mosey over to the bar and talk to him. We're work colleagues now. Maybe I can winnow out some of his secrets for you."

"Okay, call me tomorrow." Courtney pulled a twenty out of her wallet and handed it to Arwen to cover her drinks. Then she got up and sailed past the men at the bar as if she were a mighty ocean liner calmly plowing through unseen depths, deadly currents, and stormy seas. She didn't look at them or acknowledge them in any way.

Arwen picked up her nearly empty margarita glass and took it to the bar, hopping up on the stool right beside Matt. She waved the glass at Rory, who gave her a heart stopping smile that melted her insides. She quickly glanced away. Maybe she and Courtney needed to find some other bar. All of the men at the

Jaybird needed to have big yellow danger signs hung around their necks.

"Did she send you over here to spy on me?" Matt turned on his bar stool with a raised eyebrow.

"Among other things." She hooked her toes under the stool's rung and tried hard not to watch Rory, down the bar, making her margarita.

"What other things?"

"Look, Courtney is my best friend. She's had her heart broken a zillion times. So don't go there. I mean it. You and I have to work together, and if you screw around with her, I will find all sorts of ways to make your life miserable." She clutched the edge of the bar as her pulse spiked. Matthew Lyndon could easily get her fired from LL&K. But Arwen didn't think Matthew was a prick, not after seeing his reaction to last night's meeting of the Dogwood Estates Tenants Association. Those people had moved him, and Arwen had a feeling he had a heart beating somewhere inside that impressively wide chest of his.

"I have no intention of screwing around with her," he said.

"Really?" This came from Ryan, who leaned toward Matt with his right elbow planted on the bar.

Matt turned toward Ryan. "Look, man, if you and Courtney have something going on, just say so. I mean, you made it sound like you didn't have any problem with me taking her out on Thursday."

"I don't have any problem with you taking her out,

and I don't have anything going on with her. But I share Arwen's view. If you mess with her, you can expect to hear from me."

"How exactly do you define the word 'mess'?" Matt's voice sounded unworried, but Arwen noted a slight tightening in his shoulders. Men. They had more testosterone than was necessary, in her opinion.

"If, for example," Ryan said in a voice like an iron fist in a velvet glove, "you were to use her to win a bet, for example."

Matt turned away from Ryan and studied the wall of liquor bottles behind the bar, lit up with multicolored twinkle lights. After a long moment, he drew in a deep breath and spoke again in a firm voice. "I have never used a woman." He turned and met Ryan's stare.

"Good. Don't start now." Ryan stood up and threw a few dollars down on the bar to cover his Coke. He turned and strolled away, shoulders as straight as a marine on parade.

"So, does this mean Courtney knows about my bet with Brandon?" He glanced at Arwen out of the corner of his eye.

"She might."

He nodded and stood up too, leaving an unfinished beer on the bar. "See you at the office tomorrow," he said, before heading toward the Jaybird's front door.

A moment later, Rory returned with her second margarita. "Ah, it looks like you're drinking alone." He gently placed the drink before her, and Arwen spent a sensuous moment studying the backs of his broad, brown hands. She lifted her head and met his bold blue eyes. Heat prickled her skin as that gaze rubbed up against her erogenous zones. Her bones started to dissolve.

"Want to tell me your troubles?" His voice was as mellow as Irish whiskey and twice as potent. "I'm a good listener."

Yes, he was. And that made him more dangerous than any of the other men in this bar. She could fall hopelessly in love with someone who listened—truly listened—to her songs.

She picked up the drink and took a bracing swallow of sweet and salt combined, and then put it down with a hard *thump*. "Romance is dead," she said, breaking eye contact. She reached for her purse. A moment later, she pulled out enough bills to cover the night's tab. But when she laid them on the bar, Rory struck like a mythological Irish snake, snatching her hand before she could withdraw it. A jolt of pure, uncut lust hit her bloodstream.

He gently tugged her hand forward, and then the dangerous Rory Ahearn, a man with tattoos, a motorcycle, a sexy-as-sin accent, and a devil-may-care attitude toward life, turned her hand over and pressed a single, moist killer of a kiss into the palm of her hand.

He looked up, his eyes filled with fire. "Have a good night, lass."

Courtney had exactly twelve minutes before her meeting with Laurie Wilson, and she probably should have used that time to review her notes for the upcoming wedding. But this was the third wedding Courtney had planned for Laurie. Brandon had dumped her at the altar the first time around. And she'd dumped Brandon the second time around. This time she was marrying someone else, thank God. In any event, after three weddings Courtney knew Laurie's likes and dislikes like she knew the back of her own hand.

So instead of reviewing the Wilson-Lyndon file, she studied Matthew Lyndon's contact information in her iPhone, her finger poised over the telephone number. Six days had passed since she'd run into him at the Jaybird, since he'd invited her out to the Red Fern Inn. Their supposed date was tomorrow night, but she hadn't heard one word from him.

So typical.

She halfway hoped he'd forgotten about it because she didn't want a guy like Matt to pollute her memories of Dad and their dates at the Red Fern Inn. But she knew he hadn't forgotten. He was just testing her.

And even though she wanted to cancel, her finger hesitated over the phone, stopped by her clearly out-of-control libido. Courtney hadn't had sex in almost a year. The whole use-it-or-lose-it concept was beginning to worry her. What if she never had sex again? What a depressing thought.

Clearly her libido recognized a potentially great lover when it saw one. If it weren't for Brandon Kopp and his bet, she might even let it happen. Would it be so bad if she hooked up with a known Hook-up Artist?

She put down the iPhone and turned toward her laptop. Maybe she should forget about her date with Matt and think about her future. If Mr. Right wasn't ever going to arrive, maybe she should go after what she truly wanted in life—a family. Waiting for some guy seemed like a stupid plan of action.

She booted her web browser and keyed in the words "sperm bank near me." Google returned two million hits. Clearly, sperm donors were in high demand these days. Maybe everyone was tired of waiting.

She let go of a long sigh as she studied the Google list.

The Fairfax Cryobank had forty-nine Google reviews with an average of four and a half stars. She clicked on the link to the sperm bank's webpage, where she learned she could select a sperm donor by race, hair color, and eye color. She could also upload a photo of herself and use a facial matching program to select the donor that looked most like herself.

She sat there trying to process this information. Why would she want a child who looked like herself? In her fantasies, there was always a husband—a handsome one—who loved her more than life. Their baby always looked like a miniature of him in every way.

She didn't want a child who resembled her. She'd been the ugliest baby in the history of man, with a big dome head and a lazy eye. All her school pictures showed this poor child with an overbite, Coke-bottle glasses, an eye patch, and a page-boy haircut. It only got worse when her adult teeth and hormones arrived. She'd spent her teen years wearing out the road between her father's house and the orthodontist, ophthalmologist, and dermatologist. Surgery and contacts had finally fixed the lazy eye. Years of braces and losing four adult molars had fixed her teeth. And time had finally dealt a blow to the acne.

She didn't want a kid who looked like her. Never in a million years. If she were going to find a sperm donor, she'd upload a picture of Johnny Depp or Ashton Kutcher—someone with deep, soulful brown eyes.

Sort of like Matt Lyndon's.

No. Matt didn't have soulful anything, although his eyes were as dark as espresso. Her body tingled with the thought, and gooseflesh prickled her skin.

"Hey. What are you looking at?"

Courtney minimized her web browser and turned around. Laurie Wilson stood in the office's doorway, her blond hair pulled back in an easy ponytail that exposed the pearls at her ears and throat. They looked classic and beautiful with her navy and white polka-dot sundress. The expression on her face was a bit wide-eyed.

"What are you doing?" she asked.

Courtney closed her laptop completely. "Oh, nothing. I didn't expect you to come all the way up here." Usually brides checked in with the front desk and Courtney met them down in the lobby, where she treated them to tea or samples of Antonin's baking.

Laurie settled in the side chair. "I've already seen Eagle Hill Manor from top to bottom. I've sampled all of Antonin's fabulous canapés and hors d'oeuvres. I don't even know why we're having this meeting. I just want to get it over with. Honestly, I wanted to go to Vegas for a quickie wedding, but Andrew is old-school." Laurie smiled the sappiest smile when she said her fiancé's name.

And why not smile? Andrew was that rare man who knew how to treat a woman with respect. He'd stepped right up when Brandon had crushed Laurie's heart. He'd protected her, wooed her, and treated her like she hung the moon. He was the exception to Arwen's theory that romance was dead in America.

Courtney was happy for Laurie. And for Willow, Amy, and Melissa, her good friends, all of whom had found wonderful men in the last few years. But she hated that sappy look her friends got when they talked about their husbands and lovers. Envy pressed down on her heart like a giant invisible millstone.

She broke eye contact and pulled forward the manila folder containing the details for the Wilson-Lyndon reception. She needed to focus on her work, but before she could open the file, Laurie said, "Forget it, Court. I have no desire to go over the details. I'm sure it will be fine, whatever you do."

Just then Amy strode into the office carrying a vase containing two dozen long-stemmed red roses. "These just arrived for you," she said, placing them on the corner of Courtney's desk. "Everyone downstairs is dying to know who they're from." Amy turned toward Laurie with a grin. "Hey, how are you feeling?"

"Okay. How about you?"

Amy held her hand out flat and wiggled it. "I throw up every morning."

"It's every evening for me."

"Wait, what?" Courtney shifted her gaze from Amy to Laurie and back again.

Laurie grinned. "It looks like Andrew and I got the cart before the horse. Amy and I have almost the same due date, which is wonderful since our babies will be first cousins."

Courtney clamped her mouth shut on the explosion of profanity that threatened to come out of it. She gave them her best imitation of a smile and then ripped the little square envelope off the roses. The writing on the card was bold and masculine and looked as if it had been executed using a blue Sharpie. Since Courtney had never seen Matt's handwriting, she had no way of knowing whether he'd written the card himself or simply dictated it to the florist. Either way, the message was cryptic. It began with a four-line poem:

Oh how much more doth beauty beauteous seem
By that sweet ornament which truth doth give!
The rose looks fair, but fairer we it deem
For that sweet odor which doth in it live.

And it ended with a one-line signature: *Tomorrow. 6:30 p.m. at the Red Fern. M.*

"Who's M?" Amy asked, shamelessly looking over Courtney's shoulder. "And what's with the flowery poetry?"

"Oh no. Not Matt. Please tell me those flowers did not come from Andrew's cousin." Laurie looked horrified.

"Oh my God, of course they did. He quotes poetry all the time. His grandmother was much the same way," Amy said as she pulled her iPhone out of her pocket. "I bet it's Shakespeare," she said as her thumbs got busy. "Aha! It *is* Shakespeare. It's from one of his sonnets." She frowned as she read. "It says here that the meaning of the first line is that beauty is more beautiful when it comes with honesty and integrity."

"Really?" Laurie said, her face paling. "Matt has balls to send Courtney something like that. Oh my God. I'm going to kill him."

"No, don't, Courtney said. "And don't worry. I've got the situation under control." Although that was debatable. The flowers were amazing. Hook-up Artists often used flowers and poetry as tools of seduction, but they usually quoted dumb lyrics from pop music. Not Shakespeare.

"How could you get involved with him?" Laurie asked.

"I'm not involved. I'm not even dating him. I'm teaching him a lesson."

Laurie collapsed back in the chair. "I'm worried about you, Court. I come in here and you're looking at sperm banks on your laptop, and then you get two dozen roses from the biggest player on the face of the planet. Do we need to stage an intervention? What the hell is this about?"

Courtney settled back in her chair. This was going to take a while to explain. "This has nothing to do with you or the way Matt behaved when you and Brandon broke up. This is about me and a truly nasty bet that Brandon and Matt made a couple of weeks ago."

Chapter Five —————

Matt had refrained from texting or calling Courtney for an entire week, a move she probably recognized as strategic. The flowers, on the other hand, were a new tactic. He had never sent flowers to a woman before, even though he understood how much women enjoyed receiving them. Flowers were part of a courtship ritual, and Matt didn't court women.

He pursued them with unabashed joy and honesty but shied away from long-term relationships. Flowers, especially red roses, suggested something permanent, and he would never have sent them to anyone other than Courtney, because she would recognize them as a ploy. She'd probably get the Shakespeare quote too.

He couldn't wait to see how she reacted.

He strolled down Liberty Avenue carrying his suit jacket over his shoulder. The warm June sun still rode high on the western horizon, casting a golden light on the broad leaves of the sycamores lining Shenandoah Falls's main street. Their shade provided welcome relief from the day's heat as Matt sucked in a deep breath filled with a dozen familiar scents: handmade waffle cones from What's the Scoop, honeysuckle growing wild and untamed on the chain-link fence surrounding the Laundromat's parking lot, and frying bacon wafting through the doors of Gracie's Diner.

Matt missed life in the big city, but Liberty Avenue had its own home-town appeal. He'd consumed hundreds of ice cream cones at What's the Scoop, pulled dozens of honeysuckle blooms from that vine, and eaten a truckload of burgers at Gracie's Diner.

He'd also dined at the Red Fern Inn more times than he cared to remember, usually with his parents or his aunts and uncles. He'd always been required to sit up straight, keep his elbows off the table, and use the right fork for each course.

The colonial-era stone building had been a tavern for almost three hundred years, serving alcohol more or less continuously since the French and Indian War. It was the very first building in Shenandoah Falls to be listed on the historic register, probably because George Washington had imbibed there, in addition to sleeping in several of the upstairs guest rooms.

The place was small, with whitewashed stone walls, dark-beamed ceilings, and a wide-planked pine floor that listed to one side. Matt put on his jacket just before he entered the taproom's cool interior. Somewhere along the line, electricity, modern plumbing, and air-conditioning had been added to the three-hundred-year-old building, and today, someone had cranked the AC down to arctic.

He checked his watch. He'd arrived exactly on time—another break from his usual MO. He gave his name to the maître d' only to discover that Courtney had arrived before him, thereby making him late. Sort of.

No, wait. He wasn't late. And maybe Courtney had only just arrived too. Maybe they'd both decided to stop playing games.

He crossed the dining room and knew a moment of disappointment when he saw the Manhattan sitting in front of her. She'd been there long enough to order a drink.

Did that mean she was anxious? Or what?

She looked up at him with an amused twinkle in her baby blues. She'd painted her lusciously sinful mouth a bright red to match the color of her dress, which clung to every curve. The subfreezing temperature in the restaurant had affected her nipples.

"Sorry I'm late," he said as he sat down at the table with its pristine white linens that he'd never failed to soil as a kid.

Her wicked mouth quirked at one corner. "You're not late. And furthermore, you know you're not late. I got here early. It's been a rough week, and I needed a drink. What's your excuse?" She nervously fiddled with the stem of her martini glass.

"My excuse for what?"

"For being on time." She took a sip of her drink and gave him a hard stare over the rim of the glass.

He smiled because he couldn't help it. Everything about Courtney Wallace turned him on. Her shiny black hair, those big, beautiful, slightly offset eyes, the mouth he wanted to kiss more than anything. But most of all, he enjoyed her attitude. She was a total pain in the ass, and for some reason, that made him want to laugh out loud.

A waiter came over with menus, and Matt ordered a Sam Adams. When the waiter left, Matt leaned forward and caught Courtney's hand where it restlessly stroked the martini glass. Her fingers felt cold under his palm. "There's something I need to tell you," he said.

She pulled her hand away, leaving his skin tingling in reaction. She cocked her head a tiny fraction, the angle just enough to align her eyes. She scrutinized him, her expression neutral and unreadable. "I'll go first with the confessions. I know all about your bet with Brandon."

Boy, she was a piece of work. He'd spent all week working himself up to a big confession, and she stole it from him before the waitstaff had delivered his first beer of the evening. "You stole my thunder. I intended to confess."

"BS. Your big, beautiful dark eyes gave away your surprise."

"You think my eyes are beautiful?" He gave her his most seductive smile. Head tilted down, no teeth showing, mouth curled a little, and eyebrow lifted just so.

She leaned back from him and nervously laughed. What was going on in that beautiful head of hers? She seemed restless and tense across the shoulders.

The waiter returned with his beer, and Courtney announced that they were ready to order. Clearly she wanted to get this date over with in a hurry. He decided right then that he would linger over dinner if for no other reason than to allow Courtney to relax. He told the waiter that he needed a few more minutes and then sent him off with an appetizer order.

"You didn't even ask if I wanted the baked brie," she said.

"If you didn't want it, you could've said something. I love the baked brie here."

"So you dine here often?"

"If you're asking me if I bring my dates here, the answer is no." He cast his gaze around the dining room, taking in the early-American furniture and the walls covered with oil paintings featuring horses, fox hunts, and a reproduction of Peale's portrait of George Washington as a young man. "This place is popular with the horsey set, but I find it just a little stuffy."

The corners of her mouth turned down. "If you think it's stuffy, why did you invite me here?"

"To surprise you."

This earned him a tiny, Mona Lisa smile. "I'm not surprised. Taking a woman to a place with white tablecloths, sending her flowers, and quoting poetry is precisely the sort of thing a player does. Although the Shakespeare was kind of classy. Of course, you might have done all that just to win a bet."

This time he gave her a real smile because she was adorable and amusing. "I never take my dates to restaurants with white tablecloths, and you are the first woman I have ever sent flowers to."

"And the poetry?"

He shrugged. "I've been known to quote Shakespeare from time to time."

She took a long sip of her Manhattan and put the glass down before she spoke again. "Why did you send me flowers?"

"To see how you'd react?"

"Not because you thought it would help you win your bet?"

He leaned forward. "The cost of the flowers and the meal will far exceed the one hundred dollars I'd win if my seduction succeeds. So how does that make any sense?"

"Because your bet with Brandon has nothing to do with money. And I only agreed to go out with you because of the bet. I guess I'm still ticked off at you for encouraging Brandon to date other women right after he dumped Laurie. But Laurie made me promise that I would end my vendetta against Brandon and come clean with you. That being the case, I think I should go. I've already paid for my drink, and I'm not really a brie fan. If you'd ordered the crab cakes, I might have been induced to stay."

She stood up, the picture of a woman in charge of herself. She took one step toward the door before he got out of his seat and stopped her, snagging her by the arm, leaning into her, and whispering in her ear. "I've been looking forward to this dinner all week. And not because of some stupid bet. Stay. We'll order crab cakes for dinner."

Should she stay? His hand on her arm felt deliciously warm and promised so much more. The fingers of his other hand captured her hair and tucked it behind her ear right before he whispered, "Please stay." His hot breath curled around her ear and sent a pulse of lust shooting to her core. She took a deep breath and might have broken away from him were it not for the fact that he smelled so good.

Not of cologne or aftershave, or even laundry detergent or soap. Matt Lyndon smelled like himself, and it was an unbelievable aphrodisiac. She turned her head a fraction and met his gaze. Why did his brown eyes always look soulful?

He didn't have one soulful bone in his body. That

look on his face was a trap, and she was just desperate enough to believe what she saw in his eyes. Leaving was probably the right thing to do, but she'd never been one to run from a fight. So she returned to her chair, determined to win this battle, even though she wasn't entirely sure what they were fighting over.

She needed something to set him back, to surprise him, the way he'd surprised her with the flowers. And then it came to her, and even though it hadn't been her idea, it was still brilliant. It would send him spinning in an unexpected direction.

She leaned forward. "I have a proposition for you," she said, a frisson of anticipation tingling her spine.

His eyebrow arched. "Proposition?"

She stared down his smoldering look even though her insides quivered with need. He employed that look as a weapon, and he knew damn well it was effective. She wasn't about to give in to it. "Not that kind of proposition...exactly."

"Exactly? What does that mean? Are you saying you want to sleep with me?"

"Well, we could do it that way."

"What?"

She hauled in a big breath and squared her shoulders. "I'm thirty-five years old, I'm not particularly a beautiful person, and I know that I'm never, ever going to get married. So I've decided to stop waiting for Mr. Right. Instead I'm going after what I want. And the truth is, I don't want you. I want your sperm. Are you willing to be a donor? I can arrange for you to go down to Fairfax Cryobank and provide a sample, or alternatively we could..."

"What? Do it the old-fashioned way? Are you out of your mind?" Everyone in the dining room turned to stare at them.

She leaned forward and placed her finger across her lips. "Shhhhh. Not so loud. And I'm not out of my mind. I'm looking for a sperm donor with deep brown eyes, you know sort of like Aston Kutcher? Your eyes fit that bill nicely. Of course, there's also your family pedigree to consider. But don't worry. I'm not looking for any kind of commitment or monetary handout, just—"

"I can't father your child." His soulful eyes looked pretty damn angry right at the moment. That look made her feel absurdly powerful for some complicated reason.

She shrugged and rolled her eyes. "I figured as much. But you can't blame me for trying. That's what I get for being honest, I guess." She stood up again. "Sorry you lost the bet. I hate when Brandon Kopp wins anything."

She stalked out of the cold dining room and into the warm June evening, but her skin seemed impervious to the heat. She didn't know whether to cry or laugh. She'd certainly taken a sledgehammer to Matt Lyndon's calm approach to seduction. Nothing like talking about babies with a man who believed that sex was invented for his own personal gratification.

And yet she couldn't shake the disappointment. Not because he'd refused to be a sperm donor. Of course he'd say no to that. She hadn't suggested it seriously. But some small part of her, the stupid romantic part, had hoped for a different reaction. Although what that might have been remained nebulous in her mind.

She'd been utterly unreasonable with him. But then again, he'd taken a bet that was completely reprehensible and slightly misogynistic. So they were even.

She headed down Liberty Avenue toward the town parking lot, where she'd left her car, a route that took her past Secondhand Prose, her friend Melissa's used bookstore. Courtney hadn't seen Melissa in two or three weeks, which was a depressing thought. All her married friends had other interests now. Hell, all her married friends were having babies. But not Melissa. Melissa had kittens.

Courtney stopped in her tracks and turned toward the bookstore's front window. A large cat tree dominated the display case. Until last autumn, the tree had been the domain of Dickens, an eighteen-year-old cat in need of a personality transplant. Dickens had followed his longtime feline companion, Hugo, across the rainbow bridge right before Thanksgiving—an event that had depressed Melissa for months because

Dickens had been the last of her grandmother's cats to pass.

Melissa had avoided adopting any new cats until a couple of months ago, when Mary Caputo, one of her grandmother's friends and a volunteer down at the Jefferson County Animal Shelter, had shamelessly guilted Melissa into fostering three orphaned kittens.

Melissa had bottle-fed Athos, Aramis, and Porthos every three hours for weeks on end. The feline babies had kept Melissa from joining Courtney and Arwen on open mic nights at the Jaybird. For a while, Courtney and Arwen had resented the little darlings who had become stand-ins for the baby Jeff and Melissa had not yet gotten around to making.

The kittens were ten weeks old now and tumbled and pounced on each other. They were the epitome of adorable, and the sign taped to the inside of the window said they were free to a good home.

Courtney stood on the hot sidewalk watching as one of the gray and white kitties jumped from the lower shelf of the cat tree onto his littermates. That one—she had no idea whether it was Athos, Aramis, or Porthos—had lots of personality and a feisty attitude. She could almost see him coming to live in her apartment.

Wait. No. She did not want a cat. She yearned for a husband and a baby and a family, but of course that was impossible. She needed to quit before that kitten wormed its way into her heart.

She'd just pulled herself away from the abundant

cuteness when the store's front door opened and Melissa came out onto the sidewalk wearing her favorite *To Kill a Mockingbird* T-shirt.

"Hey, I saw you looking at Aramis. Wanna take him home?"

Courtney felt superglued to the sidewalk as her brain started coming up with all the reasons why a cat might actually be better than a baby. She resisted, and while she battled, she noticed something odd about Melissa's shirt.

The sleeves looked a little tight under the arms, and it stretched across her front like it might bust a seam any minute. Melissa had owned that T-shirt for at least five years and wore it every week. It was old and faded and unlikely to shrink at this late date. So if the shirt was the same size, then...

Oh crap.

"You're pregnant," Courtney said. Her words were not a question.

Melissa smiled and nodded.

Matt slept poorly on Thursday night, so he was in a grumpy mood when he arrived downstairs in his parents' kitchen the next morning. Mom had once again insisted on making him scrambled eggs and bacon for breakfast. When would she catch on to the fact that he wasn't much of a breakfast eater?

"Are you okay?" she asked as he helped himself to the cup of coffee she'd poured.

"I'm fine. Why?"

She turned her back on him. "Oh, nothing. It's just that you came home so early last night."

Damn. Most people had parents who worried when they got in late. His parents not so much. It was embarrassing to have his mother so concerned about him because he'd come home from a date at 7:30 p.m. It reminded him of his high school days—a time that held zero nostalgia for him.

Matt had most definitely not been the big man on campus in his younger days. He'd had to compete with his older brother and cousins. His cousin Andrew, the Boy Scout, had chaired the debate club when Matt was a freshman. His brother Daniel, the bad boy, had starred as Nathan Detroit in the school's production of *Guys and Dolls* when Matt was a sophomore. His cousin Edward, the foreign-policy nerd, had chaired the school's Model UN team when Matt was a junior. Even his cousin Amy, who hadn't excelled academically, had outshined him in high school by virtue of her impeccable fashion sense.

What had come naturally to his family had required years of hard work for Matthew to master. Having Mom hovering over him now, shooting him pitying looks, did nothing to assuage the toxic stew of emotions that churned in his mind and unsettled his stomach, compliments of Courtney Wallace.

What the hell was she up to? Was she crazy? Desperate? Messing with him? Cruel and self-centered like Allison? Or had she been joking? He needed to know, but a sleepless night hadn't answered any of his questions. If she'd been joking, the joke had fallen flat.

But then again, Matt probably deserved an off-color joke. He should never have taken Brandon's bet.

Well, either way, he was finished chasing Courtney. A wise man would pay Brandon his one hundred dollars, walk away, and never look back.

"You know, honey," Mom said, breaking into his thoughts, "you can talk to me about stuff. I know how hard your father is on you sometimes, and—"

"I'm okay. Really."

She gave him a skeptical look.

He needed to cut this cord. Now. Or she'd drive him insane. "Mom, you know how much I appreciate that you and Dad have let me stay here the last few weeks, but I think I need to find a place of my own."

"Hallelujah," she said, her eyes lighting up. "I thought the day would never come."

What the hell? "You're okay with that?"

"Of course I am. In fact, let me help you find a place. I'll call your Uncle Jamie's real estate person and get you a list of apartments. Would that be okay?"

He ground his teeth. Would she never stop holding his hand? "You know, Mom, I can probably find a place on my—"

"It's no problem. Let me do the first search, weed

out the unacceptable ones, and then you can look at options."

He begrudgingly agreed to this plan, mostly because she wouldn't take no for an answer. And then he finished his coffee and made a beeline to the office before she could start planning other parts of his life.

Twenty minutes after he'd arrived at work, Arwen strolled into his office, made herself comfortable in his single side chair, and asked, "So, how was your date last night? To be honest, I was impressed that you asked her out to a nice restaurant."

He leaned forward on his elbows. "Did she send you here to ask that question?"

Arwen straightened in her chair, clearly surprised. "Of course not. I'm here for our pre-meeting before Leslie Heath arrives."

"Oh yeah. I forgot. Well, if you want to know how it went, ask her." He practically snarled the words.

Arwen studied him intently for a long moment with a stare that penetrated him, and not in a good way. A slow smile curved her lips. "She scored points last night, didn't she? God, she's good."

He frowned. "Good at what? Being outrageous? Man bashing?"

"What did she do?"

"I'm not going to discuss it," he said, shooting the words like bullets. He paused a moment, leaning back in his chair, reconsidering. "It was Ryan who told her about the bet, wasn't it?" he asked.

"You and Brandon need to be careful when you shoot the breeze at the Jaybird. Juni is always listening, and so is Ryan. Juni is the biggest gossip in Shenandoah Falls, and when it comes to Courtney, Ryan is definitely overprotective."

"Overprotective how? Are they together?"

Arwen shrugged. "You need to ask Courtney that question."

"You don't know?"

She shook her head. "I don't think they're together. But sometimes I think Courtney might be willing to settle for Ryan or something. They're friends. Now, can we change the subject, please?"

"Okay, but you're the one who asked about the date." He smiled.

She nodded. "Point taken. But we need to focus. Leslie is going to be here in ten minutes, and we have nothing useful to tell her."

That was the indisputable truth.

The landlord, facing fines he couldn't afford to pay, had sold Dogwood Estates to GB Ventures LLC, an Arlington, Virginia, company that had been building single-family housing developments all over the county. The tenants would probably receive eviction notices before the summer was out. Everything LL&K had done for the tenants had come to absolutely nothing.

Worse than nothing. Instead of getting the complex cleaned up, the tenants would be losing their homes.

"You know," Matt said, "that old guy, Sid, was right. Maybe we shouldn't have gone to the county and urged them to rattle the landlord's cage. It backfired on those people."

"You may be right. But if we'd done nothing, those people would continue to live in housing that's not safe."

"I know. But here's the thing. Which is worse? Living in a low-rent apartment in need of repair or being evicted and unable to find alternative living arrangements? I feel like we ought to help those people find new homes."

"You know, Matt, the first rule of doing pro bono work is not to get emotionally involved. Trust me on this. These cases can break your heart."

"What if we sued the county?"

Arwen's frown appeared right on schedule. "On what grounds?"

He shrugged, winging it. "I don't know. Unconstitutional taking of property?"

She snorted a laugh. "You're insane. How did the county unconstitutionally take anyone's property?"

He leaned back in his chair and stroked his chin for a moment. "It's a big stretch, but maybe we could argue that by imposing fines on Scott Anderson that he couldn't possibly pay, the county essentially took his land away. Will the new owner have to pay the fines?"

Arwen blinked. "I don't know. I assume GB Ventures won't have to pay any fines since they'll be tearing down the apartments. But that's just a guess."

"Can you find out?"

Arwen nodded. "Okay, I'll take a look, but I think you're crazy." She gave him a big, genuine smile. "But it's a good kind of insanity."

Chapter Six ————————

Courtney's phone rang early on Monday morning, pulling her out of a deep sleep. She rose on one elbow and checked the caller ID. It was Lisa Brigs, Dr. Lamborn's nurse practitioner and one of Courtney's work colleagues back in the day when she'd been a nurse. She accepted the call.

"Hey. What's up?"

"Sid Miller's in the hospital," Lisa said. "He went to the emergency room with chest pains last night. It looks like he needs bypass surgery, but he's being stubborn. I thought maybe you could visit him, help change his mind."

Damn him. Courtney regarded Sid like family. It hurt that he hadn't called her. "I'm on it. And Lisa, thanks for calling."

Half an hour later, Courtney marched into Sid's hospital room, ready to read him the riot act, only to find him lying in his hospital bed with his eyes closed, looking frail and slightly gray. Her heart twisted in her chest, and she swallowed the ball of emotion that clogged her throat. She couldn't lose Sid, not after she'd lost Mom and Dad. Not after she and Sid had lost Barbara last year, following a long, expensive battle with cancer.

"When were you going to tell me about these chest pains?" she asked in a hushed voice as she gripped the bed's railing.

Sid cracked one bright blue eye. "Go away." His eyelid shut.

"No. And what's this I hear about you telling Dr. Lamborn that you don't want the bypass operation?"

Sid said nothing, but Courtney could tell he wasn't asleep. She pulled up the chair and settled into it. "I've got all day to wait. I don't work on Mondays."

"What's the point?" Sid rolled his head toward Courtney and opened his eyes.

"What do you mean, what's the point?"

"I mean that I'm ready to go."

Courtney's heart slammed against her ribs. "No. You're still young. You have a lot of life left. I won't let you give up."

"Courtney, girl, I love your grit," he said on a long, tired breath. "But I ain't got much to look forward to. Medicare will pay eighty percent for this operation, but where am I gonna get the rest of the money? Besides, Barbara's gone. Your mom and dad are gone. The hardware store is gone. And pretty soon the rat hole apartment building I'm living in will be sold right from under my ass. Where will I go then?"

"Sid, we'll find the money for this operation. And we'll find someplace for you to live. As for the rest of your life, haven't I told you dozens of times that I could get you a part-time job working for Dusty Mc-Neil's guide service? He's about to open Shenandoah River Guides, and he needs guys like you who know the fishing in the Shenandoah and Potomac watersheds. Wouldn't you love to have a job that got you out on the river as a guide?"

"I won't take no charity."

Courtney tried not to roll her eyes in frustration. She and Sid had been through this many times before. Sid's interest in life had disappeared with Barbara's death, and it was pointless to argue him out of his depression and grief.

So she changed the subject. "Arwen told me about the tenants association's battle with your landlord, but I didn't think you were being evicted."

Sid looked away and shook his head. "We haven't been. Yet. But Leslie got a boatload of bad legal advice from Lyndon, Lyndon & Kopp that blew right up in her face. Honestly, that useless law firm sent two of those Lyndon boys out, and neither one of them knew their asses from holes in the ground."

Suddenly intrigued, Courtney asked, "Oh? What did they do?"

"Well, the first feller—Andrew—thought he could *negotiate* with the landlord. Ha, that's a laugh! Scott Anderson is an SOB. He wasn't ever going to *negotiate*. And then they sent his brother or cousin or whatever—Matthew." He shook his head. "What an idiot. That boy thought Anderson would jump right to it and fix the place up when the county fined him."

Arwen had mentioned the fact that Sid had argued with Matt, but she didn't quite understand what Sid was so upset about. It seemed totally reasonable to think that something good might come as a result of county intervention.

"Why shouldn't Matt have been happy about that?" she asked.

Sid rolled his head and gave her a hard, probing stare. "You know Matthew Lyndon?"

Damn it all, why did her face get hot? "I've met him."

"Honey, by the pink in your cheeks, you've done more than meet him. I figure you're a grown woman, so I'm not going to give you a lecture."

"You know, Sid, I *am* a grown woman, and when you get to be my age and you're still living alone, you start to think about throwing caution to the wind."

"Girl, I just don't understand it. You're a smart, capable woman with a pretty nice figure. I think maybe sometimes you're a little too picky when it comes to fellers."

"Sid, let me ask you something. When you asked Barbara to marry you, were you settling? Or was she Ms. Right?"

His eyes lit up, and a dreamy smile softened his thin lips. "I fell in love with Barbara the first time I saw her—you know that."

She nodded. She'd heard the story many times, about how Sid and Dad had gone out to dinner and serendipitously met Barbara and Mom. If her parents and Sid were to be believed, love at first sight had simultaneously occurred for both of them. She idly wondered if anyone fell in love at first sight anymore.

"You hang in there, girl. You'll find a nice feller one day."

Time to get back to the main subject. "Yes, Sid, I will. And when that happens, I expect you to dance at my wedding. So, you listen to me," she said in her best take-charge, wedding-planner voice. "I'm going to go down to the nurses' station and get the consent forms, and you're going to sign them. I don't want to lose you, Sid."

"But where am I going to live?" His voice sounded strained. Clearly his living situation was a big worry, but she didn't quite understand why he thought he'd be losing his apartment. It sounded as if LL&K was doing everything they could to get the landlord to clean up the place.

She didn't want to argue with him though. So she patted his shoulder. "Look, while you're recovering, you're going to move into my spare bedroom. Okay? I'm a nurse. I'll take good care of you."

"I can't do that. What if your feller comes along? You'll need privacy."

"We'll cross that bridge when we get to it. And frankly, it's highly unlikely ever to happen. By the way, are you allergic to cats?"

Courtney spent most of the day at the Winchester Medical Center, making sure Sid signed his consent papers and talking with his doctors. She got back home in the late afternoon and planned to spend some quality time with Aramis, her new kitten. But the moment she walked into the apartment, the cat scrambled under the bed and behaved as if Courtney were a depraved cat killer.

The cat's rejection was the last straw. She refused to let a tiny kitten push her over the edge into a crying jag. So she put down a can of gourmet cat food, checked the litter box and water dish, and then headed off to the Jaybird Café. If Aramis wanted alone time, she was happy to give it to him.

When Courtney arrived at the Jaybird, she found Ryan Pierce sitting in his usual seat at the end of the bar drinking a Coke. She halted a moment, studying him. He had regular features, a strong jaw, and a buzz cut that branded him as ex-military. If she were going to settle, Ryan might be a good choice, but settling for Ryan might be dangerous unless she understood his demons.

Ryan also didn't make her heartstrings zing. She'd never met anyone who'd done that, even though she'd met quite a few men who'd awakened her girl parts, Matthew Lyndon chief among them.

She took the seat next to Ryan, and an instant later, Rory put a Manhattan in front of her. "Thanks, man. I really needed this."

"Rough day?" Ryan asked.

"You know it's bad when you're a single woman and the cat you adopt hates you."

Ryan had the temerity to chuckle.

She rounded on him. "It's not funny." She turned away and took a swig of her drink.

"I think it's hilarious. What did you do? Get a wild cat?"

Her glass *thunked* when she put it down. "No. I adopted one of the kittens from Melissa's storefront. His name is Aramis."

"Aramis? Like the cologne?"

"No, like the Musketeer. Honestly, Ryan, you should read more."

"When you brought the cat home, did you put him in the bathroom?" This advice had been said in a deep, soft voice that traveled through Courtney's eardrums and down her spine. She turned on her barstool to find Matt Lyndon, wearing suit pants and a white oxford-cloth, button-down shirt with the top button undone and a red and gray striped tie loosened. Boy, he sure had the Brooks Brothers preppy look nailed.

With all that eye candy to enjoy, Courtney momentarily lost her train of thought. What had she been talking about? Oh yeah, the cat. "Why would I put the cat in the bathroom?"

"To give it time to adjust. A new cat should always be left in a small room or the bathroom for a few days with its litter box, food, and water. It's less scary for them that way."

She blinked at Matthew for a long moment. "How did you become an expert on cats?"

He shrugged. "I've always had a cat. Well, except for the last couple of years. I was living in a pet-free house with several allergic roommates."

Somehow this detail about Matthew didn't fit. Hook-up Artists didn't have cats. Having a cat required commitment, and players wanted to be free of all encumbrances. The shock of this discovery left her speechless.

Matt gave her a slow, sexy smile. "So is this your first cat?"

His question was simple, and yet Courtney thought she heard some kind of double entendre. Was he laughing at her because of the ridiculous question she'd asked him the other night? Or was he laughing at her because she was so desperate that she'd gotten a cat? "Yes, it's my first cat."

His smile widened, and a three-alarm fire started in her core. "You know, Courtney, I distinctly remember you telling me that you had a cat. It was the day Brandon left Laurie at the altar. I think you lied to me."

Damn. She had lied to him. He'd been trying to pick her up, and she'd been leading him on a merry chase. "Guilty as charged," she said. "But now I have become one of those single women committed to her cat."

"Congratulations," Matt said as Rory placed a Sam Adams in front of him. Matt hadn't even ordered the drink.

The implications were earth-shattering. Matt was becoming a Jaybird regular.

She'd have to find some other place for cocktails, which would be difficult since only the Red Fern Inn and the Jaybird were within walking distance of her apartment. She stared down at her half-finished drink. She should never have come here tonight. Tomorrow was going to be a long day at the hospital. She should go home, capture Aramis, and put him in the bathroom.

No, wait. Why should she believe Matt about cats anyway? He was probably giving her a load of BS. The need to lash out overwhelmed her.

She turned toward him. "Did you really think that getting the county government involved would help the people living at Dogwood Estates?"

His eyes widened. "How do you know about that?"

"Sid Miller is a friend of mine."

His frown deepened, but he said nothing.

"You don't even know who Sid is, do you? For the record, he's a great guy who's fallen on some tough luck. And now he's in the hospital, and he's all upset about losing his apartment." Her voice wobbled.

Matt nodded. "I remember Sidney Miller very well, Courtney. He ripped me a new one the first time I met him."

"He told me that LL&K messed things up for the tenants at Dogwood Estates."

Matt took a long sip of beer and put his glass down carefully. "It's quite possible that we did. It's also quite possible that the situation at Dogwood Estates was never going to end well for the people living there. I don't know yet."

"You don't know yet?"

"I'm working on a theory, but I can't talk about it. It's way out there, and it will probably fail, but I'm as ticked off as you are about what's happened to those people."

Whoa, wait a sec. Who was this guy? Had an alien race snatched Matt Lyndon and replaced him with someone nicer? Or had she missed something?

Deep in the guarded part of her heart, hope awakened. Courtney wanted to push that feeling away, but it was too late. Somehow, in the blink of an eye, she'd started to see Matt in an entirely new light.

Chapter Seven ————————————

Matt's mother threw herself into his apartment search with a gusto that was surprising. Did Mom want him out of the house that badly? Or was she just looking for something new to occupy her time?

He didn't know. But either way she scored a great place on Rice Street within walking distance of the office.

The apartment building had been built in the early 1900s and had once housed a dry goods store on the ground floor. A decade ago, JL Properties, Uncle Jamie's real estate business, had renovated the building, turning it into four apartments, two on the first floor and two on the second story, each of which had New Orleans–style wrought-iron balconies.

He and Mom toured the apartment on Monday

morning, and Matt signed the lease that same after-noon. He was grateful for all her help until she said the words "interior decorator" right after the leasing agent handed him his keys.

"We'll have to get someone in to measure the rooms," she said as they left the leasing office. "I should call Pam. She has a wonderful decorator who did Andrew's apartment for him."

"I don't want a decorator."

"Of course you do, sweetie. You're a grown-up person now, and you need a grown-up apartment."

What he needed was to be left alone to figure things out for himself. Also, while he had a nice trust fund, he didn't want to spend any of it on interior decoration. That struck him as a big waste of money.

All he needed was a comfortable bed, a couch and chairs, and a dining table. And a big-screen television—the biggest he could find.

And a cat. He needed a cat to make it all perfect.

He decided not to argue with his mother. After all, she'd done a great job finding him a place he loved. Instead, he figured he could always talk to Dad and ask him to ask Mom to back off. Hadn't Dad always told him to invest the money he'd inherited from Granny Artzen? Furniture and fancy curtains wouldn't give him any return on his money.

But on Tuesday after work, Mom had a tizzy when she discovered him carrying one of his boxes of Batman comics out to the pickup truck he'd bor-rowed from Uncle Jamie.

"What are you doing?" she asked.

"I'm moving stuff to the new place."

"You can't do that. We need to have it decorated first."

"Mom, look, I don't want to spend a lot of money—"

"No, no, I don't expect you to pay for it. Let me do this for you."

Damn, she had him over a barrel, but he needed to exert his independence. "I really appreciate what you want to do for me, but I don't want to spend a ton of money decorating an apartment I might not be living in for long. And besides, I need a place of my own. I don't want to wait to move. I already adopted a cat from Melissa and Jeff, and I bought a mattress and a bed frame. They were delivered earlier this afternoon. So…"

Her face fell, leaving him feeling like a complete jerk. He hated it when Mom's eyes got all misty like that. He blew out a breath. "Okay, maybe you can help a little. But no professional decorator, okay?"

Her smile reappeared. "Don't you worry," she said. "I know exactly the look you want."

Oh boy, that didn't sound good. Who wanted their mother to decorate their apartment? No one. But instead of arguing, he ground his teeth together and continued hauling boxes of books and crap out to his uncle's truck. He didn't relax his jaw until he drove down his parents' driveway and headed off to the new apartment.

It took exactly two trips hauling stuff up the narrow staircase in the June heat while simultaneously dodging a collection of bikes and kid toys scattered around the building's front door, to make him wonder if he should have looked at a few more places. The balcony was killer, but so was the staircase and the obstacle course.

On his third trip, the owner of the toys, a scrawny freckled-face kid of about eight whose front teeth were a little too big for his mouth, materialized at his side. "You moving into Mrs. Murphy's apartment?" he asked.

"Is Mrs. Murphy's apartment the one on the right at the top of the stairs?"

The boy nodded. "Yup, that's the one. She died there, you know. The police had to carry her out in a bag." The kid had the temerity to grin. "That was pretty cool."

Holy crap. Mom hadn't told him about that. Did she know?

Despite his surprise, Matt took a seat on one of the steps and maintained his composure for the little kid. "That *is* kinda cool," he said, putting on his best fake-'em-out smile. He knew this kid. He was exactly like Matt's older brother, a gross-out artist who loved to poke at people. Matt had learned early in life never to show any weakness.

The kid's eyes grew round. "You don't care that someone died in the apartment?"

"No. Why should I?"

"Mom says Mrs. Murphy's ghost is still up there." The kid was clearly making this up. He hoped.

"Cool." Matthew broadened his smile and held out his hand. "My name's Matt, and you are?"

"Ethan Riley. I live over there." He pointed over his shoulder to the larger ground-floor apartment. "I have a little sister, Jessica."

Matt had already figured this out, since a *Dora the Explorer* tricycle was blocking the hallway and Ethan didn't look like the *Dora the Explorer* type.

"Well, Ethan, it's been nice talking to you. But I got stuff to haul up to the second floor."

He went back to work, making two more trips from the truck to the apartment while Ethan chattered at him. Eventually the boy's mother called him in and apologized profusely for the toys in the hall. She introduced herself as Alyssa, and she had the look of a harried working mother who was keeping it together only through sheer force of will. She yelled at Ethan for his toys and then helped him move the bikes out of the entryway.

After that, the hauling went a little faster, but still, by the time he'd carried up his last load, his T-shirt was soaked with sweat. He dropped the box in the middle of his living room just as the thump of footsteps on the stairs reached him through his open door. Damn. Ethan had come back.

"Ethan, didn't your mother tell you it was time to go home?" he said as he stepped into the hall.

The footsteps on the stairs stopped. "You," a distinctly female voice said.

Matt's mouth nearly dropped open at the sound of that voice. Courtney Wallace stood three steps from the top of the staircase with a couple of grocery sacks in her arms and her hair piled on top of her head in a messy knot. Sweat-dampened tendrils fell around her ears, and her breasts swelled above the neckline of her skimpy striped T-shirt. She was delicious, and he was suddenly very, very hungry.

Matt gave her a slow smile. "Me," he responded.

She finished walking up the stairs and peeked through his open door. "Are you moving into Mrs. Murphy's apartment?"

"If you mean this apartment"—he pointed at the open door—"then the answer is yes."

"This is a joke, right?"

He shook his head. "Nope."

"Did you choose this apartment because you knew I lived here?"

He leaned against the doorframe and crossed his arms over his chest. "I didn't know you lived here. But now that I do, I can't say I'm disappointed." He would never, ever tell her that his mother had picked this apartment for him.

"But you walked me home once, remember? Back in September?"

"Vaguely," he lied. Matt remembered the night last fall when he'd walked her home from the Jaybird. It was the same night that Courtney and some of her girlfriends had tried to trash Brandon's Camaro. Courtney had been more than a little tipsy, but maybe not tipsy enough. Not that he would have taken advantage of her in that state. Even drunk, Courtney had rebuffed his advances. He'd been more than a little disappointed.

She pressed her lips together, obviously annoyed. "Welcome to the building," she said in a tone that was anything but welcoming. She turned her back on him and jammed her keys into the lock.

When she opened the door, a tiny fur-covered ball of energy scampered through the threshold and raced across the landing and directly into Matt's apartment.

"Hey! Come back here." Courtney dropped her groceries and followed the kitten. "Aramis, what's the deal?" she said as she chased the cat into a corner of the living room, where it arched its back and hissed while simultaneously raising its hackles and fluffing its tail.

Matt strolled up to Courtney and gently placed his hands on her shoulders. She stiffened, but whether out of surprise or sexual awareness he couldn't tell. Her bones felt small under his hands, and she smelled delicious. He longed to place one kiss on the nape of her neck, but he resisted. Instead he gently moved her aside and let go.

"I can handle this," he said, hunkering down. "Hey, kitty, kitty," he said in a high voice guaranteed to attract the cat.

The kitten sat down and looked away for a moment and then made a show of washing himself behind the ears. After a minute, Aramis turned and walked with as much grace as a kitten could have toward Matt's outstretched hand. He scooped the furball up and scratched him behind the ears. Aramis rewarded him with a deep-throated purr that was almost too big for such a tiny kitten.

"I have a surprise for you, buddy," he said as he crossed the room to the bathroom door. Your brother's here." He opened the door, squatted down, and let the kitten go. Aramis scampered forward with a couple of loud meows and then pounced on Porthos, who'd been napping.

"You got a cat?" Courtney asked from behind.

Matt stood up, closed the bathroom door, and then leaned back on the doorframe. "Is there something wrong with a guy having a cat?"

Courtney's big blue eyes widened with a look that was so sexy it almost melted Matt where he stood. "No. I'm just surprised about you having a cat."

"I told you before, I've always had cats. The first thing I did after I signed the lease was visit the bookstore and adopt Porthos. Although I'm going to change his name. I was thinking of calling him Shredder, after the Teenage Mutant Ninja Turtles villain. Although, if I'm going to have two cats, I'll have to rethink. Maybe I'll name them both for members of the League of Justice."

"Two cats?"

He made a great show of shrugging. "Clearly Aramis likes it better over here."

The muscles along her jaw tensed. What was it about Courtney Wallace? He enjoyed teasing her, which was a little perverse, because he never teased or lied or played games.

"Okay, fine. But in my opinion, single guys with cats are kind of creepy." Courtney turned and started for the door.

"You know, Courtney, maybe you should stop reading *Cosmo*."

She whirled around to face him. "What's that supposed to mean?"

He pushed away from the doorframe. "Just that you have this tendency to put men into judgmental boxes, like some wild-eyed feminist. I'm all for feminism, but I draw the line when women try to shame men for stupid stuff. I've seen the magazine articles with ten reasons why dating a guy with a cat is a big mistake. But it's an idiotic meme."

"Well, for the record, I don't read *Cosmo*."

"Okay, but can we agree that it's a stupid meme?"

"Sure. When you give me back my cat." And with that, she turned and marched from his new apartment with her delicious hips swaying.

He ought to give the cat back, but he decided on the spot to keep Aramis and give him a super-manly name like Ra's al Ghul, the leader of the League of Assassins in the Batman comics.

It didn't take Arwen long to determine that Jefferson County had waived the fines once GB Ventures purchased Dogwood Estates. It made sense, since the buildings would be torn down. But something about the situation bugged Arwen.

So she spent three days at the county courthouse looking up deed records and matching them up with fines assessed by the Jefferson County building inspector. A troubling pattern emerged: Over the last eighteen months, the number of fines had increased threefold. And yet revenue from fines was down over the same period because the landowners were selling out instead of paying up. GB Ventures appeared to be the main beneficiary, snapping up the land at bargain-basement prices.

The properties in question were old, falling-down eyesores. Most folks in Jefferson County would probably see no problem with getting rid of them. But to Arwen, the pattern suggested an abuse of government power. And since only one company seemed to be buying up these properties, Arwen smelled a rat.

Was the County Council engaged in some kind of graft that involved GB Ventures? She didn't know. But it was troubling enough for her to compile her findings and put it all in a memo, which she planned to share with Matt on Thursday morning.

But right now, at the end of a long day, Arwen

just wanted to forget the ugliness she'd unearthed by spending the evening at the Jaybird's Wednesday open mic.

She wasn't planning to perform tonight, and she was having supper all by herself since all her married friends were pregnant and suffering from morning sickness that lasted all day, and Courtney was at the hospital with Sid. She sat at the bar, nursing a margarita and listening to Kent Henderson play "Tennessee Stud" for the umpteenth time.

"A penny for your thoughts?" Rory said as he dried glasses behind the bar and hung them in the slots above.

"I'm trying not to think at all," she said.

Rory gave her a wicked grin. "I can arrange that, lass."

What a shame he was working tonight. If he'd been another customer, she might have flirted with him. "I've already got my margarita, thanks."

"I was thinking of something a bit more mellow."

"You know, Rory, I'm not actually looking for mellow."

His eyes twinkled with devilry. "Then what are you looking for?"

She let go of a long sigh. "I'm looking for a man who's sensitive, who listens to my music, who knows how to French kiss, and who doesn't smell like marijuana." She stopped as she studied his incredibly handsome face. "And I'm not willing to settle for three out of four."

His smile deepened. "And just how do you know that I can French kiss?"

He certainly had her there. She stared into his eyes for a long, uncomfortable moment, imagining how his mouth would taste, how his stubble would feel against her cheek, how he'd really smell. No. She wasn't brave enough, or insane enough, for a man like Rory Ahearn. So she looked down at her drink and fervently hoped he would move down the bar and talk to someone else.

"I've got a break coming up in five minutes. When Kent's done boring us to tears." He delivered this line and then moved down the bar.

Thank God.

A moment later, Juni Petersen, who'd been talking to the sound engineer, crossed the room and snagged a seat next to Arwen.

"Drinking alone?" she asked.

"Yeah. I guess it's pathetic, huh? The truth is, Courtney is at the hospital visiting a sick friend, and everyone else is pregnant and throwing up."

"Well, you know what they say..."

"No. What do they say?" Her voice sounded a little bitchy even to her own ears.

Juni chuckled. *"To everything there is a season, and a time to every purpose under heaven."*

Arwen almost spewed her drink. When she caught her breath, she said, "Since when do you quote the Old Testament? Now that I think of it, I've never heard you quote the New Testament either."

Juni shrugged. "Yeah, but I hear a lot of folk music. You'd be amazed how many people cover that song on open mic night."

"Oh yeah, I guess. And you decided to quote it because...?"

"Because you're at a crossroads. I can see it in your aura. You know what you want, but you're afraid to go after it."

"And you see that in my aura?"

Juni lifted her shoulders, and her hand-knit shawl fell down around her arms. "I've known you for a long time. You come in here every week and sing your heart out. Your songs move everyone, Arwen, unlike most of the other performers. I hear you talk about making a tape and sending it to Nashville. I hear you talk about trying to make it as a songwriter. I see you looking at Rory like you want to devour him. And you never do anything about any of it. I don't need to look at your aura. Although I see plenty of murky brown in it, which is a sign of someone who's afraid to let go or to truly share herself with others."

"You know, Juni, you can pontificate all you want, but it's not so easy to let go of a well-paying job. I mean, writing songs is probably not going to pay the bills."

"Or maybe it will. You didn't learn to walk without falling down. In fact, everything valuable in life usually comes with failure. Just saying." Juni hopped down from the stool and spoke directly to Rory. "It's time for your break. I'll take over the bar."

Rory nodded and shot Arwen a look that made her panties ignite. Then he turned his back on her and headed across the bar toward the ready room. She studied his sexy-as-sin backside as Juni's words percolated through her brain. Was she woman enough to follow him?

Damn straight she was.

She snatched up her glass and gulped down the rest of her margarita. Then, filled with Dutch courage, she followed Rory and found him out in the alley leaning on the brick wall under the lone streetlamp. Shadows hid his deep-set eyes, but Arwen was more interested in looking at his wide shoulders and narrow hips and the beautiful tattoos winding up his arms.

She walked right up to him, close enough to catch his aroma, one-part leather, one-part smoke.

Good thing she didn't have to ask for what she wanted. She might have chickened out, but Rory made the first move, closing the gap between them, cupping the back of her head, and drawing her into the most erotic kiss she had ever experienced in her life.

Damn. The bad boy really did know how to French kiss.

Chapter Eight————

Courtney was so busy the rest of the week visiting Sid before and after work that she managed to avoid running into her new next-door neighbor. She also didn't have any chance to miss the cat.

Which was pathetic. It suggested that she was unlovable or something.

Not only had Aramis run away, but Sid had rebuffed her every effort to get him to move in during his convalescence. He'd sailed through the bypass surgery and would be released from the hospital on Sunday. But he insisted on going home, and arguing with him only raised his blood pressure.

So she'd given up on that idea. She planned to arrange for a visiting nurse to drop by his apartment a couple of times a day, and she'd make sure he got a good dinner every night, compliments of Antonin.

Even if Sid didn't love her enough to move in with her, Courtney still cared about him. She would not let him retreat from the world of the living. Just as soon as Sid was feeling better, Courtney intended to ask Dusty McNeil to hire him as a part-time fishing guide at Shenandoah River Guides.

But before she could accomplish all that, she needed to get through today—another Saturday in June, the day of Laurie and Andrew's wedding. Courtney would be shorthanded today because Amy was a bridesmaid in her brother's wedding. Willow would be a guest at the wedding too, since David was a member of the family.

Willow and Amy would see to the details at the church, leaving Courtney to handle a smaller afternoon wedding in the gazebo while simultaneously overseeing the setup for Andrew and Laurie's large reception in the Carriage House this evening. Thank goodness Laurie and Andrew had decided on simple decorations. Laurie had expended all her bridal angst on her first, disastrous wedding, so she was going with white tablecloths and summer flowers this time around. The arrangements arrived without mishap, and the crystal vases filled with hydrangeas, phalaenopsis orchids, and calla lilies gave the room a slightly vintage feel.

When 4:00 p.m. came and went without any frantic phone calls, Courtney breathed a tiny sigh of relief. Andrew and Laurie were supposed to say their vows precisely at 4:00 p.m. Apparently no one had been left at the altar this time.

At 4:55 p.m., the first limousine pulled up to Eagle Hill Manor's portico. The groom emerged, wearing a traditional black tuxedo, and then turned and helped his bride out of the car. Laurie had wisely decided not to retread the A-line wedding dress she'd worn two times before—for both of her failed wedding attempts with Brandon. This time around, she wore a ball gown with a creamy ivory lace bodice and a flowing satin and tulle skirt. The dress was killer, but the most beautiful thing about Laurie was the happy smile she gave to her new husband.

If only...Courtney sighed, and then stomped on the stupid, romantic thought.

After all these years, she needed to accept that she wasn't built for romance. Maybe what Matt had said was true. She was too jaded. Too cynical. Too ready to judge. At thirty-five, she was also too old to change.

Within minutes, the rest of the wedding party arrived, and Courtney ushered them through the lobby to the back lawn, where the photographer proceeded to take a million photographs of the happy couple with the gazebo in the background. Wedding guests arrived soon after, and Courtney was too busy to think about much except taking care of all the small details.

It wasn't until hours later—after the cocktail hour, the dinner, the toasts, and the cake, when the DJ had cranked the volume on the dance music—that Courtney finally took a break. She snagged a chair at one of the outside tables on the terrace and shucked off her shoes for a moment.

The June night was perfect in every way, balmy with a small breeze and not as humid as it had been the last few days. The twinkle lights over the terrace coupled with the votive candles on every table cast a warm, happy light on the handful of couples who had escaped from the loud music inside and now sat together speaking in low voices.

The setting was so romantic, and the ache in Courtney's heart returned. It seemed like the whole world had paired up into couples, and here she sat alone, with her shoes off and her back aching. Why did she do it? Why did she spend her days creating this fantasy over and over again?

She leaned back in the chair and tried to find a comfortable position. She closed her eyes listening to the muffled sound of the dance music.

"There you are."

Courtney startled at the sound of Willow's voice. Her boss looked radiant in her Audrey Hepburn–inspired brown and cream polka-dot party dress as she sat down at the table. "The wedding was lovely," Willow said. "And it's wonderful to finally see Laurie so happy."

"Well, you know what they say—third time's the

charm." Courtney did nothing to hide the cynicism in her tone.

Willow cocked her head to one side. "You want to tell me what's bugging you? You've been grumpy for days."

"Aside from Sid Miller being ill, I'd say my biggest problem is that a lothario seduced my cat."

"What? And since when do you have a cat?"

"I adopted one of Melissa's kittens, but it didn't go well. Honestly, I'm a dud as a spinster."

Willow laughed.

"It's not funny."

"Sorry, but it is...kind of. Since when do you buy into stereotypes?"

"Good point. I guess I fell for the whole single-women-and-cats thing. Imagine my surprise when the Hook-up Artist next door turned out to be a cat whisperer."

"The Hook-up Artist next door?"

"Matt moved into poor Mrs. Murphy's place next door. I haven't had the heart to tell him that the woman died there and wasn't discovered for a day and a half. But I'm thinking about it. You think it would scare him off?"

"Matt?"

Courtney nodded. "He seduced my cat. And here I've been laboring under the false assumption that single men who had cats were...well, not very hot."

"You think Matt is hot?" Willow leaned in.

Damn. She'd said too much. She blew out a sigh.

"Okay, I confess. I find him attractive. I know he's too young for me. I know he's a player. Do not give me a lecture. But the man's easy on the eye. And the whole thing has thrown me for a loop."

Willow leaned back in her chair, the lights twinkling in her eyes. "You have a crush on Matthew Lyndon."

Courtney groaned and then dropped her head to the table, where she thumped it, not so gently, several times. "Yeah," she said, "and it makes me feel exactly like I did in high school that time I crushed on Ben Katz. You remember what happened when he found out?"

"No. I can't say that I do."

"He called me a pimple freak right out loud in the middle of the lunchroom. He made me cry."

"Oh, honey." Willow reached out and squeezed her shoulder.

"You were always the one person who never seemed to notice," Courtney said. "Everyone else would try to be helpful and say stuff like 'You'll grow out of it' or recommend dermatologists. But you ignored it. If I never said thank you before, let me say it now."

"You're welcome. You were a fabulous lab partner in tenth grade. We aced every single lab assignment, which was a miracle considering my lack of aptitude for all things STEM-related. So if I never said thank you before, let me say it now." Willow paused a moment. "But, honey, this is not tenth grade."

"I know. Which makes it doubly pathetic."

"Well, if I were you, I'd go find Matt and tell him to return your cat."

"Maybe I'm not cut out to be a crazy cat lady."

Willow chortled. "I'm sure you're not. But that doesn't mean you can't have a cat."

"Good point."

"Just don't create a scene, okay? Laurie deserves a wedding completely unmarred by any sort of drama."

Matt was seated at Dad's table. This meant he had to endure his father's endless shop talk during the wedding reception. That might have been much more interesting if Matt felt comfortable raising the issues Arwen had discovered during her research into the fines levied on Scott Anderson. Her memo had been sitting in Matt's desk drawer for several days. He wanted to do something about it, but he didn't know exactly what.

Raising the issue with Dad was a waste of time. His father wasn't interested in the firm's pro bono cases. For the most part, those cases were all losers— both legally and financially. And besides, the Dogwood Estates case was pretty much a done deal. The apartments had been sold, and the residents would eventually be evicted.

Arwen's memo had nothing to do with Dogwood Estates, per se. She'd uncovered potential wrongdoing within the county government, but it wasn't the firm's job to police the government.

So he sat and smiled and listened to his father talk like the good son Dad wanted. His butt was numb by the time Mom finally intervened and literally demanded that Dad dance with her.

Finally free, Matt wandered off to the bar for a beer and then skirted the room looking for Courtney Wallace. He'd seen her a few times, dressed in her little black dress. And he was looking forward to proverbially tugging her pigtails. When he couldn't find her, he strolled out onto the terrace, coming to a stop when he saw Willow and Courtney deep in conversation.

Over the last few days, he'd knocked on Courtney's apartment door several times, but she always seemed to be out. What the hell was she up to? Going out with all of her Match.com daily matches? Checking out potential sperm donors? What?

He wanted to know.

And that desire threw him for a loop. What was happening to him? Was he turning into the nosy next-door neighbor?

He hung back in the shadows, waiting until Willow got up and walked away before he headed in Courtney's direction. But he didn't get far before Brandon Kopp came stumbling down the walkway from Eagle Hill Manor's main building. His shuffling gait said it all. The guy was drunk out of his mind.

Matt altered his trajectory and intercepted Brandon at the edge of the terrace. He was pretty sure no one at this wedding wanted to see him, especially the bride.

"Matt, hey, buddy, 's'up?" Brandon slurred.

"Did you drive here on your own?" Matt asked.

"'Course I did. Brought the Camaro. Now, step aside. I need to kiss the bride."

Brandon attempted to walk past, but Matt grabbed his friend by the shoulders. "I don't think so."

"Let me go." Brandon unsuccessfully attempted to shake Matt off.

Instead Matt pulled him into a semi-embrace, turned him around, and marched him off in the direction oi the gazebo. "The bride's already gone," he lied. In fact, the bride had just tossed her bouquet. The newlyweds were almost ready to leave the reception.

"Damn," Brandon huffed.

"But good news. I owe you a hundred bucks."

"What?"

Matt stopped on the footpath and released Brandon while he dug in his pocket for his money clip. He pulled off two fifties and slapped them into Brandon's hand. "You're right. I was unable to seduce Courtney."

"I told you so. Didn't I tell you so?" He laughed like a braying jackass. And then he shouted at the top of his voice, "Matthew Lyndon thinks Courtney Wallace is an ice queen bitch."

Damn. He should have walked Brandon all the way back to the parking lot. Courtney didn't need to hear Brandon's drunken profanity. And the small, anguished sound she made broke his heart. He wanted to strangle Brandon right on the spot.

But he didn't get the chance because the bride and groom stepped out onto the terrace, clearly ready to make a run for the honeymoon suite at the Hay-Adams Hotel in Downtown DC, where they'd be spending the night before getting on a plane to Mallorca for their honeymoon tomorrow.

"Come on, Brandon, let's get out of here," Matt said, pulling his friend down the footpath.

But Brandon dug in his heels. "Laurie?" he said in an utterly dejected tone as he stared toward the terrace where Andrew and Laurie stared back in shocked silence, their getaway route blocked by their worst nightmare.

The horrible moment seemed to spool out in slow motion until Courtney sprang into action, barreling down the walkway, grabbing Brandon by one arm and issuing the order, "Let's get him out of here."

Matt knew a command when he heard one. He grabbed Brandon's other arm, and between the two of them they dragged Brandon off toward the lawn and the gazebo, clearing a path for the bride and groom.

Brandon wailed once, but when they got to the gazebo, he fell to his knees and hurled.

Once Brandon's father had retrieved his drunken son, Matt pulled Courtney into the gazebo. The situation was hopelessly romantic. A stand of honeysuckle growing along a nearby fence perfumed the air, and fireflies sparked above the lawn. A thin sliver of moon hung in the midnight sky.

Courtney wanted to escape. But Matt insisted that she sit down and talk to him.

"I'm sorry about what Brandon said. It's not true. And it's not what I think." Matt settled his back more comfortably against the gazebo's bench and took a gulp of his long-necked beer. The darkness hid his face.

"Okay. But be honest, what *do* you think?" she asked bravely. A small part of her wanted to know, while the rest of her was certain the truth would hurt.

"I think you're careful." He took another long sip of beer, and Courtney wished she had a drink of her own.

"I have good reason to be careful," she said, trying to find a more comfortable spot on the bench without getting too close to him.

"Don't we all?"

"Ha!" She leaned back, increasing the distance between them. "What do you have to be careful about?"

He shrugged. "I'm not exactly the guy you think I am, Courtney."

"Oh? Then who are you?"

"The quintessential middle child."

"I feel so sorry for you, really." She heaved a dramatic sigh. "You know, I can see through what you're doing. You're telling me what I want to hear. You probably already know that I was the dorky, insecure girl at Jefferson High, the one with zits and braces and an eye patch. But I have—"

"Eye patch?"

"I had a lazy eye. And even though I had surgery to correct the problem, I was required to patch my good eye in order to force my brain to use the lazy one."

"That explains it."

"Explains what?"

"The thing I like so much about your eyes. They're not quite symmetrical. It's sexy as hell, you know."

The man was exasperating. "You know, Matt, I've been around. I know how this works. You compliment me on all the things I'm insecure about, and it makes me go mushy inside, and I drop my barriers."

He stabbed his hands through his hair in a gesture that conveyed a certain amount of frustration. "You're right. I do that. All the time. And it really sucks now that I'm trying to tell the truth. And the truth is, I love your slightly asymmetrical eyes."

The wounded romantic who lived deep in her heart started seeing rainbows. Courtney tried her best to yank that foolish girl back, but she failed. A tiny chink formed in her wall of protection. Something warm and sweet and utterly intoxicating flowed through her blood, making her suddenly aware of the moon and the man and the scent of summer on the wind.

She should go. Now. Matt would hurt her, and she hadn't been hurt in decades. She stood up. "I want my cat back," she said, retreating a step.

He stood too. "Okay. I stopped by your apartment several times last week to give him back, but you haven't been home. What are you up to? Where have you been? Not interviewing sperm donors, I hope."

Her face flamed hot, and she sincerely regretted the things she'd said that night at the Red Fern Inn. "I was visiting a friend in the hospital."

"Oh, I'm sorry. I didn't know—"

"A friend of my parents. He's going to be okay."

He took a step forward. Was he going to kiss her? Oh, please.

When his right palm cupped her cheek, she leaned into the touch, closing her eyes and savoring his warm skin. Her heart exploded in her chest right before his lips brushed hers.

His kiss was so incredibly soft and gentle that she opened for him without even thinking about it, and when his tongue met hers, the pleasure was so intense that she groaned out loud.

She expected him to come in for the kill, but instead he backed up. "Nice," he said, and then turned and walked away.

Chapter Nine

Weekends were always hard on Courtney, working late on Saturday and then sometimes having to show up on Sunday for yet more weddings. But this Sunday she'd have to do it on almost no sleep. Matt's brief, erotic kiss had left Courtney tossing and turning all night. Why had he walked away?

Easy answer. He was luring her. And she was stupidly falling for it. In fact, she'd spent most of the night thinking about crossing the landing and knocking on his door. After all, she had a good excuse. She wanted her cat back. But he might have seen through that at three thirty in the morning.

So she was grumpy when she arrived at the Winchester Medical Center at 9:30 a.m., and discovered that the café in the hospital's lobby didn't open until 10:00 a.m. Was this some kind of joke? People needed caffeine. And in her case, the caffeine she'd ingested with her first cup this morning had worn off.

She strolled into Sid's room and found him sitting in the chair by the bed wearing a bright green and orange Hawaiian shirt with birds of paradise plastered all over it. His skin tone looked brighter today, but whether it was the shirt or his improving health Courtney couldn't say.

"Good morning. Since when do you wear Hawaiian shirts?" she said in her best happy voice. Barbara, Sid's late wife, had disapproved of loud shirts, so the birds of paradise were a big surprise. But maybe not an unwelcome one.

"Since I talked him into one. With my employee discount, I was able to buy a whole bunch of them at ten percent off."

Courtney turned to find a sixtysomething woman with beautiful white hair and big hazel eyes standing in the doorway. Her lips glistened with poppy-pink lip gloss, and she wore a pair of slim white slacks and a chambray shirt open at the neck to expose a turquoise necklace. Matching earrings dangled from her ears.

The woman stepped forward, her hand out, the nails painted a shade of pink that matched her lips. "Hi. I'm Leslie Heath."

"I'm happy to meet you. I'm Courtney. Sid is like—"

Leslie waved her hand, silver bangles clinking. "Oh, honey, I know all about y'all. And I think it's so sweet the way you've been visiting Sid, especially with you so busy over at Eagle Hill Manor. Don't you worry. I've got my car, and I'll take Sid home. I'll keep an eye on him and make sure he takes his meds. He lives right across the hallway from me. And I don't want you worrying about his groceries, now. I can pick up anything he needs at Walmart. I'm there three days a week as a greeter."

"Uh, thanks," Courtney managed. Who was this woman? And why hadn't Sid mentioned her?

Courtney turned toward Sid, who refused to make eye contact. "Are you okay with this? Because my guest bedroom is ready for you if you want it."

Sid looked down, studying his big hands, and nodded. "Leslie is a busybody. She chairs the tenants association, you know. She knows everyone at Dogwood Estates and looks after all of us. I told you I'd be all right."

"He's right about me. I am a busybody. Nosy as the day is long." Leslie strolled into the hospital room on a pair of flip-flops that showed her poppy-pink toenails. She leaned over Sid, resting her hand on his shoulder. "Don't you worry about him, honey. I'll take good care of him."

Sid finally raised his head and met Leslie's gaze. He gave her the tiniest of smiles.

Damn. Where was the depressed, gray man from

a week ago? And after all these months of grief...
What the hell?

Courtney felt a moment of selfish envy, which she
immediately quashed. Had love found him a second
time? Damn. He seemed utterly besotted with the
beautiful, age-appropriate, apparently single Leslie.
Courtney was happy for him and utterly demoralized
about her own single life.

She spent twenty minutes with Leslie and Sid
before concluding that her father's best friend
was in capable and loving hands. She left them,
grabbed a second cup of coffee from the shop in
the lobby, which had finally opened, and headed
back to work.

Where she once again spent her day making fairy
tales come true for everyone except herself.

Charlotte's Grove, the Lyndon family's centuries-old
home, perched on a rise of land northeast of town
with spectacular views of the Shenandoah River.
Built in the early 1700s, the Georgian mansion and
the land surrounding it had always belonged to a
member of the Lyndon family. On Sunday, Senator
Mark Lyndon and his wife, Pam, the current occu-
pants, held a family brunch to celebrate Andrew's
wedding.

The bride and groom were not in attendance, since
they'd departed for a week-long honeymoon in Mallorca, but everyone except Amy, who was managing
a big wedding at Eagle Hill Manor, was there. Matt

had overslept because his night had been disturbed with erotic dreams featuring Courtney Wallace, so he was the last to arrive.

Although it was an overcast day, he found his kin on the back terrace enjoying a buffet of eggs, bacon, bagels, and smoked salmon. His younger brother, Jason, handed him a mimosa, and he dived into what was left of the food. The Lyndons were a hungry crowd when they gathered, and the smoked salmon had been demolished. He'd started filling his plate with eggs when Dad sneaked up behind him.

"You have a minute, son?" he asked in that stern-father voice that always sent a shiver of dread through Matt. Plus, he hated it every time Dad called him "son" like that because it almost always preceded one of Dad's fatherly lectures, which were peppered with plenty of criticism and disapproval. So not on Matt's list of things he wanted to do on his Sunday off.

But saying no wasn't an option either, because in addition to being his dad, Charles Lyndon was now also his boss and the managing partner of the Virginia office of LL&K. Family members who worked at LL&K huddled during family get-togethers—a behavior that Matthew had always thought rather rude.

Apparently Dad expected him to behave exactly like his older cousins, David and Andrew, which was hardly new. Dad had been expecting him to behave like his older cousins for most of his life, and Matt had been falling short for just as long.

"Come on," Dad said, ushering him across the patio to the table where David sat with August Kopp. Uh-oh, it was worse than Matt thought. Dad was going to lecture him in front of the firm's senior partner.

Matt snagged a seat and greeted David before he turned toward August. "Is Brandon okay?"

"He was still asleep when I left him this morning. I'd have more sympathy for his feelings were it not for the fact that he behaved like such an idiot last fall."

Matt was hardly surprised by August's comments. Brandon and his father had an uneasy relationship. In fact, Matt and Brandon had spent a lot of time talking about their respective fathers during their trip to Bermuda last year—the trip that was supposed to have been Brandon's honeymoon.

"Well, don't be too hard on him," Matt said. "I don't think he expected Laurie to find someone else."

Dad scowled. "He should have expected it. And he should have stayed far away from Laurie yesterday."

"Laurie's better off with Andrew," August said. "But we're not here to talk about Brandon."

Holy crap. August Kopp's tone suggested that the partners of LL&K had been sitting at that table waiting for him to arrive. What had he done? He could think of so many possible missteps over the last week, but he swallowed down his discomfort and asked, "What exactly are we here to discuss?"

"The Dogwood Estates Tenants Association," David said.

"What about it?" He cast his gaze from David to Dad and then finally to Mr. Kopp.

David leaned forward with an intense gaze. "Arwen gave me a copy of her memo, the one she wrote at your suggestion."

Was there an accusation in his tone or his words? Matt couldn't tell.

"Look, all I asked her to do was to find out if the county had forgiven the fines once GB Ventures bought the apartment complex. I didn't expect her to come back with a memo suggesting something deeper and more nefarious."

"But why did you ask her to do the research in the first place?" Dad asked.

He clamped his back teeth together for a moment before he forced himself to relax. It was always this way, being called to account for decisions he'd made. "I was curious," he finally said.

"Curious?" Dad said in an incredulous tone.

"Okay, I had this crazy-assed idea that we could go after the county for violating property rights."

"What?" Dad's eyebrows reached up toward his hairline. "Since when are you a constitutional lawyer?"

Of course he wasn't a constitutional lawyer. And the idea of suing the county was totally crazy. He'd been grasping at straws when he'd suggested it. Why did Dad always go out of his way to make

Matt look like an idiot? He was tired of it, so he looked Dad right in the eye and said, "I was just looking at every option. The people living at Dogwood Estates are going to lose their homes. They are our clients, and I wanted to find a way to stop that from happening. But clearly suing the county would be stupid."

Mr. Kopp chuckled. "I don't know," he said. "It's not that stupid."

Everyone turned in the managing partner's direction.

Red crept up Dad's cheeks. "Explain."

"Well, I wouldn't want to argue the case, but if the county was using punitive fines to force landowners off their land in order to upgrade the buildings and the tax rolls, it might violate the Constitution. It would depend on the facts in the case, I think."

Matt met August Kopp's gaze. The senior partner had been a Supreme Court clerk and had gone on to argue dozens of cases before the highest court. He was a noted constitutional scholar. Matt was blown away to see a twinkle in August's eye.

"Well," Dad said before Matt could figure out his next move, "I don't care whether it's constitutional or not. The truth is that we're all better off without Dogwood Estates. It's an eyesore. Getting rid of it is a win in my book."

Matt was about to challenge his father by asking him whether he cared about the people who lived at Dogwood Estates, but he was saved from that mistake by Aunt Pam, who came up behind his chair and rested her hand on his shoulder.

"Matt, honey, your mother just told me that you've rented a new apartment and need an interior decorator."

It was like being tossed from the frying pan right into the fire. "Um, no, really, Aunt Pam, I don't need a decorator. I was just going to buy some furniture, you know, nothing fancy, and—"

"Oh, no, you can't do that. You need a decorator."

Out of the corner of his eye, Matt saw his father's face go a deeper shade of red. Great, just great. He could not win. Dad would think he was blowing through his trust fund the way Danny had.

Well, at least he could take a stand on this issue. He stood up and faced his aunt. "No, Aunt Pam, I don't need a decorator. Thanks. I don't believe in wasting my money on stuff like that."

"But—"

"You heard the boy," Dad said from behind him. Matt could hardly contain himself. For once in his life, Dad actually had his back.

"Really, Charles, do you think Matt has any sense when it comes to buying furniture and putting up curtains?" Pam asked, giving Dad one of her determined-at-all-costs looks.

The silence behind Matt was ominous. Then Dad cleared his throat. "I suppose you've got a point there."

❦

Arwen always did her chores on Sundays.

It was a habit, formed in her childhood. In the Jacobs household, Friday and Saturday had always been devoted to the Sabbath. Mom had cleaned house like a fiend on Fridays before sunset. And then she'd always gone to the grocery store on Sunday.

Arwen no longer kept the Sabbath as her parents did, but she still shopped for groceries every Sunday. This Sunday she also planned to do her laundry and visit The Home Depot for a few pieces of hardware she needed to finish a DIY project she'd started last week—a front-hall storage unit built out of reclaimed barn wood.

But before she got busy, she needed her weekly fix of waffles from Gracie's Diner.

Gracie's place had been a fixture on Liberty Avenue for at least two generations of Shenandoah Falls residents. Its mid-century ambience had become fashionable once again, but Gracie's main claim to fame was the inexpensive, down-to-earth food, always served with a smile.

Arwen strolled into the diner with a copy of the Sunday *Washington Post* tucked under her arm and took a deep breath filled with the scent of bacon, waffles, and maple syrup. There wasn't anything that smelled better than Gracie's place on a Sunday morning.

She waved at Gracie, found a spot at one of the two-person tables in the back corner, and settled in to read the newspaper. Gracie appeared a moment later with coffee. "Your waffles will be out in a minute," she said as she filled Arwen's cup.

"Thanks, Gracie." One of the best things about Gracie's Diner was that Arwen never had to order. Gracie just knew, or remembered, or had some unexplained gift for determining what people wanted. Of course, Courtney had been having waffles at Gracie's every Sunday for at least five years, so maybe Gracie wasn't a mind reader.

Maybe Arwen had become completely predictable.

"I don't know why you read the news anymore," Gracie said with a shake of her head. "It's all bad all the time."

This was true, but Arwen had always read the paper on Sunday. She'd been doing it since she was a kid in middle school. "I guess I'm a creature of habit," she said.

"Aren't we all? Gotta run." Gracie turned and made a quick circuit of the dining room, topping off coffee cups as she went.

Arwen pulled out the sports section and started to read Tom Boswell's Sunday column about the Washington Nationals. She loved baseball, and she loved Tom Boswell, so she didn't see trouble coming.

But it arrived at her table, sat down, leaned forward, and said, "I haven't seen you at the Jaybird these last few days. You wouldn't be after avoiding me, would you?"

Rory's lilting accent was like an instant aphrodisiac. It rubbed up against her erogenous zones, making her feel crazy and trapped at the same time.

"I've never seen you in here before," she said, looking up into the endless blue of his eyes.

"I like to cook my own breakfast."

Wow. Rory didn't look like someone who could cook. She imagined him rolling out of bed naked and heading immediately for his refrigerator and a beer. Or maybe some weed.

"Okay, so why are you here?"

"Looking for you. You haven't been down to the bar in a while now. Why not?"

Had she been avoiding him? Maybe. A little. She'd also been working overtime on Matt's side project. She shook her head. "I've been busy at work."

"So you haven't been avoiding me?"

He wasn't going to give up, was he? Did she want him to give up? Her pulse quickened. No. But he needed to understand that she wasn't one of those easy girls.

She leaned forward. "I meant what I said the other night. You know what I'm looking for. I want old-fashioned romance, Rory, not party time, not—"

She was interrupted by the arrival of her waffles, smothered in syrup and butter. Her stomach growled just as Gracie turned toward Rory. "Hello, handsome," she said. "Can I get you something, or are you just visiting?"

Damn. Arwen had never actually heard Gracie ask a customer what they wanted.

"Cup of tea?" He turned those baby blues on Gracie, and she wasn't immune.

"Nothing else? Really?" Gracie asked. "No eggs, no bacon, no sausage, no potatoes? No wonder you're so thin."

Rory's face softened, and the bad boy disappeared for a moment. He might even have sighed.

"I thought so," Gracie said, then turned and bustled away.

"You've never been to Gracie's before, have you?" Arwen asked.

He shook his head. "I have a feeling I've been missing something."

"You have been. And I have a feeling that your full Irish breakfast will arrive momentarily."

He eyed her waffles. "I'm surprised to see you eating waffles. I always took you for a cereal and fruit sort of person."

"I indulge myself once a week," she said, cutting a piece of waffle and popping it into her mouth. The burst of sweetness on her tongue almost made her groan.

"I have a feeling that's your problem."

Arwen swallowed her waffle. "You think waffles are a problem?"

"No, but eating them only once a week is."

"What, and you eat a full Irish breakfast every morning?"

"Bacon and eggs are not the same as waffles." He delivered this line as if he were handing out some kind of deep philosophy. But hey, what the hell, the guy was a bartender. It came with the territory.

"Why are you here?" she asked.

"To seduce you into doing something different. Whatever it is you've got planned for today, I want you to give it up and do something crazy. Have you ever ridden on a motorcycle?"

Her girl parts, which had always longed for that quintessential bad-boy experience, were totally down with the idea of a motorcycle ride. And her brain, which was probably drunk on maple syrup, suddenly thought a ride on his bike sounded like heaven. "No, I haven't. Is this an invitation?"

He gave her a winning smile. "Only if it sounds like more fun than whatever you were planning to do today. What were you planning to do today?"

"Errands. And then a DIY project."

"On a beautiful Sunday in June? Love, you need to get out and live a little."

Yeah, she did. It was a tiny bit pathetic that her one and only weekly indulgence had become a habit, like everything else in her life. "Okay. I'm game," she said.

The smile on Rory Ahearn's mouth sent her girl parts into an ecstatic happy dance, which was both wonderful and scary at the same time. She could see where this was leading, and she almost wanted to go there, but not quite.

Rory wasn't the man of her dreams. He would never court her or send her flowers or take her to a restaurant with cloth napkins. He wasn't safe or sane or stable.

But he was incredibly exciting. And maybe that was enough for now.

Another late Sunday night at the Jaybird Café, unwinding from a long weekend at Eagle Hill Manor. It was well past ten o'clock, and Courtney sat at the bar facing the fact that her life had settled into a definite rut. Nobody needed her, unless she counted the endless lineup of demanding brides.

Leslie had called her tonight at ten o'clock to say that Sid had retired for the night and it would be best not to disturb him. Clearly Sid didn't need her.

Nor did Willow, Melissa, or Amy. They were home with their husbands. Gone were the days when Courtney and her friends would gather here at the Jaybird after work and commiserate about single life.

Even Arwen seemed strangely absent. She'd been putting in long hours at work lately, and she hadn't answered her cell phone this evening. Maybe Arwen had found someone too and didn't want Courtney to know about it.

She stared down at her Manhattan and wished she'd ordered something different. Something she'd never tried before. Something without cherries maybe. Or without whiskey.

"You've hardly touched your drink. And your aura is ominously gray." Juni leaned on the inner side of the bar and gave Courtney a gentle, dark-eyed gaze. Juni's curly brown hair seemed wilder than usual, probably because of the killer humidity outside. Her vintage lace top fell low over her shoulders and exposed a tiny bit of midriff above her faded jeans.

"I do not wish to talk about it," Courtney said, lifting her drink and taking a sip.

"Okay, but I'm just saying that a thread of dark gray is threatening the yellow around your head."

Courtney put her drink down with a *thump*. "Not tonight, okay? I concede that my life is crap. I don't need anyone to read my aura to give me that newsflash."

"What's wrong?" Juni asked, cocking her head to one side. Real concern radiated from her sober gaze.

"All my friends are married, and all of them are expecting babies, and my kitten fell for a lothario. I mean, how pathetic is that? I'm even a failure as a crazy spinster cat lady."

"Ah. I understand." Juni nodded.

Courtney hated when Juni behaved like some kind of Buddha, enlightened but unwilling to share. "You know, Juni, I don't see you going out on any dates."

"Maybe I don't want to go on dates." Her eyes drifted to the left.

Courtney wanted to get right up in her face and

say, "Liar, liar pants on fire." Instead, she said, "That's what we all say."

Juni nodded. "Yeah, I guess we do."

Courtney pointed at the Jaybird's owner. "You need to find a manager. As long as you're stuck behind that bar, you're never going to have a life."

Juni nodded. "I've come to that conclusion myself, and I'm already taking steps to change my life. So the question is: What about you?"

"Well, I tried to adopt a cat."

Juni rolled her eyes. "That doesn't count. That's just trying to conform to some stupid meme that isn't true anyway. And besides, not everyone is a cat person."

"I was making progress with Aramis until Matt Lyndon moved in next door. Honestly, the guy seduced my cat."

"Really? I don't see him with cats." Juni's eyebrow arched, and for some reason—probably Courtney's frustrated libido—the angle of that arch reminded her of Matt. She envied Juni's ability to move her eyebrows in two different directions at the same time. Oh, the things she could accomplish with recalcitrant brides if she could stare them down that way.

Courtney pulled the cherry from her drink and popped it in her mouth. A moment later she said, "Now that Aramis has moved into his house, Matt has two cats. And you know what?" Courtney picked up her drink and took another healthy swig.

"What?"

"Single guys with cats is a thing. Who knew?"

"Really? I always thought guys with cats were, I don't know, kinda wimpy or something. But I guess you're right—if the single cat lady meme is stupid, then so is the single cat man meme, right?"

Courtney nodded her head. "I kid you not, there are articles all over the Internet about men with cats. The new consensus is that these men are hot. I don't know what to do with this. I mean, Matt is clearly a Hook-up Artist, but he also classifies as a Cat Guy. And according to many sources, a girl could do worse. I mean, think about it. A Cat Guy would have to clean the cat's litter box and pick up hair balls. That has huge implications."

"You're right. I never thought of that before."

"And a guy with a cat isn't always trying to prove how macho he is either."

Juni nodded. "Uh-huh. That's true. Matt's very confident in his masculinity."

"And, when you think about it, a Cat Guy is probably super sensitive to people's moods."

"You mean like when we get grumpy on a monthly basis?"

"Uh-huh. I think that's important."

"Yeah, it probably is."

"And a Cat Guy isn't super needy either. I mean he has a cat, not a dog, right?"

"Yup, definitely." Juni continued to nod with a goofy smile on her face. The evil eye had disappeared.

"Damn. I could probably go for a Cat Guy, if it weren't for the cats."

"Since when do you have a problem with cats?"

"Since Aramis. The little stinker." Courtney propped her head on her fist and drew circles in the condensation from her glass. "He ran away after only five days in my care."

"You know, that's not long enough to draw any conclusions."

"You're probably right. And Matt said he'd tried to return him. But who knows if he was truly sincere. Maybe he only tries when he knows I'm at work. Maybe I should assert my rights to the cat."

"Honey, I think you should do more than that."

"Really?"

"What have you got to lose? And besides, if Cat Guys are a thing, then research is required. And who's going to do the research if not you? I mean, you may have to add Cat Guys to your list of man types."

"I never thought of that before." Courtney sat a little straighter in her chair.

Just then Ryan Pierce strolled through the front doors. "Okay, my work is through here," Juni said. "Let me know how it works out."

The Jaybird's owner turned, her lacy top billowing as she moved to the far end of the bar, away from Ryan Pierce's usual spot. A moment later, Steve, the Sunday bartender, returned from the stockroom, and Juni disappeared into her office.

Ryan watched this ballet, his eyes focused on Juni with a yearning that was so clear it was hard to ignore. Courtney had seen him look in that direction before, but he never did anything about it. And Juni was clearly uninterested.

Courtney gulped down the last of her drink and then glanced at her watch. It was almost eleven o'clock. Did Cat Guys go to bed early on Sundays?

She hoped not.

Chapter Ten —————————

Matt left the family brunch at Charlotte's Grove determined to head off his mother and aunt before they foisted some kind of sissy decorator on him. Neither of them seemed to understand that he didn't want their help or their money. For once in his life, he wanted to be a normal guy, furnishing his first solo apartment the way anyone else would. By taking a trip to IKEA and buying some stylish but inexpensive furniture.

Just because he had a trust fund didn't mean he had to behave like a trust fund baby. And he sure as hell wasn't going to let Mom pay for his furniture. If he wanted to earn Dad's respect, he would do this on his own.

The way Dad had. Mom came from a wealthy

family, but Dad had never touched one penny of Mom's money. This explained why Matt and his brothers had grown up in a modest split-level home instead of a big mansion like Charlotte's Grove or the sprawling hilltop compound that Uncle Jamie had built for himself.

Dad would appreciate the fact that Matt stood up to Mom and Aunt Pam. And even though it might hurt Mom's feelings, he had to do it. He had to be independent.

So he asked Uncle Jamie if he could borrow his truck a second time, and Jamie agreed, no questions asked. Matt drove down to the IKEA in Woodbridge and filled the truck with a ton of boxes containing housewares, a dining room table, four dining room chairs, a coffee table, two end tables, and two reclining chairs. The couch would be delivered on Thursday.

It took all day to buy the stuff and haul it up the stairs. By eleven o'clock that evening, Matt had managed to put together the basic rectangular dining room table and straight-back chairs, but everything else sat stacked in boxes, and his living room had become a sea of discarded cardboard—a veritable playground for Dr. Doom and Ra's al Ghul. To be precise, Doom hid, and Ghul stalked and pounced. The cat formerly known as Aramis had attitude, ex-Porthos did not. Doom was destined to become a fat, lazy lap cat.

Matt pulled a Coke from his mostly empty fridge

and watched the cats for a long moment. He ought to take Doom across the hall as a peace offering. Doom and Ghul looked a lot alike. Maybe Courtney wouldn't notice the switch. All in all, Doom would make a much better chick's cat. Ghul was the sort of cat that didn't give a damn what his human did, so long as food arrived on a regular basis. A perfect guy cat.

He let go of a long sigh and rubbed his eyes. He was tired, and thinking about Courtney wasn't much better than thinking about the tenants of Dogwood Estates. His mind flashed back to that moment in the gazebo when he'd first tasted her. Sweet. Salty. Hot. Like fudge and nuts on creamy ice cream. She was delicious, and he had a craving.

He checked his watch. It was too late. Maybe tomorrow.

He finished his soft drink and tossed the can into the recycling bin. He was too tired to clean up. Too tired to finish the job. "Come on, you guys, it's bedtime." He chased after the kittens, snagging Doom without much trouble. Ghul tried to hide behind the unopened boxes, but Matt managed to corral that kitten too.

He was about to take them back to the bedroom when someone knocked on his door. He didn't have to guess who it might be, not at this hour.

Well, damn. When he'd kissed Courtney and walked away, it was with the hope that she might make the next move. But he hadn't expected her to come knocking. She'd built a big wall around herself and then dug a moat. A single kiss seemed unlikely to breach those barriers. But maybe he'd underestimated her.

He tucked the kittens under his arm and opened the door. Courtney stood in the buttery glow of the hall lights with her big, slightly asymmetrical eyes wide. She wore a little black dress that did nothing for her curves, and she'd pulled her hair back into a tight granny bun. Her shoes were flat, and she looked as if she hadn't slept well last night.

The last detail gave him reason to smile. "If you've come to borrow a cup of sugar, I'm afraid I don't have any."

Her gaze traveled down and then up, stalling at the kittens cuddled in his left arm. "Cute," she said. "I have a question."

"The answer is yes."

"I haven't even asked my question yet."

"The answer is still yes."

She sighed, the sound conveying her exasperation. Man, he loved pushing her buttons. "Okay, wiseass," she said, putting her hands on her hips, "if you want to play Jeopardy that's fine with me. What's the question?"

"What is, can I have my cat back?"

She shook her head and made a sound that resembled an obnoxious buzzer. "Wrong."

"Wrong? You don't want your cat? Really?"

She shrugged. "I'm willing to negotiate on that point, but that's not why I knocked on your door."

His heart slammed against his ribs. Holy crap, was this his lucky night? No, wait, stop. Even if she had come to ask *that* question, maybe he wanted to play hard to get. Maybe he should make her work for it.

No. Bad idea. Besides, if she'd knocked on his door looking for sex, he'd be an idiot to turn her away. He wanted her in the worst way. He wanted to touch those incredible breasts. He wanted to feel the silk of her skin beneath his hands. He wanted to bury himself in her. And not just because it had been a couple of months since he'd hooked up with anyone. This want wasn't a general longing. It was quite specific. He wanted her because she was Courtney.

"You want to come in?" he asked.

She bit her lip, and even though she wasn't wearing lipstick, the sight of that plump lower lip caught against her teeth made him hard. She had no idea how she drove him to distraction.

"So," he asked into her hesitation, "are you coming in or not?"

She straightened her shoulders as if girding herself for battle and then nodded without a word. He stepped aside and let her pass into the cardboard chaos that was his living room.

"You went shopping."

"Yeah, I've always lived with roommates. So I needed a few things."

"This is a bad idea," Courtney said under her breath, and turned back toward the door.

He blocked her path and then bent down and gently turned the kittens loose. They scampered away into their cardboard playground. "What's a bad idea?"

"I don't know, really. I was at the Jaybird, having a conversation with Juni about Cat Guys, and somehow I came to the conclusion that it would be okay for me to knock on your door tonight. Because I've never met a Cat Guy before, and there's all this stuff on the Internet about how great Cat Guys are. You know, how they're comfortable with their masculinity, aren't very needy, and clean up after themselves..." She scanned the mess in his living room. "Obviously I was wrong."

"Cat guys?"

"Single men with cats. As opposed to single men who are Hook-up Artists. The truth is you're sort of interesting."

"Well, that's nice to know." He took a step toward her. She didn't back away.

"I'm babbling, aren't I?"

He took another step that brought him within kissing range, and she still hadn't backed up. "Maybe, a little. So I take it you're here to learn the truth about Cat Guys?"

"Um, yeah, kind of." Her eyes went wide and dark, and a blush crawled up her cheeks that was so sexy and adorable it almost made him groan out loud.

"You're a funny girl, Courtney Wallace."

"Not really. The thing is…it's been years since I've kissed a guy who was moving into his first apartment."

He dipped his head. "Are you gonna bring up that age thing again?"

She shook her head. "No. Yes. I—"

"Make up your mind."

"Yes," she said on a puff of air, but she didn't move away from him. If anything, she swayed a little in his direction.

He smiled. "See, I knew the answer all along." He slanted his head and moved in.

Courtney froze, enthralled by the heavy-lidded look in Matt's gaze. The outcome of this chase was no longer in doubt. The irony, of course, was that she'd put herself at his mercy.

Would he live up to expectations? Or would he turn out to be like so many other guys, selfish, in a hurry, and essentially clueless about sex.

Courtney could count on the fingers of one hand the number of times any guy had given her an orgasm. So, really, the odds were stacked against her.

But she'd never taken a Hook-up Artist to bed. And she'd never even dreamed that a Hook-up Artist could simultaneously be a Cat Guy. It was worth a shot, wasn't it?

She didn't move as he advanced, and when his lips finally met hers, she surrendered. His kiss started out as soft as a butterfly's wing, sweet as nectar, and strangely unsatisfying.

Damn. She hadn't knocked on his door for sweet kisses. She'd come to see if Matt was capable of giving her the full monty. So she took the offensive, stepping into the kiss as she cupped the back of his head. The silky texture of his hair brushed along her palms as his body heat overwhelmed her. Her pulse roared in her ears as she parted her lips and invited him in.

All at once, the sweet, soft kiss morphed into something fiercely carnal. Matt spiraled in, his tongue circling and dancing instead of invading. Holy crap, he really knew how to kiss.

And he tasted good. He smelled even better—an intoxicating blend of woodsy soap and man. She ran her hands down over the hard bones and muscles of his shoulders and then rocked up to get better traction. He rewarded her with a deep, inarticulate grunt that made her burn more fiercely. Nothing turned her on more than knowing that she'd turned on some guy. It felt like a validation in some deep part of her psyche.

She fell into that kiss and lost all sense of time and place. She wanted it to go on forever and almost mourned when he pulled away. But then he linked smaller kisses and nips down across her jaw to the corner of her neck, right below her earlobe.

He nuzzled her there, his tongue still drawing lazy circles, igniting an inferno inside her that threatened to melt every single one of her bones. It was her time to cry out, but even that release did nothing to diminish the coiled energy that Matt's kisses created inside her.

Suddenly, he was too far away.

"I want to feel you," she murmured, as her hands journeyed down his back, over the bumps in his spine to the bottom of his T-shirt. She continued the exploration under the soft cotton, splaying her palms on the warm skin of his back for a moment, before she drew the shirt's hem up so she could touch his chest. He was hard muscled, all male, with just the right amount of chest hair.

Matt undid her dress' zipper and then drew the shoulders down her arms so he could link more kisses over her clavicle. She wiggled out of the dress, letting it fall around her ankles.

She expected him to move in on her breasts like an invading army. Guys always did that. But not Matt. Instead he concentrated on that spot right below her ear, while his hands seemed to be counting the bumps in her backbone.

Damn. Her breasts ached for his touch, but he seemed intent on denying them. She ought to say something. But she didn't. She held back, like she always did. Afraid that the moment her breasts were exposed, he'd lose interest in everything else. And right now that thing he was doing to her neck was so nice.

Maybe she should take the initiative. That would

be different. It seemed like the right thing to do, so she reached for the button on his jeans. Then she dipped her fingers below his waistband. His breath caught, and she wondered if she should stop.

No. She was going to take charge this time. So she drew down the zipper, a move that elicited a soft, erotic groan that made her feel strangely powerful. That feeling didn't last very long because, in the next instant, she found herself shoved up against the door as he ground himself against her.

She could have predicted that result, but for some reason, it felt good to have him pressed up against her. Almost perfect, but not quite.

"Take off your shirt," she whispered. He complied, tossing the garment over his shoulder into the pile of cardboard boxes. His chest was wide and solid and utterly drool-worthy.

"Nice," she said.

This earned her a cocky grin. She glanced into his espresso eyes, blown away by the dark fire she saw in them. He was beautiful and aroused. She ran two fingers down along his jaw, his stubble abrading her fingertips, until she found the pulse point at the base of his neck. She didn't bother counting the beats. She'd checked enough pulses to know that his heart was racing about as fast as hers.

He moved in again, making short work of her bra, which he tossed over his shoulder into the mess on the floor. He gazed down at her girls, and she braced herself for the moment she stopped being a person and became a collection of body parts.

She waited. But he didn't do the expected. Instead he leaned against the door, his hands on either side of her head, as he moved close enough so that the tips of her breasts brushed against his chest.

A tidal wave of lust swamped her. She arched against the door, hungry for more, but he denied her. Instead he dipped his head and kissed her again until she couldn't think about anything else except the fact that she might explode any minute if he didn't touch her.

"So," he murmured, drawing back, "if the answer is yes, what's the question?" One of his eyebrows arched.

"What is *will you touch me, please*," she rasped.

His eyes sparked with a wicked, amused gleam. "Ding. You win."

He stepped closer, taking the weight off his hands as he trailed hot, moist kisses down her chin and neck to her breasts. Finally one of his broad, warm hands cupped her left breast as his mouth found the nipple of its twin. He didn't tweak or knead. He didn't grope. He touched with such unbelievable skill that she could hardly bear it.

"Oh, God," she hissed, arching against his touch and giving him unfettered access. "Don't stop, please." She had never begged a man before. But she'd never been teased so unmercifully either.

"I have no intention of stopping until I touch every square inch of your incredible body," he said.

There was nothing incredible about her body, but in that moment, she believed him. And then he started kissing her again, from her mouth down her neck to her breasts, and then Matt fell onto his knees and drew her panties down and started all over again with his touches and kisses until he'd turned Courtney into a quivering mass of sexual longing.

Courtney was delicious in so many ways. Her curvy bod, the soft skin over her belly and thighs. Her unbelievable scent, musky and sweet at the same time. Her taste. Salty, womanly, and utterly unique.

He wanted to give her an orgasm but not here, not against the door. So he left her right on the brink.

"No," she said. "Please don't—"

He was a total jerk to leave her like that, but he wanted her to have the best possible memory when she walked out of here tomorrow, and his instincts told him that taking her into the bedroom and starting all over again would be better.

So he stood up, breathless and aching for her.

"Why did you stop?"

He didn't answer the question. Instead he performed the He-Man maneuver, pulling her up into his arms and carrying her across the threshold of his bedroom. Which, now that he'd entered it, was not as neat as it should have been for a night between the sheets. But it was too late now. He hadn't exactly put his bed frame together. His mattress and box spring sat directly on the floor, surrounded by boxes and suitcases he'd yet to unpack.

She didn't seem to notice, thank God. Instead she had her arms around his neck, her head on his shoulder, and her gaze locked firmly with his.

Matt believed that every woman was a beautiful creation, but Courtney was more than beautiful. That slightly skewed gaze gave her a sultry innocence that made him want to introduce her to every possible nuance in the *Kama Sutra*. Of course she wasn't a virgin; she just looked like one. And he had a feeling she might even be willing to venture beyond the restraints of convention.

Not that he was into kink particularly. But he had a very specific fantasy that involved cheerleaders, and Courtney would look outstanding in a tight little sweater and a short little skirt.

She looked outstanding naked too.

He gently placed her on the bed. "Now, where were we?" he asked, but before he could climb in after her, she rose on one elbow and put up the universal stop sign with the palm of her hand.

"Stop," she said. A wave of untamed frustration washed through him, but he stopped.

"What? Did you change—"

"Strip. I want to see the goods," she said, a wicked glimmer in her baby blues.

"The goods?" He gave her a supremely confident smile.

She nodded and bit her lip, sending uncontrolled lust coursing through him. The next time they did this, he was going to ask her if she'd suck on a lollipop while he watched. She'd probably slap him if he asked for something like that, especially since she was so hung up about being older than him. Oh, if she only knew.

"Okay," he said, his voice husky.

She'd already unzipped his zipper, so it was easy to shuck out of his jeans and boxers all in one quick motion.

"Oh," she said on a little breath.

"Do I pass the test?"

She nodded. "Absolutely." Her smile was wonderfully naughty.

"Okay, your turn. Take down your hair while I watch."

She seemed surprised for a moment, but then she smiled like Botticelli's Venus emerging from her shell. She raised her arms and slowly pulled out bobby pins, scattering them across his bedroom. He groaned as her dark hair tumbled down over her shoulders.

"How's that?" she asked as she settled back into his pillows, stacking her arms behind her head.

She left him speechless and breathing hard.

"Come on, Matt, a girl can't wait forever."

Neither could a guy. He climbed into the bed

with a clear agenda in his mind. But he lost all control over his mind when she rolled him over and proceeded to fulfill several of his most intimate fantasies. After which he returned the favor. Several times. Well into the wee hours of the morning.

Chapter Eleven————————

Courtney's cheek peeled away from Matt's warm, sexy chest as she raised her head to identify the noise that had awakened her. The kittens raced up and down the hallway from the bedroom to the living room and back, their tiny paws thumping over the wide-plank pine flooring.

Out beyond the French doors, the June sky had turned the deep lavender of morning twilight. She braced herself on an elbow and stared down at Matt in the half-light. His hair curled down along his forehead, and his thick, dark lashes lay against his cheeks. He looked peaceful, content, unworried. And so very young...

She resisted the urge to touch his hair or kiss his sleepy mouth. No matter how much she lusted after his body—and she needed it like an addict craves his next fix—kissing him awake would be a huge mistake.

He was a terrific lover. That shouldn't have surprised her since he'd had so much practice in his young life. But practice didn't always make perfect. She'd had lots of practice and had never experienced anything like last night. He'd been so generous in bed, so interested in giving pleasure as well as receiving it, that it would be so easy to believe he cared about her. But she was too smart to fall into the trap of mistaking pleasure and passion for true love.

She could no more imagine Matt Lyndon in a stable, long-term relationship than she could imagine finding a unicorn in Eagle Hill Manor's backyard. It wasn't going to happen. Ever.

It was time to leave.

She slipped from the bed and tiptoed into the living room, where she found her clothes scattered across the discarded cardboard. She slipped on her dress without bothering with her underwear or shoes. She found her purse where she'd dropped it the night before and dug for her keys. Just as she was ready to open the door, one of the kittens scampered up to her and curled itself around her ankle. She had no idea if this was Aramis or Porthos because the two kittens were so alike. But the kitten meowed and looked up at her with such an adorable face.

How could anyone call these little fluffballs Doom

and Ghul? Short answer: a twentysomething guy just moving into his first apartment. It was like a sign or something, reminding her that Matt Lyndon was basically a well-educated frat boy.

She stared down at the kitten, torn by her conflicted emotions. Should she take him home? She wanted a cat. But a small part of her brain whispered that leaving the cat at Matt's gave her an excuse to knock on his door some other time. Plus, leaving the cat here meant that he'd have to scoop the litter box.

She picked up the kitten and snuggled it against her cheek. He rubbed his head against her and started to purr. A lump formed in her throat for no reason she could truly explain.

"It would be dumb to leave you here where you'd be called something horrible like Ra's al Ghul," she whispered to the adorable creature snuggled against her neck.

It was settled. Better to go, leaving nothing behind. She'd satisfied her curiosity once, and if she allowed herself to satisfy it again, she might end up hurt or broken. Curiosity killed the cat, and in this instance, it might destroy the cat owner's heart.

Besides, she'd had a wonderful night. That was all she needed. A wise woman would leave it at that.

She didn't feel very wise as she crossed the short distance between his apartment and hers. She opened the door and headed into her own bedroom with the kitten, where she fell into her bed, snuggling the furball until she fell asleep. Thank God Monday was one of her off days.

She woke up hours later, the kitten still curled next to her. "You've definitely had a personality transplant," she said to the kitten, giving him a little kiss on his tiny head. She reached for her cell phone and checked the time. Holy crap, it was almost noon, and she had promised Sid she'd be there in the morning.

Guilt and remorse washed through her, along with a familiar sense of shame. What had she been thinking? The last thing she wanted was another one-night stand, and even though it had been a memorable one, sex with Matt Lyndon was not what she wanted.

She wanted a relationship. She wanted to find someone who would rock her world the way Jeff rocked Melissa's, and Dusty rocked Amy's, and David rocked Willow's. She wanted the fairy tale. Instead she got twenty-first-century sexual liberation, which wasn't all that.

She raced through her shower and headed out to Sid's place, stopping at the Food Lion to do a little grocery shopping for him, focusing on food that was low salt, low-fat, and low-calorie.

But when she knocked on Sid's door, Leslie Heath answered it, wearing a purple and green dashiki shirt and looking like a Baby Boomer fashion plate. "Oh, hi, Courtney, we were just about to call you. Let me take those groceries." She snagged the plastic bags from Courtney's hands and continued talking. "I'll put them away. You come on in and visit. We've been commiserating and plotting."

"Commiserating and plotting?"

Leslie waltzed off without any further elaboration. She moved into the kitchen as if she lived there. She seemed surprisingly familiar with where Sid kept pantry items. Courtney watched for a moment, emotions churning. Who was this woman? Leslie was as unlike Barbara as a woman could be. Barbara had been reserved and conservative. Leslie was anything but.

Courtney held her resentment in check and turned toward Sid's small living room, crowded with Barbara's big, traditional furniture, which he'd been unable to let go of when he'd sold his house in town. Courtney found Sid sitting in the big wing chair, wearing yet another Hawaiian shirt—this one in the same shades of green and purple as Leslie's dashiki. Despite the loud shirt, or maybe because of it, he looked surprisingly well, considering that he'd had coronary bypass surgery less than a week ago. His color had improved dramatically, and the twinkle had returned to his deep-set blue eyes.

And why not? Three other sixtysomething women occupied Barbara's gigantic, rolled-arm sofa. Sid and his coterie of women appeared to be having a party of some kind. Plastic cups in various shades of pink sat on the mahogany end tables, and a platter of half-eaten crudités took up most of the space on the claw-footed coffee table.

The moment Courtney stepped into the living room, one of the women hopped up from the sofa and spread her arms. "Courtney, sweetie, we're so glad you came." Linda Petersen, Willow and Juni's mother, enveloped Courtney in a fierce hug. Linda had apparently gotten the hippy-dippy apparel memo, because she was wearing a loose-fitting, blue-and-white India-print dress, and she smelled like the lavender she grew out on her farm, where she made the soap and other natural lotions featured at Eagle Hill Manor.

"I didn't know you and Sid were friends," Courtney said as Linda released her.

"Oh, I just met Sid today. I'm one of Leslie's friends. She put out an all-points bulletin late last night, so we assembled the gang." She gestured toward the other ladies in the room. "These are my friends Alice and Susan. Y'all, meet Courtney. She's the wedding planner at my daughter's bed-and-breakfast place. Leslie, Alice, and Susan are my best organizers, and if we're going to fight this eviction, we'll need everyone."

Leslie and Alice looked like a couple of suburban grannies, not organizers. Courtney waved in greeting, and they waved back. "What evictions?" she asked.

"The ones I predicted," Sid said.

Leslie cleared her throat from behind. "Yes, you did warn us all. But I had hoped that maybe Scott Anderson would finally get his act together."

"But he didn't," Sid said. "He sold out, and that bastard who bought the apartments from him had all the notices hand delivered on Saturday. Dogwood Estates is going to be torn down."

"It's a dark day, I'll agree to that," Leslie said on a sigh. "But as the chair of the Dogwood Estates Tenants Association, it's my duty to fight this thing. So I figured we could have a meeting in Sid's living room, and that way we can plot and scheme and make sure he takes his medicine at the same time."

Courtney was a little alarmed. She wasn't sure Sid needed all this excitement. Besides, Linda had a reputation for fighting lost causes. Sid didn't need to get his hopes up, although clearly he didn't sound very hopeful, which might be a good thing at the end of the day. Sometimes being a realist was called for. And wasn't that why she'd left Matt's bed this morning?

She turned toward Sid. "I'm not sure protesting is going to change things. And I told you before, Sid, if you need a place to stay, you can have my spare room. I'll take care of you."

Sid's lips thinned, and the twinkle dimmed in his eye. "Girl, I truly appreciate the offer, and I know you'd do a good job looking after me, what with you being a nurse and all. But I'm not an old man, and I don't need a nurse." His gaze shifted toward Leslie, and his expression softened ever so slightly.

Courtney knew when to stop arguing. She nodded and said, "Okay." But a painful wave of loneliness washed through her. Sid was moving on with his life. And she was being left in the dust.

"Sweetie pie," Linda said, pulling Courtney out of her self-pity, "we can't let Leslie get pushed around."

"Okay," Courtney said, "but I don't know if protesting is going to change anything. Maybe you should have another conversation with your lawyers or something."

Sid waved his hand in dismissal. "Those lawyers from LL&K are as useless as tits on a bull. You're right, a protest won't change one damn thing, but it might make some people in government sweat a little. It might stir things up. Not that I expect anyone working for LL&K to be happy about that."

"What are you trying to say, Sid?" Linda asked.

He let go of a long breath. "Linda, I know your girl's married to David Lyndon. But I don't trust any of them."

Linda helped herself to several pieces of broccoli. "You're entitled to your own point of view, but I can say, in all honesty, that my son-in-law has been a huge surprise to me. He's a good man. I'm sure he cares about what's happening here. It couldn't hurt to get his advice."

"Go ahead. Waste your time. But none of them Lyndons has impressed me yet. That last one, Matthew? He was the biggest jerk of them all."

Matt jolted awake at the sound of his cell phone alarm. He raised his head, still unfamiliar with his new bedroom, and squinted at the bright morning sun streaming through the French doors. He hauled in a deep breath, filled with Courtney's incredible scent—something wild and musky and deliciously sweet. His groin tightened as he propped himself on one elbow.

There was no sign of her. No sounds coming from the bathroom or down the hall in the kitchen. And Ghul lay curled on the pillow where Courtney had slept beside him for part of the night. He ran his hands over the rumpled sheets. They were cool.

So she'd left without a word. And judging by the single cat on the pillow, she'd absconded with Doom, who was not exactly her cat, but he could see why Doom might prefer living with Courtney. Did she know she'd taken the wrong cat? Maybe not. And maybe Doom would be happier with her. She'd probably change his name to Fluffy, or something stupid like that.

Damn, he missed Courtney. It might have been nice to wake up beside her. He had no doubt that morning sex with Courtney would be as awesome as evening sex had been. In fact, in his expert opinion, sex with Courtney was utterly mind and body blowing. And for some strange reason, her absence made him feel hollow inside, which was odd because usually he appreciated it when a woman departed before the sun came up.

He hauled his ass out of bed and stood in the shower for longer than was absolutely necessary, let-

ting the warm water sluice over his body while he
told himself not to be such a wuss over a woman.
There were plenty of fish in the sea, and the one next
door wasn't interested in a purely physical relationship with him.

Courtney Wallace had a romantic streak a mile
wide. She was a wedding planner, and hadn't she told
him last fall, in a moment of weakness, that she'd
been waiting for Mr. Right all her life?

Of course she had.

She had also come knocking at his door last night
looking for something else, but she'd left and taken
a cat with her. It was time to move on. He loved
women, and he would love to have sex with Courtney
again, but he was honest about himself. He was no
good for Courtney. It would be better not to repeat
what had happened last night.

So he shaved and dressed in one of his gray suits
and put on his conservative blue-and-white striped
tie and headed off to the office. It was another humid
June day, and even though the walk was short, he was
sweating by the time he entered his cubbyhole and
found a new stack of folders sitting on his chair.

These papers had nothing to do with any of the
pro bono cases he'd been working on as LL&K's
contribution to the Blue Ridge Legal Aid Society.
They appeared to be background information pertaining to several of David's clients who were scheduled to meet with him later in the day. The cases
involved one custody dispute, two divorces, and a

client who needed a living trust. Sticky notes had been attached to each file, in David's handwriting, noting the time of each meeting.

When he opened his e-mail, he found a message from David indicating that henceforward he would be relying on Matt to track progress on client work and to manage his client meeting schedule.

On some level, Matt knew this was typical first-year associate work, but he felt as if he'd been demoted, which was odd because these cases involved real, billable hours, in marked contrast to the work he'd done for the Legal Aid Society in general and the Dogwood Estates Tenants Association in particular. He ought to view this as a vote of confidence, that his partners trusted him to do something with real, paying clients. But he just couldn't see it that way.

Matt couldn't help but wonder if Dad had pulled him off the pro bono work because he'd gotten too deeply involved with the clients—a mistake Arwen had warned him about. And yet, as he parsed through the conversation on Sunday, Dad had seemed most upset by Arwen's memo and Matt's wild idea of suing the government.

An idea that August Kopp had not ridiculed.

Matt was trying to figure out if Mr. Kopp had been trying to encourage him when Arwen herself strolled into his office looking as if she hadn't slept in days. "Are you okay?" he asked.

"I'm fine. Why?" Her response seemed tense, just like her shoulders.

"Nothing." Matt knew better than to tell a woman that she looked as if she'd rolled right out of bed. Arwen usually showed up every morning bright-eyed and buttoned-down. Today her hair looked slept on, and her eyes looked bloodshot. Maybe she'd tied one on at the Jaybird last night.

She dropped into his side chair and leaned forward. "Have you heard the news?"

"What news?" He braced for something bad.

"GB Ventures has sent eviction notices to everyone living at Dogwood Estates. Leslie left a message on my cell Sunday afternoon. She's pretty upset."

"I'm sure she is. But we saw this coming, and I was told pretty explicitly that we needed to cut our losses on this," Matt said on a long sigh as he leaned back in his squeaky chair.

Arwen gave him the Frown of Disapproval. "I thought you cared about those people."

"I do. But the senior partner of this law firm, also known as my father, has made it clear that we're all better off without Dogwood Estates because it's an eyesore."

A big hollow place opened in his chest. He wanted his father's respect, but he didn't respect his father. Not on this issue. Dad had shown no compassion for the people who were losing their homes.

Arwen's frown disappeared, replaced by another look he couldn't quite decipher. She leaned back in the chair and folded her arms. "I know it's not wise for me to say this, but in my opinion, you should ignore your dad."

"Is that why you showed your memo to David?"

She nodded. "I was worried that you might sit on it...because of your Dad."

"You know, if Dad knew how you felt, he'd probably fire you."

She nodded. "Probably. But here's the thing. Something unethical is going on. I can feel it in my bones."

"I can too. But what can we do? We aren't crusaders. And the unethical appearance of insider trading has nothing to do with Dogwood Estates. So we don't actually have a client. And, you know, Dad is right about that. If we want to pursue this, we need to actually represent someone."

"Maybe that's what we should do."

"What, go looking for a client so we can expose corruption in the county government? Somehow I don't think Dad would be happy with me for doing something like that."

Arwen's frown returned. "Okay."

She got up, and the hole in Matt's chest grew so large it felt as if it might swallow him whole. "Wait," he said.

Arwen stopped and turned. "You've changed your mind?"

He gestured toward the files on his desk. "Look, my chain has been yanked. David has me working on a bunch of divorces. And based on the e-mail he sent me this morning, I've been promoted. I'm now in charge of his schedule, which makes me a glorified appointment secretary. How on earth can I possibly find this mythological client?"

"By just doing it."

"Okay. So how would we go about finding a client who's been fined by the county?"

She smiled, and some color returned to her face. "I have a friend in the building department. I'll see if I can get him to give us some information. And by the way, first-year associates always manage their partner's schedules. And they also work more than eight hours a day." She turned and stalked from the office.

Damn. Of course first-year associates put in long hours, and David seemed to be intent on keeping him busy if for no other reason than to keep him far away from the crap Arwen had discovered in her research.

But he couldn't stay away and maintain any kind of self-respect. Something rotten was happening in Jefferson County. And deep in his soul, Matt wanted to be more than just a charming guy with a last name everyone recognized. If he truly wanted to compete with his brother and cousins, sitting back and following Dad's rules was probably not the way to do it.

Chapter Twelve

Courtney stayed at Sid's house until the early afternoon. His collection of girlfriends, all of them widows, tried to ease his worries. And by the end of her visit, Courtney had concluded that Sid's annoyance at LL&K, while possibly misplaced, might be doing him a world of good. At least he had started to care about something again.

And he certainly wasn't going to lack for attention and care. Courtney made sure that each of his girlfriends had her cell number and instructed them to call her right away if Sid needed anything or if they thought he was not taking care of himself.

Still, his situation depressed her. He had exactly thirty days to move out of his apartment. Where was he or Leslie or any of the other tenants going to live?

And it sure didn't ease her mind to know that Leslie was thinking about moving all the way to Arizona, where she said a person on a fixed income could live in much better style than here in Virginia.

She hated the idea of Sid moving halfway across the country. But she had a feeling he might do just that, following after Leslie. And then she'd be alone. The last of Dad's friends would be gone.

An aching loneliness settled over Courtney that afternoon. She called Melissa to see if she'd be interested in an evening at the Jaybird, but Melissa and Jeff were doing inventory at the store.

She called Arwen and couldn't get her on the phone, even though it was Monday. What the hell was up with that anyway? Her cell phone had also been off for most of the weekend.

Finally, in the late afternoon, Arwen called back.

"Where have you been? I was trying to reach you all day on Sunday," Courtney accused.

Silence greeted Courtney for a very long moment before Arwen said, "I got busy and let my cell phone die."

"Busy with what?"

"I was finishing up that storage rack I started. You know the one out of reclaimed wood."

"Oh. How'd it come out?"

Another long, suspicious pause. "Great," Arwen said without much conviction.

"So, you want to meet at the Jaybird tonight?"

"No!" Arwen's refusal was more than emphatic; it sounded almost panicked.

"What's the matter?"

"Nothing's the matter. I just have work to do, okay?"

"Tonight?"

"Big case. I have to work late. And I really, really need to go. The senior partner just walked into my office." Arwen ended the call without even saying goodbye.

Courtney stifled her irritation. Arwen was a good friend—her last remaining single friend—and she couldn't afford to lose that friendship.

Oh well. It certainly looked like a Netflix and chill evening, in the original meaning of that phrase. Courtney decided to make the best of a lonely situation by spending some time in her kitchen. She headed off to the grocery store for the ingredients needed to make her mother's lasagna.

An hour later, as she hauled groceries up the stairs, she ran into Pam and Julia Lyndon, who were standing in the hallway outside Matt's apartment looking as if they'd stepped right out of the pages of *Town & Country* magazine.

Pam was dressed for a polo match in a powder-blue and white polka-dot dress with matching spectator pumps. Julia, on the other hand, would have fit right in at a fancy garden party in her vintage-look flowered sundress.

The only times Courtney had ever come face-to-face with Pam or Julia was at work, where she always dressed in a conservative, usually black, suit, which was basically like the uniform she used to wear as a nurse. But today she had on a pair of old cutoffs, a tank top, and flip-flops. It was three million degrees outside, and it was her day off.

Damn. If Matt's family was going to drop by unannounced, she would have to improve her wardrobe. These women made her feel small and insignificant and... nerdy. The way she'd felt as a kid in high school, when, in addition to having braces and glasses, she'd worn a lot of hand-me-downs. Dad had been a wonderful man, but he hadn't been a rich one, and he hadn't had much of a fashion sense.

"Oh. Courtney, is that you?" Pam asked as her gaze traveled down Courtney's legs and back up to her face, which was a little sweaty right at the moment because of the heat. Pam clearly never sweated and probably didn't even perspire much.

"Hi," she said. "I, um, live next door." She continued up the stairway and edged around Pam and Julia.

It seemed odd that Matt's mother and aunt would be here in the late afternoon while Matt was at work. What were they up to?

"Oh. That's nice," Pam said. Courtney interpreted her disinterested tone as a slap in the face. If these women knew what she and Matt had done last night...

A blush crawled up her face. Thankfully they would never know. And she'd have to be careful.

They were busybodies. She jammed her key into her door, trying to make a quick escape.

"So, you won't tell Matt that we were here, will you?" Julia asked.

Courtney turned around. "We're just neighbors," she said. It came out sounding exactly like the line: *We're just friends*. Damn.

"Of course you are, darling," Pam said. "Which is why we need you to keep the surprise."

"Surprise?"

They nodded in unison. "We're doing something about his apartment."

"Is there something wrong with it?"

Pam chuckled. "He went off to IKEA and bought furniture. Can you imagine?"

Yes, she could imagine. She had a couple of IKEA pieces at her place because Ethan Allen was out of her price range. She thought back to last night. But Ethan Allen wasn't out of Matt's price range, was it?

Warmth spilled through her. Matt was a lot of things, but he wasn't a snob.

She gave Julia and Pam a smile. "No, I can't even imagine," she said, trying to keep a straight face.

"So we've measured the place and we're going to redo it for him. You won't tell, will you?"

She shook her head. "No," she lied. "We hardly know each other. And my lips are sealed. You ladies have a nice afternoon." She turned back toward her door and escaped as quickly as she could.

Should she text him with this news? Or should she wait until she saw him again? She decided to wait and spent the rest of the afternoon making lasagna and weeping over *The Notebook*, a movie she'd seen at least twenty times.

After the movie, she dined alfresco on the balcony as the June sun slipped low on the horizon. It was still humid and warm, but the balcony was shaded and had a ceiling fan that cooled and kept the mosquitoes at bay. She sipped some Chianti and started a John Grisham book she'd been meaning to read while Aramis pounced at her feet.

She could do this. She thrived on being alone.

She swallowed the lump in her throat as twilight settled in. Who was she kidding? She'd come out here on the balcony hoping to catch a glimpse of Matt when he returned from work. But here it was, almost 9:00 p.m., with no sight of him.

Where was he? Arwen said they were busy at work. Maybe she'd been telling the truth. But Courtney couldn't shake the idea that he was probably out with some other woman. Maybe she wouldn't tell him about his mother's plan to redecorate his apartment.

She hated herself for thinking like that. She'd crossed the hall last night knowing how things would end. In fact, now that she thought about it, cats were the perfect pets for guys like Matt. Cats weren't needy, and it didn't take much to commit to a cat. She stared down at the adorable Aramis.

Of course, it didn't take much to fall in love with one either.

"I'm hopeless," she said to the kitten as she put down her book. The days were long this time of year, but at nine o'clock, the light had faded to a deep purple-blue. It was too dark to read on the balcony, so she stood up and started collecting her dinner dishes.

"But soft, what light through yonder window breaks?
It is the east and Juliet is the sun!"

The words floated up on the summer air from the sidewalk below in a voice that kissed her eardrums and wrapped around her chest like a warm, romantic hug. She leaned over the railing, and there he stood in the light of the streetlamp, wearing a wrinkled white shirt with the sleeves rolled up and his tie undone. He carried his suit jacket over his shoulder, and his unruly hair curled over his forehead, making him look vaguely Byronic.

Her pulse jumped. Never in her life had any man quoted Shakespeare to her. She wished she could remember Juliet's comeback line. It was something about the moon being inconstant. Something about Romeo's love being untrustworthy. But she couldn't quote it directly.

So instead she said, "I bet you say that to all the girls."

His mouth quirked on one side. "Busted."

His response disappointed her on some level. But she knew damn well that normal, twenty-first-century guys didn't quote poetry...ever. They talked about the Redskins and UVA football.

Only a Hook-up Artist quoted poetry. And this particular Hook-up Artist seemed to have a plethora of Shakespeare to fall back on. "So, what? Did you memorize a bunch of quotes in order to impress the ladies?"

"You'd be surprised how impressive it can be when you quote Elizabeth Barrett Browning or Emily Dickinson." His deep espresso eyes danced with amusement. He was teasing her.

"Wow, you know more than Shakespeare?"

"I do, actually."

"Really? Why do I not believe you?"

He let go of a long sigh. "Oh. So you want only the truth?"

"Yeah, I do."

"Okay, I'll give you the truth but on one condition."

He was such a player. She cocked her head. "And that is?"

"That you tell me the truth first."

"What is this? A game of truth or dare?"

"No. Just honesty. Are you ready?"

She nodded.

"Okay, so...were you sitting out here waiting for me?"

She should have known this was coming. Thank

goodness it was almost full dark. Otherwise he might have seen her blush. "Absolutely not. I was reading this John Grisham book." She held up the book.

"Really? In the dark?"

"It's the third week in June. The sun just went down." A semi-truth. "Besides, I answered your question. Now you answer mine. Did you specifically memorize that line from *Romeo and Juliet* in order to impress the ladies?"

"I memorized a great deal of poetry to impress one special lady in particular."

A frisson of pain knifed through her. One lady? Since when had he cared about one woman? "Really. Who?"

"My grandmother," he said, his smile widening into a grin. "I was a little boy, and she was a very old lady whose eyesight was fading. I had a date to read to her every afternoon. And I'm afraid my grandmother loved romantic poetry."

A tiny bit of mortar crumbled from the wall around Courtney's heart. In her mind's eye she could see a young Matt, with a head full of wild curly hair, sitting beside his grandmother, reading Elizabeth Barrett Browning. "That's sweet," she said.

He shrugged, and for a tiny moment he looked slightly uncomfortable. It had cost him something to share this secret.

"To be utterly honest," Courtney said, "I did kind of hope you might walk by while I was reading." And then she took a wild and crazy leap off a very tall precipice. "Are you just getting home from work? If you haven't eaten, I have a ton of homemade lasagna."

"*Homemade* lasagna?"

"Yeah." It struck her then that she was having her own balcony scene with a very handsome man, but instead of talking about the moon and the stars, they were talking about lasagna. "What if I bring you a plate?" She almost cringed. Was she going to become *that* neighbor? No. She would not.

"Okay. You can bring Doom back too."

"His name isn't Doom. It's Aramis."

"Nope." He shook his head. "The cat formerly named Aramis is still at my house. You've got Doom, the cat formerly named Porthos."

"Does it matter which is which? And for the record, I'm trying to square the guy who quotes Shakespeare with the guy who names his cats after comic book villains instead of the Three Musketeers. The inconsistencies worry me."

His eyes twinkled. "I guess that makes you like Juliet, then."

Damn. He knew about Juliet's comeback line. "You mean that line in the balcony scene where she talks about the moon being unreliable?"

"You don't remember the specific words, do you?" he asked.

She shook her head. "No, but I'm not a player either."

"O, swear not by the moon, the inconstant moon,
That monthly changes in her circled orb,
Lest that thy love prove likewise variable."

His voice was low and deep, but it carried up to the balcony and swept away her carefully placed barriers.

"Yeah, that's the one," she said, trying to keep her heart from racing away with her. She needed to stop this. Now. She'd take a plate over to him, tell him about his mother's plans for his apartment, and turn right around and come back home.

Yes, she most definitely would do just that.

Matt shouldn't have told her about Granny Artzen. Courtney was the kind of woman who might use that knowledge against him.

Why had he done it?

Easy answer: When he'd seen her sitting out on her balcony reading a book with her bare legs propped up against the railing, something eased inside him. He'd had a truly awful day at work. The Dogwood Estates case had ended in disaster. All those families would have to find new homes and Matt couldn't do one thing about it. Instead, he spent the day following David around while he dealt with no less than four divorces. And then he'd had to sit in Dad's office for a full forty-five minutes while he pontificated about the law.

The only good thing that had happened was Arwen's news that her contact in the Jefferson County

Building Permits Division wanted to meet with them. Arwen was excited about this. She thought she could find them a client.

This made him a little nervous. For one thing, Dad had practically prohibited this sort of thing. And for another, Matt didn't have the skills to bring a property rights case. He'd have to win David and Dad's approval. And that seemed remote.

Or barring that, he'd have to go to August Kopp, the managing partner, who would probably eat him for lunch.

So when Courtney knocked on his door for the second time in two days, he welcomed the diversion. She stood on his threshold like a voluptuous angel of mercy, holding a plate of lasagna that smelled deliciously of cheese and marinara. Her cutoffs exposed her shapely legs, and her tank top clung to her breasts.

Instant hard-on. Especially with her hair piled on top of her head in a messy bun with tendrils falling down around her ears. His fingers itched to take that hair down one bobby pin at a time.

Damn. He should send her back across the hallway. He wanted her too much, and nothing good had ever come from wanting a woman too much. But the aroma of the lasagna did him in. He was starving. "That smells amazing," he said.

She grinned like the proverbial casserole-bearing neighbor. "It's my mother's secret recipe. I used to make lasagna for my dad all the time."

Wow, that seemed like an odd detail. But her reference to her father made him suddenly curious about her parents, a scary thought. He didn't want to get in too deep.

"Enjoy," she said, handing him the plate. She stood on the threshold, either waiting for an invitation or preparing to make a quick escape. He should send her back across the hall.

"Come on in," he said, backing away from the door. Damn. He was not thinking with the head on his shoulders.

She hesitated a moment, as if considering her options. As if she was having second thoughts about the game they played. She understood the rules better than most.

That should ease his conscience, but it didn't.

She didn't move. "Um, I need to tell you something."

Uh-oh, was she about to have some long-winded talk about last night? "Okay," he said, bracing himself.

"I caught your mother and aunt coming out of your apartment this afternoon. They think you need a decorator. I got the impression they were going to redo your apartment behind your back."

"Goddammit," he said, turning to head toward his dining room table.

"I'm sorry."

"Not your problem. Thanks for warning me." He looked at her over his shoulder. "Are you coming in or not?"

She finally crossed the threshold and closed the door behind her.

He placed the lasagna on the table and said, "I've got some silverware somewhere, in one of these shopping bags."

"Let me help," she said, as she started peeking into one bag after another.

Damn. His mother was meddling in his life, and now the girl next door was sticking her nose into all his stuff. He almost told her to stop, but she found the package of knives and forks before he did.

"Here you go," she said, handing him the package.

He retrieved a fork and sat down at the table, but before he could dig into the lasagna, she said, "Aren't you going to wash that first?"

She plucked the fork from his fingers and walked into his kitchen as if she owned the place or something. His skin started to itch. She returned a moment later. "All clean," she said, and then sank into the chair facing him.

Their gazes met across the table, and all his blood went south. Forget the lasagna and the silverware and his misgivings about the women in his life. Maybe he could tackle her like a cave man and drag her back to the bedroom and bury himself in her.

"About last night," she said, just as he lost himself in her incredible blue-eyed stare.

"Yeah." He almost grunted the word as he tore his gaze away and focused on the lasagna. He took a bite, closing his eyes to savor the mouthwatering taste. Holy crap. Courtney Wallace could cook.

"I think it would be better if we were friends, and not lovers," Courtney said.

His eyes sprang open, and he swallowed down the pasta. What the hell? Hadn't she admitted that she'd been hanging out on her balcony waiting for him? Hadn't she come across the hall with food? Then it occurred to him that she might have been waiting all day just to tell him that his mother had been sniffing around, meddling in his life. Maybe she'd been waiting to tell him she just wanted to be his friend.

Did he have any female friends?

Sure he did. He had women friends in Washington. Work colleagues and the girlfriends of guys he knew. And Arwen was becoming a friend too.

Could he be friends with Courtney?

No way. On the other hand, being friends with her might be better than letting her get too close.

"Okay," he said, looking back down at the lasagna.

"Good. Now that we're friends, I need to ask you a question."

He ground his teeth. She was poking him sort of the way he sometimes poked her. "Sure. Whatever. I might not answer it though."

"Fair enough."

"So?"

"Who are you? I mean, you're rich but you bought furniture at IKEA. You have a cat named Doom after some comic book character, but you also quote Shakespeare. You're a player with cats."

"What's the matter? Don't I fit into your man classification system?"

She shook her head. "No. That's not it. You actually fit the definition of a Hook-up Artist perfectly. But for some reason I still like you."

"You do?"

"Yeah. And I'm trying to figure out why a guy like you, from a wealthy family, who has had everything in life, ended up becoming a player. I mean players are guys who have low self-esteem. And you're not like that."

Whoa. That came way too close to the truth. He gave her an intent and sober stare. "First rule of friendship: no psychoanalysis."

She snorted a laugh. "Sorry. That's fair. But for the record, just so you feel comfortable with your insecurities, I'm pretty sure they won't ever rival mine. See, I was the girl no one loved in high school. I had zits, braces, a slightly crossed eye. So I'm naturally defensive. Especially after what happened at senior prom."

His hearing faded away as blood rushed through his veins. He had the strong, almost overpowering urge to give her a hug. A hug! "What happened?" he asked instead.

"A guy I really liked asked me to the prom. I was over the moon, and then he turned out to be the high school equivalent of a player, or something. He took me to the dance, but he didn't sit with me, he didn't dance with me, and he didn't take me home. He sat with the popular kids, pointing at me and laughing."

Matt blew out a long breath. "I'm so sorry."

She pushed up from the table. "I wanted you to know that because I think that prom incident warped me in some deep way. It's not that I don't like guys. It's not that I push them away on purpose. It's just that I don't quite trust any of them. I guess I never have. So really, I think it would be best if we were friends, because I do like you, Matt, and that's a huge surprise."

Before he could say another word, she turned and walked with an astonishing amount of dignity out of his apartment, leaving him stunned and utterly adrift.

"So, I'll see you later, at the open mic?" Rory tucked a strand of Arwen's hair behind her ear, the gesture so kind, so surprising.

She sat on the edge of his bed, in the apartment he shared with Steve, one of the Jaybird's other bartenders. It was four in the afternoon, and she needed to get back to work. Her life would be so much simpler if Rory didn't work nights, and if he didn't live here, at Dogwood Estates.

For the last four days, she'd been skulking around, leaving the office for a few hours every afternoon, sneaking in here, scared to death that someone would see her.

How had she missed this essential fact about

Rory? All these months, visiting with Leslie and the tenants, never once had she come face-to-face with him. But then, most of the tenants association meetings had been held in the evenings when Rory was working. And Rory's name wasn't on the lease. He was Steve's subtenant.

"I can't make it tonight," she said in answer to his question.

"Why?"

"I have something important I need to do tonight."

"Really? What's more important than your songs?"

She stood up, moved to the grimy window, and looked out on the weed-choked parking lot. The coast was clear right at the moment. "It's none of your business," she said, trying to infuse her voice with conviction. In truth, what she had to do tonight *was* his business in a roundabout way.

She let go of a long sigh and turned around. Rory reclined in the bed, his dark hair tumbling across his forehead in a ridiculously romantic fashion. He was also gloriously naked, and every fiber of her body wanted to climb back into bed with him.

"You're fooling yourself, love," he said with a knowing spark in those deep blue eyes.

"About what? You? I already know that."

He chuckled. "No. About your songs. You're running away from them."

"How?"

"By doing whatever it is you think you need to do tonight instead of showing up for the open mic."

"No one listens to me at the open mic."

"That isn't true. I listen. Courtney listens. Juni listens. Ryan listens. A lot of people listen. And even more people would listen if you would do something about those songs. We should get on the bike right now and go to Nashville. What do you say? I'm going to have to leave soon anyway, now that everyone here is being evicted. Let's go today. Right now."

"I can't. I have things to do."

"Things that aren't as important as your songs?"

She turned away and hauled in a huge breath redolent with his scent: smoke and whiskey and something else that made the crazy part of her come alive. How easy it sounded, to pick up and move, to bet her future on a handful of songs no one ever listened to. It was seductive.

And it was a pipe dream.

She turned toward him. "I have to go. I won't be back."

He sat up in bed. "But—"

"I mean it. I won't be back. I won't be back to the open mics either. I need to get my life back together. I can't go on lying to people at work. To my friends. To myself. I know it's only been four days, but honestly, I'm not cut out for this kind of life. I need structure. I need routine. I need habit."

She turned and raced out of his apartment, down the rusty iron stairs, and out into the parking lot, where her worst nightmare awaited her. Just as she reached her sensible Honda Civic, Leslie Heath pulled her classic red Volkswagen Bug in to the adjacent spot.

There was no escape this time. Leslie climbed out of her car with a smile. "Arwen, I wasn't expecting you today. Do you have news for us?"

Oh crap. Now what? "I, um, I—"

"She wasn't here to see you, Leslie," Rory said from his apartment's concrete stoop. He'd thrown on a pair of jeans, but no shirt or shoes. He looked gorgeous and romantic and dangerous all at once. He was an addiction Arwen could not afford.

Leslie's gaze snapped from Arwen to Rory and back again before a big smile spread on her face. "Oh, I didn't know you two were acquainted."

"You should come down to the Jaybird some Wednesday," Rory said. "Arwen is an amazing songwriter." Rory's deep-set blue eyes pierced Arwen like a pair of twin lasers.

"It's not true," she said. "I'm a much better paralegal. And, um, I, uh, really need to get back to the office." Arwen pulled open her car door and escaped before Rory tried to convince her to stay. She needed to keep away from that man. He was not good for her. He was messing with her mind.

She peeled out of the parking lot, but instead of heading toward the office, she turned left onto Route 7 and drove toward Winchester. She hadn't been lying to Rory about the open mic tonight. She had a meeting with Tom McClintock, a clerk in the Jefferson County Building Permits Division.

But even if she hadn't been busy, she would have begged off the open mic. It was stupid to believe anything Rory said. After all, he was hardly a success in life. He tended bar in a small backwater café, and he lived in a room he subleased in a rundown apartment. He wasn't living a dream life.

In fact, he was wasting his life on cigarettes and weed. Where did he get off telling her what to do about her life?

But then again, did it make a difference if your cell was gilded or rusty? Either way it was still a cell.

Tears formed in her eyes as she drove. She wanted to be wild and adventurous, but four days of sex with Rory had done nothing except make her crazy. The hours of lost sleep. The deep questioning of her beliefs. The yearning for something she couldn't even articulate.

Damn. It wasn't healthy. She needed to get back on track. And tonight's meeting was the first step back. After that, she'd find some other bar where she and her friends could hang out. There were a few chain restaurants up at the highway interchange not far from downtown Shenandoah Falls. She would get over this momentary lapse of judgment.

She forced herself to focus on tonight's meeting. Tom was a good guy and an old friend from high school. And in true whistle-blower fashion, he hadn't wanted to meet in the county offices. In fact, he hadn't wanted to meet anywhere within the boundaries of Jefferson County. So at 5:30 p.m. Arwen pulled into the parking lot at Jim Barnett Park in Winchester and waited until Matt joined her twenty minutes later.

Then the two of them hiked to a remote picnic area, where they sat down with Tom, who had a lot to say about the Jefferson County Council, and its chairman, Bill Cummins.

Chapter Thirteen —————

Courtney arrived at Eagle Hill Manor at 9:00 a.m. on Saturday. Allison Chapman's wedding and reception were the only events on the calendar today. Thank God.

No less than three hundred guests were expected. The Carriage House, Eagle Hill Manor's largest function space, wasn't big enough to hold three hundred wedding guests, so a tent had been erected over the adjacent terrace to create covered space for five additional ten-person table rounds.

The ceremony would take place at 4:30 p.m. on the lawn adjacent to the gazebo. The guests would start arriving a little before 4:00 p.m., so Courtney had plenty of time to get ready.

Her first stop of the day was to check on the

tent and tables for the reception, but she needn't have worried. The tent was up already, and staff were setting up the thirty tables required to hold the crowd. The thirty centerpieces and the flowers for the gazebo and wedding party were scheduled to arrive at noon, and Amy had already confirmed delivery with the florist. Courtney spent twenty minutes with Amy going over a checklist and had just started to think that maybe Allison Chapman's wedding would be perfect when her cell phone jangled.

"Is that the bride?" Amy asked.

"Of course it is," Courtney said as she punched the talk button.

"Hi, Allison. How's it going?" Courtney held her breath, prepared to hear yet another conversation about the canapés.

"I have a few minutes before I need to go to the hairdresser. I'm having breakfast. Can you join me?" Allison sounded somber.

Courtney agreed and then gave Amy an exaggerated eye roll.

"Drama?" Amy asked.

"I don't know yet."

Five minutes later, Courtney strolled into Eagle Hill Manor's dining room, where breakfast was served to the inn's guests on a daily basis. Allison, wearing a University of Virginia sweatshirt and looking surprisingly calm for a bride, sat alone at a two-person table near one of the windows.

Something bothered Courtney about this. A bride

usually didn't eat breakfast alone on her wedding day. Where were Allison's bridesmaids? Her mother? For that matter, where was breakfast? Allison's table was bare except for a half-empty coffee cup.

Courtney slipped into the facing seat and immediately attempted to reassure the bride. "I was just down at the Carriage House," she said. "The tent is already up, and the tables are being set. Amy says the flowers are on the way. We'll have the corsages, bouquets, and boutonnieres delivered to the Churchill Suite when they arrive." Courtney gave Allison a professional smile. "Are you excited?"

The bride nodded and took another sip of coffee. Her smile wavered.

Courtney leaned in, concerned. "Are you all right?"

"It's terrifying," she said on a shaky voice. "I mean, I think Erik is the right man. After all, he's a hedge fund manager. So I'm probably set for life. But still…"

Courtney tried mightily not to snap at Allison. Without question, this woman was the most spoiled, the most calculating, the most annoying bride she'd ever worked with. "And you love him, right?"

"I suppose."

She supposed? Arwen was right. Romance and true love had died somewhere in the 1990s during the Clinton administration.

"Are you having cold feet?" Courtney asked, dreading the answer.

Allison vigorously shook her head. "Of course not. I mean, Erik is great."

Yep, she was having cold feet. Brides and grooms with second thoughts were becoming a real occupational hazard. "I'm glad to hear that you love your fiancé. Relax, girl. It's going to be fine."

Allison put her coffee cup down on the table and stared at it. "Are you still dating Matt Lyndon?"

Dating Matt Lyndon?

Courtney's heart went on a wild trip before settling back into her chest. It wasn't a new sensation. Ever since that night when she'd chickened out and pushed Matt into the friend zone, thinking about him had become a hobby. Thinking about him, lusting after him, and reliving their one night of breathtaking sex was not the same as dating him though. And she'd never told Allison that she and Matt were a thing, had she?

No. She'd told Allison that she had a plan for Matt. And at the time, three weeks ago, that had been a true statement. It wasn't anymore. Her desire to put Matt in his place had disappeared.

"We're not dating. We're just friends," Courtney said.

Allison looked up, the expression on her face morphing from uncertain bride into evil-eyed Maleficent. "You're friends?" She delivered the words like a slap to the face.

Courtney probably deserved that. "I know. How could I possibly be friends with a player like him?

But he moved in next door, and we've become…
neighbors, okay?"

"And what? Are you taking casseroles over to him
on a nightly basis?"

The comment hit perilously close to the mark.
"Allison, did you ask me here so we could talk about
Matt Lyndon?"

Allison leaned back in her chair and stared out the
window. "I must have told you that we hooked up in
college."

Courtney nodded. "Yes, you did." Where was she
going with this?

"I knew him in high school, of course, but he was
such a dork back then," Allison said.

Damn. Matt had told her he'd been short and fat,
but she hadn't believed him. How was it possible?
The Lyndons didn't do dorky. Did they?

"I know it's hard to believe when you look at
him now. In high school, he was short and kind of
chubby. And he liked poetry. Although, to be honest,
he still liked poetry when we hooked up in college.
I thought the whole poetry thing was a little gay, to
tell you the truth. But Matt's not gay." She paused a
moment. "He's better in bed than Erik."

Allison whispered the last sentence, and suddenly
Courtney understood. Not ever having been a bride,
Courtney had never actually experienced this emotion. But Allison wasn't the first bride to freak out
at the thought that her fiancé would be the last man
to share her bed. And she could understand why any

woman would look back on her encounter with Matt with a certain amount of nostalgia. Still, she didn't need to know that Allison had slept with Matt.

"Sex isn't everything," she said, but her voice sounded pretty damn insincere.

"I was going to marry him."

"What?" How gullible had Allison been?

Allison finally looked away from the window. "You heard what I said. He proposed to me, and then he broke it off…"

"What? He left you at the altar?"

Allison shook her head and sighed like a drama queen. "No. It never got that far. He broke off the engagement. But to be honest, I don't think he wanted to break it off."

"Why not?" Was this woman delusional?

"His family made him do it."

"Why?"

Allison shrugged. "I don't know. But I should have found a way to make it stick, because I'd be a Lyndon now. Instead I'm marrying money, which isn't bad. But Matt has the last name, you know, like American royalty."

WTF? Had Matt left her at the altar, or had his family refused their blessing? Either way, Courtney should have felt some deep sympathy for Allison, but instead a profound sense of relief washed over her. The idea of Matt with someone as selfish and craven as Allison seemed all wrong somehow.

But then, she was hardly a disinterested party.

Allison waved her hand in dismissal. "I guess I should get over it. It's all ancient history anyway. So, tell me, how have you fared with him? How many casseroles have you taken over? And what have you done to put him in his place? Isn't that what you wanted to do? Or have you changed directions and decided to go after him? Be honest."

"I haven't taken him any casseroles." A true statement, even if it was a tiny bit dishonest.

Allison arched a brow. "None? Really? Are you an idiot? If I lived next door to a Lyndon, I would be all over him with casseroles. And I'd make sure the condoms got lost, if you know what I mean. Honey, you've been handed an opportunity. Don't blow it the way I did."

What the hell? Had she tried to trap Matt into a marriage? It sure sounded that way.

Courtney stood up, her hands balling into fists. She was done with this idiotic, spoiled brat of a bride. "Look, Allison," she said. "If you're looking for advice, I suggest that you go back upstairs and decide whether you love Erik Smith or his money. Because as far as I'm concerned, the only reason to get married is for love."

Allison threw back her head and laughed. "You're such a romantic. If that's the way you approach things, you'll never land a Lyndon. Of course, you're unlikely to land one anyway. I tried, and I failed. I can't see you doing something I couldn't accomplish."

In that moment, Allison Chapman became the

face of every snotty girl in high school who ever put
her down, called her zit faced, or teased her because
she wasn't pretty enough for the in crowd or coordinated enough for the cheer squad. They'd taught
her a few lasting lessons: Smart girls were nerds, and
cross-eyed smart girls were pathetic.

But Courtney was done feeling pathetic, so she
leaned over the table, got right up in the bride's face,
and told her where she could take her opinion and
shove it. Then she turned on her heel and marched
from the dining room.

She felt strong, empowered, and almost kick-ass
for about two minutes. But by the time she reached
the back terrace, reality set in. Allison wasn't one of
the mean girls from high school. She was a mean
girl who was also a client. And clients were always
right—even when they were wrong.

Deep in Courtney's head, the ghost of her father
whispered words he'd said to her a thousand times:
Beauty is as beauty does.

And Courtney had just been unforgivably ugly to
one of Eagle Hill Manor's brides.

It didn't take long before Willow heard about Courtney's *faux pas*. An hour later, Eagle Hill Manor's
owner cornered Courtney in the gazebo, where Rick,
the sound guy, was connecting the PA system for Allison's ceremony. "What's the matter with you?" she
said, then scowled at Rick and told him to take a five-
minute break.

When Willow scowled, people jumped.

Once Rick had left, Courtney turned toward her boss and said, "I'm sorry, Willow. She's..." Words failed her.

"What? What is she? Aside from being one of our clients and a bride?"

Courtney let go of the breath she'd been holding seemingly for the last hour and collapsed on the bench that ran the gazebo's circumference. "She's a snob. And a bully. And I could call her other names..."

Willow sat down beside Courtney. "Don't. Honestly, you do fabulous work for me, but I'm tired of dealing with your anger issues."

"Are you firing me?" A sharp pain pierced Courtney's chest. What would she do if Willow fired her?

"I can't decide that until I know what the hell happened."

Courtney leaned back and rolled her neck, trying to ease the tension. "Honestly, Willow, she's kind of psycho. I mean..." She took another long breath and started again. "Okay, this is what happened. I found out that she knows Matt Lyndon. She told me she had hooked up with him in college. And to tell you the truth, until this morning, I was sure she was another one of his victims. So I told her that I was going out on a date with him in order to put him in his place.

"But then this morning, she tells me some other story about how Matt proposed to her but his family broke up the relationship."

"What?"

Courtney nodded. "She said a lot of mean, selfish things, the way she always does. But the gist of it was that she's marrying Erik for his money, but if she had her choice, she would prefer to be marrying someone with money and the Lyndon last name."

"So she's a fortune hunter. But we've always known that. Why lose your temper now? If I didn't know better, I'd say that you were jealous of her. That this had more to do with your feelings for Matt than anything else."

Courtney took a deep, calming breath and nodded. "Yes, it's about Matt. But not the way you think."

"Okay, why don't you explain it to me?"

"You know he's my neighbor, right?"

Willow nodded.

"So I just want to make it clear that I'm not the kind of neighbor who takes over casseroles every night."

"Oh." Willow elongated the word as if a lightbulb had just flashed in her brain. Willow cocked her head and studied Courtney for a long moment. "What happened? Did Allison suggest that you weren't good enough for a Lyndon?"

Heat crawled up Courtney's face, and when she spoke again, her voice trembled. "I'm not in love with Matt Lyndon, okay? He's too young for me, and he's not looking for commitment right now. We're friends.

"But when Allison suggested that I'd be stupid not

to bring over casseroles every night and try to trap him into marriage...I don't know, I—"

"What? She suggested you should trap him in a marriage?"

Courtney nodded. "Worse than that. I got the feeling she had tried to trap him and failed. And when I realized that, I just saw red." She blew out a breath. "I know I was in the wrong. And I know I need to apologize."

"Okay. I expect you to do that. And I also want you to be very careful with Matt."

"I told you, Matt and I are friends. Besides, he's what? Twenty-five. He's a baby."

Willow stood up. "Courtney, if you want to lie to yourself, go right ahead. But you and Matt are not friends. If you were, you wouldn't have lost your temper the way you did."

Chapter Fourteen ———————

Over the next week, Matt argued with his mother about his apartment no less than ten times. And when he wasn't arguing with Mom, he was spending long hours at work as a means of distracting himself from the woman living next door. Work seemed to be the only panacea for the daydreams that distracted him whenever he let his concentration slip. He'd imagined himself making the journey across the hallway hundreds of times, but he never could decide what he should say if he knocked and Courtney answered.

Would he explain that he'd also been a social outcast during high school? Would he tell her about his broken heart and Allison Chapman's endless cruelty?

No. He. Would. Not.

So instead he followed David around, writing

meeting notes, proofing filings and motions, and preparing his cousin for every meeting and every court appearance as well. After regular office hours, once he'd finished any work David had assigned him for the day, Matt chased down the leads Arwen's whistle-blower had provided.

By Monday of the following week, Matt had found a potential client—a landowner who had been assessed an absurd fine and now faced a choice between forfeiting his property to the county or selling out to GB Ventures. But even though the situation was unfair, the facts made the potential case difficult. And besides, Matt wasn't a litigator.

He needed advice, and he couldn't go to Dad, and he wasn't about to call up the managing partner. So on Monday afternoon, during a lull in David's schedule, Matt strolled into his cousin's office and shut the door behind him. "You have a minute?" he asked.

David looked away from his laptop screen. "What? Is there a problem with Klempert vs. Klempert?"

"No." Matt crossed the room and sat in one of the leather-covered wing chairs. David's office was sumptuous in comparison to Matt's small cubbyhole. David had two gigantic windows overlooking the parkland in front of the county courthouse a block away.

Matt swallowed hard. "I have something I'd like you to see." He handed David a folder that contained all the relevant facts pertaining to Avery Johnson's property, located north and west of town.

Mr. Johnson was a hillbilly from a long line of hillbillies who had lived up on the ridge since before the Civil War. He owned a parcel of land off the unpaved section of Good Shepherd Road, where his family had been raising chickens and pigs for more than a hundred years.

But a year ago, on a three-to-two vote, the County Council outlawed the raising of pigs in that area. Not too surprisingly, Avery Johnson refused to comply with this rule. So the county fined him, and now the fines amounted to more than Johnson's land was worth. GB Ventures had already approached Mr. Johnson with an offer to buy his land. Mr. Johnson was holding out for more money.

On its own, that wasn't much of a case. But it turned out that GB Ventures had bought a huge parcel of land off the paved section of Good Shepherd Road, adjacent to Mr. Johnson's land, six months before the County Council outlawed pig farming. For the last eighteen months, GB Ventures had been building million-dollar homes right next to Mr. Johnson's pig farm. Clearly GB Ventures wanted Mr. Johnson and his smelly pigs out of the way, and they'd gone to the chairman of the County Council, Bill Cummins, to make it happen.

David read these facts while the grandfather clock in the corner of his office ticked the minutes away in ominous fashion. As he read, David's eyebrows lowered in a frown Matt found difficult to read. Was he angry or outraged? Or possibly both?

Minutes passed with no other sound except for the ticking clock and David's methodical turning of pages. Matt's hands started to sweat, and he wondered if he'd done the right thing.

Finally, his cousin looked up. "Didn't Uncle Charles tell you not to pursue this?"

Damn. He'd hoped David would see the injustice. Matt nodded. "And August Kopp also said there was a potential case here. I told Avery Johnson to contact the Blue Ridge Legal Aid Society, and he's done so. So, we have a client if we want one. And for the record, I did this after hours. On my own time."

"How did you get the information about the penalty amounts?"

"Arwen knows someone."

"So Arwen spent time on this too?"

Matt nodded. "She's the one who discovered this, David. You know that. But she's only worked on it after hours."

"What do you want me to do about it?"

"I want us to take Avery Johnson's case pro bono. And I want to sue the county for abuse of power, or maybe the unconstitutional condemnation of private property."

David let go of a long breath and leaned back in his chair. "Matt, I understand your outrage, but you have no experience in this sort of thing. And neither do I."

"Mr. Kopp does."

David nodded. "Yeah, he does. And he only takes paying clients. You do understand that this case wouldn't be anything like our normal pro bono work. A case like this could go to the State Supreme Court. Who's paying for our time?"

"No one, but that doesn't mean we shouldn't take the case." Matt said.

"No. It doesn't. But this is the kind of case that requires help from the American Civil Liberties Union or, better yet, the Institute for Justice. Those guys live for cases like this. And they have independent funding to pursue them. You should talk to those guys."

"Don't you live for a case like this?"

David pressed his lips together. "Look, here's the thing. In the long run, farmers like Avery Johnson are going to get squeezed out of Jefferson County no matter what we do. And the people buying those mansions on Good Shepherd Road will be happy to see the pigs go."

"So you think justice is reserved for those who can pay for it?" Matt stood up, too angry to sit.

David shook his head. "No. I'm just saying that your solution isn't a legal one. You're likely to win the case, at enormous cost, but lose the war."

"What's that supposed to mean?"

"If you really wanted to change the world, you'd have to run Bill Cummins and his cronies out of office. That means you'd have to elect two or three additional council members who don't care about the property tax base, which, as you know, affects the quality of our schools."

Matt sat back down. "You're saying it's hopeless, aren't you?"

David shook his head. "No. I'm saying that it's hard. I don't like the way Bill Cummins runs this county. But I'm not going back into politics. And if I touch this case, it will lead me right back into that rat race. I have no heart for it, Matt. It's not who I am. And it's not who Uncle Charles is either." He handed the file back to Matt.

"So you think I should give this up?"

David scrubbed his face with his hands. "No. But if you do this, you do it on your own. I admire you for tilting at windmills, but remember that if Charles hears you're spending regular office hours doing this kind of thing, he's going to be furious."

"So that's it? You won't help?"

His mouth twitched. "Feel free to ask for advice anytime. But with another baby on the way, I'm out of the windmill-tilting business for the foreseeable future. When Natalie was a baby, I was chairing the County Council and I never had time for her. I missed out on a lot. I'm not going back to that life. This time around, I want to be there for my child."

Another Monday night and Courtney was walking into the Jaybird Café and Music Hall at 6:00 p.m. so she wouldn't be home when Matt returned from work. Mondays and Tuesdays were the hardest because she had all day to think about ways to avoid Matt. Workdays were easier because they both worked long hours. She'd only heard him once, last Wednesday.

And even though the weather had been unusually beautiful, with bright sunny days and low humidity, Courtney had refrained from dining alfresco on her balcony for fear of another reenactment of *Romeo and Juliet*.

Willow was right. She and Matt Lyndon were not friends. But they weren't lovers either, which was probably a good thing, even if Courtney was having a hard time forgetting about their one-night stand and the pleasure he had given her.

It was like she'd told Allison—sex wasn't everything. But maybe when it came to Matt, sex was the only thing.

She needed a drink. And she probably needed to join a group for middle-aged singles. Not to find Mr. Right, but to find a few girlfriends she could commiserate with. Arwen had officially abandoned her. Had she found someone?

What an awesome and depressing thought.

She battled against the self-pity, and since she was flying solo, she bypassed her favorite table and took a seat at the Jaybird's bar, where she ordered guacamole and chips and a Manhattan. Thank goodness Rory was tending bar because Courtney wasn't in the mood to have Juni reading her aura tonight.

But when Rory placed the Manhattan in front of her, he leaned against the back edge of the bar and asked, "Where's the lovely Arwen tonight? We've missed her at the open mic these past two weeks."

Funny. In the two years Rory had been tending

bar for Juni, Courtney had never once had a real conversation with him. She'd ordered drinks from him. She'd said hello to him. But that hadn't been the same as actually talking to him. And since when had Rory started to notice Arwen's comings and goings?

"She tells me she's crazy busy at work," Courtney replied with a shrug.

"It sounds to me as if you don't believe that's true." Rory cocked his head and studied Courtney the way bartenders study drinkers the world over.

Great. Just great. Maybe it would have been better if Juni had read her aura after all. She didn't want to talk about Arwen to the Jaybird's bartender. So she gave him a long, hard stare, which bounced right off.

"Ah," he said, "so I'm right. You don't think she's been busy at work. What is it, then? Has she finally found her kind and sincere man?"

"Are you telling me that you actually listen to Arwen when she sings? I mean, she's always singing about that mythological man who is both kind and sincere."

"Of course I listen. Why would that surprise you?"

She took a sip of her drink and thought about his question. "I thought I was the only one who listened."

His gaze narrowed. "Aye. I know that. But I think you've been filling Arwen's head with the idea that no one ever listens. And you're wrong about that, Courtney Wallace. The people who matter have always listened to Arwen."

Courtney didn't know how to respond. Was he suggesting that she'd been holding Arwen back somehow? How was that possible? She showed up every time Arwen screwed up the nerve to sing in public. And she held her hand. And she loved her songs.

Rory's black Irish smile widened. "The people who matter aren't the ones who clap for Kent Henderson and his tired rendition of 'Tennessee Stud.'"

Courtney finally found her sense of humor. "And that would be who? You, me, Juni?"

He shrugged. "And one or two others." He leaned a little closer. "I've missed her music these last few weeks. Would you tell her that for me?"

Whoa. Wait. What was up with Rory? Did he have a crush on Arwen? In a million years Courtney would never have seen that coming. Arwen was so middle-of-the-road about everything except her music. And Rory...well, he was the walking embodiment of a black Irish rebel.

"I'll tell her. But I have to be honest, something's up with that girl. She's been avoiding me."

"Has she, now?"

Courtney looked down at her drink and played with the cherry for a moment. "I miss her too. And I have a feeling someone has swept her off her feet. Someone romantic. You know the kind. A guy who sends flowers, takes her out to nice restaurants. She's hungry for that sort of thing."

"Is she, now?"

What the hell? She hardly knew Rory, so pigeon-holing him into one of her ten male types would be wrong. But the tattoos, earrings, and leather suggested a guy who was carrying around lots of pain and anger. If she had to bet, he was probably another example of the Emotionally Unavailable Man. Or maybe an Irish version of a Man Baby—one of those guys who thinks his emotions are more important than anyone else's.

"Yeah, Arwen's a sucker for romance. She's also a nice Jewish girl. You might want to keep that in mind."

"I'll do that," Rory said as his gaze drifted toward the door just as Ryan Pierce arrived.

Oh, great, her night was complete. She should have stayed in and ordered pizza.

"Drinking alone?" Ryan asked as he took the stool next to hers.

"Not now."

Ryan ordered a Coke. Rory headed down the bar to fill the order while Ryan scanned the dining room as if he were looking for someone.

"Juni hasn't shown her face tonight, if that's who you're looking for," Courtney said.

Ryan stilled. "I have no idea what you're talking about," he said.

Suddenly the world made no sense. "You know, Ryan, you come in here almost every evening. You sit at the bar and drink a Coke, and you watch Juni. But for all her aura reading, she's utterly unaware of your focus."

"You're a fine one to talk," he said. "By the way, did Matt Lyndon ever win his bet?"

She said nothing, but she had the horrible feeling that Ryan Pierce was as good at reading body language as she was. So she took a huge gulp of her drink.

"I thought so," he said as Rory placed the soft drink in front of him. Thank God Rory didn't stay to chat. Instead he moved down the bar and started filling drink orders for a group of guys at the corner. "I think Rory has a crush on Arwen," she said.

"You've just now figured that out?"

"How did I miss that?"

"Maybe because you're too busy passing judgment on people."

Ryan's criticism was justified. She did pass judgment on people, especially men. And she probably needed to stop. People were more complicated than her man classification system.

Ryan Pierce might not be the emotionally unavailable one. Maybe that label fit Juni even better. And any man who truly listened to Arwen Jacobs's songs couldn't be a Man Baby.

Was Matt really a Hook-up Artist when he hadn't brought a single woman home with him over the last week? She knew because she'd been listening for just that sort of thing. And besides, he quoted Shakespeare, had apparently adored his grandmother, and loved cats. And once, he might have proposed marriage to someone who might have played him.

Damn it all, she loved every single one of Matt's inconsistencies. Despite all her efforts to keep him at arm's length, to push him away, to be careful with her heart, she'd fallen for him anyway.

If only she were braver. But she was as big a coward as Ryan Pierce. The object of her desire lived only five steps away from her front door, and she didn't have the courage to make that journey. But if she didn't take a risk on someone soon, she'd be spending the rest of her Mondays here at the bar alone.

On Monday evening, Matt walked home slowly, turning over David's advice in his mind. Was he tilting at windmills?

Maybe. David was right, though, about one thing. Matt was a fool to think he could stop the development that was changing Jefferson County. The sad fact was that Shenandoah Falls was becoming a suburb of Washington, DC. Its rural character was disappearing.

Still, that didn't give the county the right to work hand in glove with GB Ventures. The close connection between the fines and the land sales suggested graft. Or even abuse of the public trust. Matt hadn't found evidence of real corruption, like kickbacks, but there was the possibility of that. Maybe he should get his younger brother, Jason, involved. Jason had just finished the FBI training course, so he had to know more about how to run an investigation than Matt did.

No. Matt couldn't leave things alone. Something had to be done about the cushy relationship between Bill Cummins and GB Ventures. But what?

Should he run against Cummins in the next election, which was only a few months away? The party hadn't put up a candidate yet. And the filing deadline was looming. Should he run for office?

No way. Who would vote for him?

The sun hung low in the sky as he walked down Rice Street. The mockingbird who lived in the tree on the corner serenaded him with evening song. A trace of something sweet, like honeysuckle, hung in the air, and a soft breeze blew away the day's heat. He'd come to love this walk from the office to his apartment, especially on nights like this, when the humidity wasn't so bad.

Tonight, as in every night over the last week, he glanced up at Courtney's balcony half a block before he reached home. And tonight, as in every night for the last week, he was disappointed. She hadn't come out on her balcony once since the night of the lasagna.

But she was at home most nights. He usually arrived after dark, and her living room lights shone through her French doors like a beacon guiding him safely home and unleashing a deep longing for something more than his lonely apartment. But today her windows were dark, leaving him oddly adrift. Where was she at eight thirty on a Monday night?

The answer came to him as he started up the stairs. She was probably having dinner with her friends at the Jaybird. He hesitated midflight. The Jaybird was a short walk. It wouldn't break any rules for him to go down there for a drink. Plus he could really go for one of the Jaybird's Swiss burgers.

He jettisoned the idea. Ambushing Courtney at the Jaybird would be stupid and immature. If he wanted to have a conversation with her, he'd have to cross the hallway and knock on her door.

He climbed the rest of the stairs and entered his apartment.

So it wasn't like some place out of a magazine. It was still comfortable, and he hadn't spent much money on furniture. He'd even gotten creative over the weekend—buying some slate-gray paint and rolling it on the long wall as an accent. He liked it. And it gave him a sense of pride that he'd done it himself instead of calling up some chichi decorator.

He paused a moment, just inside the door, taking it all in.

He should enjoy it while it lasted. Because he knew darn well Mom had not given up. One day he was going to step inside his front door and feel like he'd walked into someone else's world. When would Mom—and Aunt Pam, who was clearly egging her on—get out of his life?

Short answer: never.

But for now, his apartment was neat and tidy, the way he liked it. And best of all, Ghul came racing out of the bedroom to greet him as if the cat had missed him while he was away.

He dropped his briefcase and snagged the cat for a quick cuddle and a scratch behind the ears. Ghul wasn't all that into affection though. Not like Doom, who'd moved in next door. Or more precisely, the cat who had been stolen from him.

The thought annoyed him for some reason, and so did his empty refrigerator. He grabbed a beer and ordered a pizza and then fired up the fifty-inch flat-screen TV he'd bought over the weekend. He flipped through several channels and settled on the Nats game, which was tied in the bottom of the fourth inning.

He collapsed on his couch. Waiting.

Waiting for the pizza man to arrive. Waiting for the Nats to score. Waiting for his father's respect. Waiting for Mom to swoop in with fabric swatches. Waiting for real life to begin. Waiting for Courtney to come home.

Dammit.

Courtney wasn't going to bridge that gap between his apartment and hers, was she? If Matt wanted her, he'd have to go after her. But how could he do that honorably? He'd never lied to any woman about his intentions, and he wouldn't lie to Courtney.

Of course, he'd been perfectly happy to let women lie to themselves. But Courtney didn't do that sort of thing. Courtney was always so honest with herself.

Restlessness consumed him. He popped up from the sofa and paced the length of his living room a few times before he threw open the French doors and stepped onto his balcony. The midsummer sun had finally set, leaving the world in twilight.

Dammit. He wanted to cross the divide between them. He wanted to feel Courtney in his arms and sink himself into her body. He also wanted to talk to her and share things with her. He wanted her to trust him. And he wanted to trust her.

But none of that would ever happen if he stood here waiting for it. In fact, nothing in his life was going to happen if all he ever did was wait around for it.

Chapter Fifteen ————————

Courtney should have stopped after her second Manhattan. If she had, her walk home would have been less harrowing. She could have floated along on a buzz instead of stumbling a tiny bit.

And she would have been better prepared for what awaited her at home in the form of the ridiculously handsome Matt Lyndon lounging on his balcony with a long-necked beer in his hand.

If she'd been sober, she could have ignored him or even pretended that she didn't see him. But no. Her brain was semi-pickled, and so she stood there looking up at him and said, "Hi," and then giggled like an idiot.

He leaned on the railing. "You've been drinking," he said, his eyebrow doing its thing.

She stumbled slightly because looking up messed with her balance. "Did you take lessons?"

His mouth tipped into a smile. "I took a lot of lessons. Which ones are you talking about?"

"The one where you learned how to do that thing with your eyebrow."

He chuckled. "No. Everyone in the family does that. You should see my father. It's very intimidating."

She nodded. "I'm going up now. Have a nice night." There. She'd been adult. Polite. Now all she had to do was make it to her apartment in one piece.

She dug in her shoulder bag, searching for the key that would open the building's outer door. Damn. Her keys were in here somewhere. She shook her purse, satisfied by the metallic jingle. She stumbled sideways a little. Damn, it was dark out here.

She squatted down and rested her purse on the pavement as she dug deeper. She almost fell over on her ass. This was not going well.

The apartment building's door opened. Thank God it was Matt and not Alyssa Riley, the ground-floor tenant.

No, wait. Something was wrong with that thought. Maybe it would have been better if Alyssa had come to her rescue.

Matt stepped onto the sidewalk looking delish in a golf shirt and jeans. He offered his hand. "Here, let me help."

She stared at his hand for a long moment, trying to decide what to do next. He had beautiful hands, square fingered, broad palmed. Beautiful, talented hands that knew precisely where to touch, where to stroke. A little inarticulate sound escaped her throat.

"Come on. I'll walk you up," he said in that deep voice of his.

"Will you quote poetry?" A warm, intense yearning coursed through her.

"Come on, Courtney. It's time to go up."

He sounded so stern, and maybe a little disappointed. She was an idiot. He probably saved his poetry for the women he seduced. She turned back toward her purse, digging deep, and the keys finally made their way into her hand.

She pushed up from the sidewalk, ignoring his hand, and would have been fine if she hadn't stumbled again. Matt was right there, putting his talented hands on her shoulders.

She looked up at him then, the streetlamp sparking in his espresso eyes. She leaned in, overwhelmed with the desire to kiss him.

But he kept her at bay. He shook his head. "Not like this," he said.

Damn. She was making an idiot of herself, but just as she decided to pull away from him, he started reciting in that deep, incredible voice.

"She walks in beauty, like the night
Of cloudless climes and starry skies;
And all that's best of dark and bright
Meet in her aspect and her eyes:"

So instead of pulling away, she leaned a little closer. "Have I ever told you that your hair is vaguely Byronic?" she asked on a ridiculous sigh.

He barked a laugh. "No. But I'm impressed that you recognized Lord Byron. I didn't think of you as a romantic, Courtney."

"Bull. You know I'm a romantic. I'm just a jaded one." She really should get the hell out of his arms. "I bet you quote that poem to all the girls."

"No." He shook his head, and for some reason, the light in his eyes grew sharper or something. She wanted to believe him.

"I think of that poem every time I see you."

"Really?" She was melting in his arms when she should be freezing him out and running like hell.

He tucked a lock of hair behind her ear, and Courtney's body caught fire. "Really. You have such dark hair and such bright blue eyes." He cupped her jaw and ran his thumb over her cheek. "I love your eyes. They always make me wonder about what's going on inside that head of yours."

Damn, damn, damn. She couldn't resist. Even if she'd been sober, she would have succumbed. She closed her eyes and leaned into his touch, another groan escaping from her.

"Come on," he said in an entirely different tone of voice. "Let's get you upstairs."

He took her keys and guided her through the door and up the stairs. He even unlocked her front door for her. And right there the fantasy unraveled. Aramis sat inside the doorway and gave out the feline equivalent of a lovesick howl the moment Matt crossed her threshold.

"Doom, bro, wazzup?" Matt let Courtney go and scooped the kitten into his arms. Damn. Damn. Damn.

She almost accused him of loving the cat more than he loved her, which, on reflection, was the absolute truth, since Matt Lyndon was not the kind of guy who did relationships. Except with cats. And she, on the other hand, sucked at being a spinster cat lady.

Her love triangle could be summed up this way: He loved her cat, she loved him, and the cat was a turncoat. It was enough to make anyone cry. Especially if the person had overindulged in alcohol. Tears overflowed her eyes, and Courtney wasn't able to stop them. The sudden glimpse of a life lived utterly alone flashed through her brain, and it was more than she could bear. The sob she tried to hold back overwhelmed her, and she fled, utterly humiliated, into the bathroom.

She locked herself in right before she tossed every single one of her cookies.

"Go away," Courtney said through the locked bathroom door.

Matt sat down on the floor outside the bathroom, settled his back against the wall, and let Doom circle his lap looking for a nice, comfy spot. "Sorry," he said. "I can't leave you locked in the bathroom. It goes against my moral code."

"This is my apartment. Please leave."

Matt took Courtney's annoyed tone as a positive sign. He was also glad that she'd stopped coughing and gagging. If that had gone on much longer, he would have broken down the door. As it was, he had to hold himself back. Sometimes a woman needed privacy, but he had never abandoned a woman in distress. He was happy to give Courtney all the privacy she wanted, so long as he could make sure she was all right in the end.

He and Doom settled in, prepared for a long wait.

After five minutes she said, "Are you still there?"

He said nothing. Telling her the truth would only prolong the situation. She was moving around in the bathroom, washing her face, brushing her teeth. When the noises faded, she said, "I know you're still out there. I can hear you breathing."

He kept silent, and another few minutes passed.

"Go away."

Doom, being a young cat with little patience, took matters into his own paws. The cat stood up, gave a sinewy stretch, and then pussyfooted out of Matt's lap. He sat in front of the bathroom door looking up at the knob and meowed.

"Aramis?"

The cat meowed again and scratched at the door.

"Has he gone, Aramis?"

Matt found this both adorable and amusing even if he hated the name Aramis.

The cat meowed again, right on cue. Matt was going to have to find some way to get this cat back. Doom had a bright future ahead of him...as a therapy cat.

When the doorknob rattled, Matt scrambled to his feet and took a step to his left so Courtney wouldn't see him immediately. The door swung open.

"You stayed," she said to the cat, bending down to scoop him up. "I was so sure he'd seduce you into leaving me. And then I'd be all alone." Her voice wavered at the very end.

Damn. She was still drunk and upset. Evidently about the cat.

He peeked around the door, but not before securing it in order to head off any retreats. She looked beautiful even with a swollen red nose and mascara rimming her puffy eyes. "I would never seduce your cat," he said in a soft tone. "In fact, I've been taking good care of Ghul over at my place. You're the one who abandoned him and absconded with Doom."

"I did not. You seduced him, and I simply brought him back home." She sniffled, and her lips trembled. "But he still misses you," she said.

"Does he?"

She nodded. "He sometimes stands at the front door and meows, like he wants to go visit you."

"He can come over anytime," Matt said, releasing the door and taking a step toward her.

"I guess we'll have to arrange a playdate for him." She looked down at the cat, refusing to meet Matt's gaze.

"You can come over too."

She frowned. "Not a good idea."

He put his finger under her chin and lifted it so he could stare down into her incredible eyes, which were still brimming with tears. "Why not?"

She blinked, and one of the tears escaped. He brushed it away. "Because..." Her shaky voice trailed off, and her lips trembled.

He didn't press her for an answer. "Come on, it's time for bed."

She blinked again. "Are you going to take advantage of me?"

He snorted a laugh. "I don't do that sort of thing. I was thinking more about making sure you're tucked in nice and safe, with a couple of aspirin for the headache you're going to have tomorrow."

"Oh." She frowned. "That's a little disappointing."

"You want me to take advantage?"

She shrugged. "Does that make me desperate?"

He shook his head. "No. But you might hate yourself in the morning."

"I wouldn't." She took a tiny step in his direction and leaned her head on his shoulder. Doom snuggled down between them and started to purr.

Matt couldn't just stand there, could he? No. So he put his arms around her shoulders and pulled her a little closer, tucking her head under his chin. He buried his nose in her hair, drinking in the scent of wildflowers and whiskey. He wanted her.

"I need to tell you a story," he said, speaking the words against her temple.

"Is this going to be like a bedtime story?"

He chuckled. "You have a one-track mind, don't you?"

She looked up at him. "And you don't?" The frown she gave him was nothing short of adorable.

"Get this straight. I'm happy to tell you bedtime stories. In fact, I need to tell you this particular story. But no sex. Not tonight. You've had too much to drink."

"Damn. And here I thought you were a scoundrel."

Doom decided he'd had enough of his people. He launched himself out of Courtney's hands and then scampered away in the general direction of his food bowl. The cat's exit gave Matt a chance to move Courtney toward her bedroom.

He'd never been in her bedroom before, and he'd expected a wedding planner to have something lacy and frilly and pink. But Courtney's bedroom was none of those things. It looked like something out of a magazine captioned with the words BEDROOM OA-SIS. It was contemporary and done in various shades of calming gray. Damn.

Had she hired an interior decorator? Or did she have mad skills? Maybe he could ask her for a few tips on how to make his apartment look this nice. Maybe if she helped him, he could reassure Mom that he was going to be fine.

He guided her to the bed. "You want your bedtime story now, or do you want to put on a nightie or something?"

She fluffed the pillow before hopping into bed and ·leaning back. "It depends. Are you going to watch me put on my nightie?"

"Maybe I should just tell you the story."

She patted the bed beside her. "Climb in. Make yourself comfy."

Dangerous territory. But hadn't he decided that he was tired of waiting around? So he accepted her invitation—with only the best of intentions. The mattress was soft and comfortable, like the woman and the room. He leaned back on a pillow. "Are you ready?"

She looked up at him with her tear-ravaged face. "Is this going to be a sad story? I don't think I could do sad tonight."

"Like all stories, it has its ups and downs."

"Okay." She snuggled back into her pillow. "You may begin." She closed her eyes.

She would probably be asleep in thirty seconds. So maybe it wasn't the best moment to bare his soul. But he'd crossed the bridge and it was time to set fire to it.

"Once upon a time," he began, "when I was fourteen and a freshman in high school, I weighed about one hundred and fifty pounds, but I was only five foot three."

"So it's true. Wow," she murmured, but didn't open her eyes.

"Wait a sec. Did someone tell you that I was short and fat in high school?"

She nodded. "Yeah. She said you were dorky."

"She? Who?"

"Allison Chapman," Courtney murmured on a long, sleepy breath.

The name was like a prizefighter's punch to the gut. It took a moment before he could collect his breath. "What did she say about me?" he finally asked, his pulse suddenly racing.

But Courtney didn't answer; she'd fallen fast asleep.

Courtney startled awake. Something was different. She rose on one elbow, pushing her hair out of her eyes as she checked the digital clock on her bedside table. It was 2:30 a.m., she was fully clothed, and someone was hogging her blanket.

She sat up, her eyes as gritty as sandpaper. A gibbous moon spilled a ghostly, silver light through the French doors and revealed the blanket thief. Matt sprawled on the other side of the bed, also fully clothed but sleeping on top of the bedspread, pinning it down.

He looked peaceful in sleep, and so incredibly handsome. Like a Michelangelo statue, with the moonlight turning his skin to pale marble. But he was warmer than stone. And it seemed almost miraculous that he was here, in her bed.

Memories of the evening's events spilled through

her mind. Heat crawled up her cheeks. She'd lost it last night and in so many ways: her cookies, her dignity, her cool, and her mind. Why was he still here? Hook-up Artists always ran from drama. And hadn't she been the quintessential drama queen last night?

And now what? She'd fallen asleep on his story. Damn. He'd been talking about his dorky past—also unusual for a Hook-up Artist. In fact, staring down at his gorgeous face and killer body, Courtney could only conclude that she'd been wrong about Matthew Lyndon.

He was not a Hook-up Artist. She ran through her list of man types, jettisoning each one as she tried to apply it to the man snoring softly in her bed. He wasn't a Man Baby, or a Nice Guy Not, or a Space Invader. He wasn't Clueless. He'd never belittled or shamed her. He wasn't Too Selfless to Be True, and while he did work hard, he didn't strike her as a Workaholic. And finally he was not an Ogler. The few times she'd been out with him, he'd never once even looked at another woman. In fact, Matt had a way of focusing in on her that made her feel special and beautiful and wanted.

Last night, he'd even tried to talk about something deeply emotional. Something that had probably scarred him early. As a high school ugly duckling herself, she could totally understand the pain of being fourteen and overweight. Negative body images were hard to overcome, and any man willing to open himself up to talk about those painful times simply couldn't be Emotionally Unavailable.

So the question was: If he wasn't any of the standard man types, then what the hell was he?

An emotion, tender and warm, spilled through her. A woman needed to be careful, but a woman also needed to see the truth when it knocked on her door. Matt was a man worth risking everything for.

She leaned over him and brushed his hair back from his brow before placing a small, heartfelt kiss on his forehead. He voiced a sweet, inarticulate noise that arrowed through Courtney. She truly wanted this man, on any terms.

She pressed against his chest and continued her assault on his face, linking tiny kisses from his temple down across his cheeks and jaw to the sweet spot under his earlobe. He responded by snaking his arms around her waist and giving her a small upward flex of his hips.

Yes. That was more like it. Fully clothed or not, there was no mistaking the fact that Matt was waking up, and with consciousness came that coiled male energy that had always turned Courtney on. He flexed his hips again while his hand ran across her butt in a sleepy exploration, right before he pulled her a little closer.

This time Courtney let go of a deep, throaty noise as Matt's hands worked their magic. He echoed her then, with a gruff noise halfway between a purr and a growl, which told her he had awakened. She scrambled up onto his body, settling more firmly against him.

She took heart and courage from the fact that he didn't stop her from exploring his neck with her mouth and tongue and teeth. Maybe he was too sleepy. Or maybe, like her, he'd gotten tired of waiting for this. Whatever the reason, her first tentative touches and kisses morphed into something more carnal, involving arms and legs and hands and hampered by clothing.

"I need to feel you," she finally said, frustrated by his clothes. She sat up, straddling his hips. She looked long and deep into his eyes, which managed to twinkle even in the fading rays of moonlight. She unbuckled his belt and unbuttoned his jeans.

He stacked his hands behind his head and watched as she freed him. But his watchfulness disappeared when she went down on him. She reveled in the taste and smell of him and in the way he enjoyed this pleasure-filled moment. But he didn't allow it to go on for too long.

Courtney found the tables reversed as he rolled her over, pinned her to the bed, and kissed her senseless right before he efficiently stripped both of them of their clothes.

And after that, Matthew Lyndon showed Courtney Wallace just how incredible sex with Mr. Right can be.

The scent of coffee and frying bacon awakened Matt.

He cracked his eye, suddenly alarmed by the angle of the sunlight pouring through Courtney's French doors. He checked his watch: 7:45 a.m.—late for a weekday if you worked at a law firm.

He sat up and stopped himself from reacting to the time flashing on the clock. Instead, he took a big breath and let himself enjoy the combined scents of bacon, coffee, and Courtney that filled his head. It would be nice to wake up to this every morning.

The thought engendered no panic. Courtney was not Allison Chapman. She wasn't cruel or selfish. Of course, she'd jacked him around at first, but that was because she'd known about his bet with Brandon. That bet was way in the past now. Trust had somehow grown between them despite everything.

So racing off to work would be the wrong move.

Besides, what was he racing off to do? Every day, Matt sat alone for hours at a time in his little cubbyhole office, working on divorces and trusts and wills. Every day David and Dad found ways to remind him of his inexperience. No one at LL&K appreciated his quixotic need to expose Bill Cummins and his cushy relationship with GB Ventures.

No, he didn't need to dash off to work. The firm's office hours were nominally nine to five, so he had some time. Who was he trying to impress anyway, getting to work every day before 8:00 a.m.?

He put on his jeans and shirt and followed the scent of bacon. Halfway down the hall, a pair of identical gray and white kittens greeted him. He checked his pockets. Sure enough, Courtney had stolen his keys.

That took him aback for a moment. Had she violated his privacy or crossed any of his unstated boundaries? Probably. But on the other hand, Ghul seemed happy to be reunited with Doom. And since Matt usually fed Ghul before 6:00 a.m. every morning, Courtney had saved the kitten from going hungry and being lonely. She'd also allowed him to sleep in. How could he fault her for any of that?

He entered the apartment's main room, with its open kitchen and dining area, and found Courtney wearing a short, flowery robe that barely covered her ass. She'd piled her hair on top of her head in a messy bun, and she bustled in the kitchen with her back toward him. Oh man, she looked like a sweet morning morsel. His mouth watered, and his groin tightened.

If it weren't for the hour and the smell of bacon, he might have snatched her up and carried her back to the bedroom.

Instead he cleared his throat. "Morning."

She turned, her blue eyes sparkling in the sunlight, her cheeks slightly pink either with a blush or beard burn. Either way, the effect was devastating. Delight filled him to overflowing. Last night, she'd been sad and lonely. Now look at her. Radiant, happy, and deliciously well-used.

"Hi," she said, her plump lips curving a little like Mona Lisa's. His mind flashed on those lips and the pleasure they had given him. "I made eggs and bacon. And I hope you don't mind. I borrowed your keys and brought Porthos over to play with Aramis. I fed both of them. Your keys are on the counter." She pointed.

"I don't mind." He sat down at the breakfast bar. Her apartment had a different layout than his. It was more up to date, and her furniture had more style and character. He liked the bold orange and yellow of her throw pillows, and the artwork on the walls. He should ask her for pointers. His walls were barren, and he hadn't even thought about buying pillows for his couch.

"It's okay if you don't have time to eat breakfast. I understand," Courtney said in a rush as she placed a plate in front of him containing two sunny-side-up eggs, toast, and several strips of bacon. How the hell did she know he liked his eggs sunny-side up?

"I have time," he lied. He didn't have time, but he would make time this morning.

Her smile was so wide that it lit up the room more than the sunshine. "You want coffee?"

He nodded. "Black, please."

She placed a mug in front of him and then leaned against the countertop. "About last night..." she began, a little frown folding up the skin of her forehead.

He put up his hand to stop her. "No need to explain. We've all overindulged at one time or another."

"I'm officially giving up Manhattans," she said. "And I'm seriously thinking about giving up the Jaybird. None of my girlfriends go down there anymore.

Not even Arwen. Drinking alone isn't healthy anytime, but drinking alone with Ryan Pierce is pathetic."

A mysterious and heretofore unknown muscle deep in his chest twisted tight, stealing his breath. What the hell? He still didn't fully understand Courtney's relationship with Ryan. And he suddenly wanted to know.

Damn. He'd never cared about that sort of thing before. The women he'd hooked up with had been temporary. If they had other relationships, it didn't matter.

He didn't like this tight feeling in his chest. Not one bit. And Ryan Pierce was an idiot if he'd been stringing Courtney along. He took a bite of bacon and chewed for a long, thoughtful moment. No wonder she'd had a crying jag last night.

"There's nothing to be sorry about," he finally said, once he'd swallowed the bacon.

"Yes, there is. I didn't need to drag you into my pity party. With all my girlfriends married and Sid moving away, I don't know, I felt as if life was leaving me behind."

"So you know that the Dogwood Estates tenants have gotten eviction notices."

She nodded, biting her lip. "Yeah. I've been trying to get Sid to move in with me, but he and Leslie seem to have something going. They were talking about moving to Arizona, where it's warmer and cheaper." She gave him a watery smile and continued. "Can I ask you a favor?"

He nodded. "Sure."

"Would you ask Arwen to call me? I mean, she's been avoiding me or something. She never wants to go down to the Jaybird anymore. You know, she's probably like Sid. She's probably found someone or something."

"Um, I don't think so." He shook his head.

"No?"

"She's been putting in a lot of extra hours at the office. And I'm probably the reason for that. We've been working on something."

Courtney cocked her head. "On what?"

He shrugged. "It's not that important. I thought I could figure out a way to stop the county from abusing its power and throwing people off their land and out of their homes, but yesterday David made me see the truth."

"Abusing its power how?"

He looked up from his eggs into her curious face. And it struck him right then that Courtney could be so much more than a bed buddy, although God alone knew sex with her was nothing short of incredible. Maybe the sex was so good because there was more to Courtney than a curvy body and a pair of killer blue eyes. She had heart. She had soul. She was smart and accomplished, and sometimes she had the ability to see right through him.

"Matt?" Her voice pulled him from his thoughts. "Is something wrong?"

He shook his head. "No. It's just that I'm frustrated in my job right at the moment." He took a deep breath and spent the next fifteen minutes filling her in on the way Bill Cummins and several members of the Jefferson County Council had been using zoning and safety regulations to help GB Ventures acquire land at rock-bottom prices.

When he came to the end of his explanation, he shook his head. "Of course, with all this research into the County Council, I seem to have forgotten that my client is the Dogwood Estates Tenants Association. The truth is, none of the dirt I've dug up on the county is going to help them. I feel so utterly useless when I think about Leslie and Sid and all the rest of the tenants."

"Oh my God. You need to do something with this information about Bill Cummins. He's running for reelection. This stuff could be dynamite."

"Or it could give him a boost," Matt said. "David pointed out yesterday that a lot of people are happy to see eyesores like Dogwood Estates disappear."

"You have to give this information to Linda Petersen."

"Willow's mother?"

Courtney nodded. "Linda and Leslie are great friends, so she's already involved in the Dogwood Estates issue. Sid told me that Linda and Leslie are planning some kind of protest for later this week. They were going to picket GB Ventures headquarters in Arlington, but now I'm thinking maybe they should picket city hall. They could use this stuff,

Matt. And you know what? I'll bet Linda has friends at the *Winchester Daily* who would love to have your research. The *Daily* has never liked Bill Cummins's pro-growth-at-any-cost agenda."

Her shining eyes reflected an image that had nothing to do with scorn or disappointment or mistrust. She believed in him. She believed in his cause.

He leaned across the counter and snagged her hand. "Courtney, I want to make something clear. Last night wasn't a one-night stand. I'd like to see where this goes, okay? And I will be here precisely at six thirty to pick you up for a nice dinner date. Where would you like to go?"

The corner of her mouth ticked up. "Could we try the Red Fern Inn again?"

Chapter Sixteen ————————

June was almost over, thank God. The last weekend was almost upon them with a flurry of weddings that kept Courtney crazy-busy with half a dozen demanding bridezillas. Her days were long and hard, but her nights were romantic and steamy and incredibly erotic.

Sleeping with Matt would have been enough. The man knew how to give and take pleasure. But Matt gave her so much more than that. He took her to dinner at the Red Fern Inn on Tuesday night and behaved like the perfect gentleman. He treated her to a candlelight dinner at his place on Wednesday night featuring linguine and clam sauce that he made himself. And on Thursday, he blew her mind by sending a bouquet of cupcakes, exquisitely decorated to look like small nosegays of violets.

"Oh my God," Amy exclaimed when the deliveryman put them on the corner of Courtney's desk. "Those are amazing. Are they from that new bakery in Winchester?"

Courtney nodded, although she wasn't entirely sure. She'd mentioned the bakery to Matt last night when she'd been talking about a bride who wanted cupcake centerpieces. Good thing she intercepted the small white card that came with them before Amy got to it. Matt never failed to impress when it came to cards. She recognized his handwriting now. And of course there was a poem.

A violet by a mossy stone
Half-hidden from the eye!
—Fair as a star, when only one
Is shining in the sky.

~Wordsworth

Looking forward to seeing you shine for me
    tonight.

"Holy crap. I've never seen you blush like that, girl. What's in that card?"

She almost told the truth. But some instinct for self-preservation stopped her. Matt was more than a Hook-up Artist, but was he Mr. Right? She wanted to believe that she'd found true love, but who could make a decision like that based on less than a week of mind-blowing sex, a couple of nice dinners, and a bouquet of cupcakes?

There were so many ways this could go wrong. And when it did, she'd probably fall apart. And if she told her friends, they would all tell her she was stupid to have gotten involved with a Hook-up Artist like Matt. And then they'd tell her to grow up and settle. Or get used to living alone.

She didn't want to settle, but by the same token, she wasn't some naïve girl who could be swept away with fancy gifts and dinner at a nice restaurant. So she turned toward Amy and lied. "They're from Bethany Carr." Bethany was the bride who wanted cupcakes at every table.

"Oh." Amy sounded so disappointed. "They're kind of cute, but they aren't as pretty as real flowers."

"That's only because you're biased in favor of real flowers."

Amy gave her the stink eye, and Courtney shut up. She also slipped the card into the pocket of the dress she was wearing. No way Amy would ever get her hands on that card. Not after she'd read Matt's first card.

Willow proved far more difficult. She dropped by Courtney's office late in the afternoon while Amy was consulting with a client, took one look at the cupcakes, and shut the door. She sat in the single side chair, her face sober.

"Those are cute, but I have a feeling you didn't order them yourself. And if you tell me you're sleeping with Matt, I'm going to wring your neck."

"They're from Bethany Carr. She wants us to use that new bakery. For her centerpieces."

Willow gave her the evil eye. "Have I ever told you that you are a terrible liar? Amy told me all about them. About how you blushed when you read the card."

Pleading the fifth would not work, so she remained silent.

"Oh, my God. They *are* from Matt. You know this is what he does, right? I'll bet he quoted poetry or something. Probably about violets."

Willow had been around the block a few times. She'd suffered her share of jerks and players before finally finding the love of her life in the most unlikely of places. She meant well, but Courtney still resented the intrusion.

"You know, a few weeks ago I had this conversation with Arwen about how romance is dead in America. And here you sit staring at these cupcakes as if they are toxic or something. Why do we have to suspect every man who sends gifts?"

"I don't suspect every man who sends gifts. But I don't trust Matt any farther than I can throw him. Courtney, you know he's a player. And besides, since when are you a cougar?"

Whoa, that was a low blow. "Can we leave my age out of it, please?"

"No. The last time we talked, you were the one

telling me that he was too young for you. That you were just friends. I was worried then, and even more worried now. You've always been so clear-headed when it comes to guys like Matt. What changed?"

Everything had changed. She'd stopped looking at him that way. Now all she saw was a man with a pretty big heart and a strong set of shoulders, and a wicked-smart brain.

Willow's gaze softened. "You've fallen for him, haven't you? Damn, I saw this coming the day of Allison Chapman's wedding."

Courtney shrugged and looked away. "If I've fallen for him, it's nobody's business but my own."

Willow nodded. "I guess that's right. And I sincerely hope it works out. But just know that I'm here in case it doesn't." She paused a moment and leaned in. "And just a word of caution. Navigating the Lyndon family can be very difficult. Don't expect them to be happy about you."

"So you agree with Allison Chapman then?"

Willow's eyes widened as she shook her head. "That's not what I meant. If you and Matt really are in love, then you have my blessing. And of course I think you're good enough for him. I'm just not sure he's good enough for you. But if you and Matt really do become a couple, I'm just saying that the Lyndon family can be challenging at times."

Courtney let go of a long breath. "Look, Willow, I'm not ever going to marry Matt Lyndon. But I've decided to enjoy the cupcakes while they last. Is that so wrong?"

Willow shook her head. "You sell yourself too short, Courtney. Don't settle for anything less than true love. It's worth the wait."

One by one, the tenants at Dogwood Estates began to move out and move away from Jefferson County. By the first week of July, fewer than half of them still remained, among them Leslie Heath, who had rattled a few sabers by suggesting that she and several others might not move out at all—a position Matt had counseled against.

But Leslie was a fighter.

And so was Linda Petersen, who accepted his file with a certain amount of glee. Linda, it turned out, hated Bill Cummins because the chairman of the County Council had thrown her in jail a number of years ago for carrying signs at a council meeting. Linda practically salivated as she read through the information Matt and Arwen had compiled.

It also turned out that Linda knew a lot of Avery Johnson's neighbors—hillbillies who'd been living up on the ridge for generations, raising pigs and chickens. She nominated herself to go up there and clue those folks in on what Cummins and GB Ventures had planned for them, and in the space of a few days, she single-handedly screwed up at least two land sales.

Linda was a whirlwind all right. And at 9:00 a.m. on Monday, July 2, Linda and more than a hundred protesters showed up at city hall in order to picket the regular first-Monday-of-the-month County Council meeting. And since Linda had coordinated her efforts with Sally Hawkes, an investigative reporter for the *Winchester Daily,* an exposé of Bill Cummins and his relationship with GB Ventures appeared in the July 2nd edition of the paper.

That morning, Matt stood in David's office watching the protesters through his gigantic windows while his cousin sat fuming at his desk.

"What on earth were you thinking, giving that information to the *Winchester Daily*?" David snarled. "Sally Hawkes is a hack. A couple of years ago, she tried to destroy Dusty's reputation. I can't believe you did this."

"I haven't had any conversations with the *Winchester Daily.*" A statement that was entirely true. Matt had handed the file to David's mother-in-law, and Linda had done all the talking.

"That was a nondenial denial. I'm starting to think you have a future in politics."

"I gave the file to Linda," Matt said.

"Damn." David pounded his desk with his fist.

"I had to give it to her. She was working with Leslie and the tenants. They had a right to know."

David blew out a long, exasperated sigh and leaned back in his big leather chair. "You're right, but did you have to involve Willow's mother?"

"I'm right?" Matt turned from the window. "You think I'm right?"

David nodded. "I hate it when my mother-in-law starts protesting. It almost always upsets someone in the family. But I guess that's my cross to bear, not yours." He gave Matt a long, sober look.

"I'm happy to take the heat for you this time."

"Thanks. Your father is probably going to be furious."

"Why? I didn't think he was a big Bill Cummins fan."

"He's not, but he wants to turn you into a small-town lawyer. And mounting crusades is not exactly what small-town lawyers do."

"Unless they're Atticus Finch," Matt muttered under his breath. Although the protagonist in *To Kill a Mockingbird* hadn't intended to mount any sort of crusade. He'd just been trying to get justice for his client. Matt turned back to stare at the protesters. "Do you mind if Arwen and I go out there and say hi?"

"I have a feeling I couldn't stop you even if I tried."

"Thanks." Matt turned and hurried down the hallway into Arwen's cubbyhole office, which was even smaller than his. She looked up from her laptop as he entered, and it struck him that she looked a little haggard and pale. What was up with her anyway? She'd been grumpy for the last two weeks. "You need me for something?" she said in a less-than-welcoming tone.

"Yes. I need you to get up and leave this office."

"What?"

He took two steps into her cubbyhole, gently snagged her by the upper arm, and gave her a tug. "You need some fresh air. Besides, there are more important things than the next divorce case. Get up." He yanked her out of her chair.

"Matt, stop. What are you talking about?" Arwen dug in her heels.

"Have you read the *Winchester Daily* today?" he asked.

"Uh, no. Why?" She shook her head.

"Because the front page is an exposé of Bill Cummins, his high-handed tactics, and his cushy relationship with GB Ventures."

Arwen's eyes grew round. "Oh my God. Did you give our file to the *Daily*?"

He shook his head. "No. I followed the advice of a very smart woman. I gave our file to Linda Peterson. She's out there in front of city hall right now."

Arwen grinned. "I knew I liked you, despite your reputation. Does your father know you did this?"

"Not yet. But he will eventually. Come on, let's go join the fun before he rains on my parade."

Matt took Arwen by the hand and pulled her down the hallway, through LL&K's front doors, and out onto the sidewalk in front of city hall. Along the way he stopped at a newspaper dispenser, where he purchased a copy of the paper for Arwen.

She took one look at the headline—JEFFERSON COUNTY COUNCIL CHAIR HAS CUSHY DEAL WITH GB VENTURES—and squealed.

"Oh my God. I love you. Thank you for not giving up on this. Especially since I've been so out of it these last few weeks. I'm happy someone had a little courage." And then she threw herself into Matt's arms and kissed him right on his cheek.

A mixed bag of emotion slammed into Courtney's chest as Arwen threw her arms around Matt's neck. The sound of Arwen saying "I love you" to Matt Lyndon traveled across the space between them like a nuclear missile.

Courtney froze where she stood amid the protesters. Fury, jealousy, confusion, shame, and a healthy dose of self-loathing combined into a toxic brew that buckled her knees.

It was almost as if God had decided to punish her for something.

A moment ago, Sid had announced that he and Leslie were going to elope to Vegas and then move to Phoenix. He'd seemed so proud of himself for arguing Leslie out of her foolish last stand at Dogwood Estates.

Courtney had been searching for something nice to say about this news when she'd seen Arwen and Matt giving each other intimate face time.

What an idiot she'd been. All that tender love-making. All those words whispered in the dark. The flowers. The cupcakes. Dinner at the Red Fern. All of it was a sham. A game. The usual BS that any Hook-up Artist knew how to manage.

The pieces of the puzzle suddenly locked into place.

Poor Arwen. She was so hungry for romance that Matt's flowers and cupcakes had probably turned her head. And she was probably too ashamed to admit it. No wonder she'd been avoiding Courtney. She probably didn't want to hear any lectures about sleeping with a player.

Who did?

And, of course, since they'd hardly spoken the last few weeks, Arwen didn't have any idea that Matt had moved in next door or that Courtney had broken her own set of rules when it came to Hook-up Artists.

An icy pain lanced her heart. How could she have been so stupid? How could Arwen have been so stupid?

"Hey, hon, are you okay?" Sid asked.

She shifted her gaze. Unable to speak, all she could do was shake her head.

"Honey, don't be sad. Please. For the first time in more than a year, I feel as if I have something to look forward to."

And Sid looked that way too. He carried a poster board sign bearing a picture of a bulldozer with the red circle-and-slash symbol superimposed on it. Dressed in a pair of madras shorts and a Grateful Dead T-shirt, Sid bore no resemblance to the ghost of a man he'd been just a few weeks ago. Leslie had changed all that. And Courtney was happy for them, even as her own heart shattered into a million pieces.

"I'm fine. I'm glad you found a reason to go on living." She turned away from him so he wouldn't see the tears welling up in her eyes.

"No, you're not fine. What is it?"

She brushed the tears away with the palm of her hand. "I should have brought my sunglasses," she said. "Maybe I should go home and get them."

"Courtney," Sid said to her back, "don't be sad."

"I'm not," she said in a watery voice as she took off across the street, giving Arwen and Matt a wide berth. Not that they would have noticed her. They were holding hands and smiling as they came down the walk from their office building.

By the time she got home, her tears had dried up and her reeling emotions had settled into a stone-cold fury. She scoured her apartment collecting the stuff Matt had left there—a T-shirt, a pair of socks, a UVA sweatshirt, and a David Baldacci paperback. She dumped them in a heap in front of his door.

Then came the hard part. Would she give Doom back to him? Or would she keep both cats?

She spent the next thirty minutes consuming a pint of Ben and Jerry's Chocolate Therapy ice cream as she considered this question.

No. For this betrayal, Matt had to lose his cat. There had to be consequences.

Besides, Melissa, who had hand-raised these kittens, wouldn't want Porthos to end up with someone who would name him Dr. Doom. And Melissa wouldn't be happy with Matt for coming into Courtney's life and ruining her long-standing friendship with Arwen. And for another thing, a woman in Courtney's predicament needed more than one cat.

Especially with Sid moving away. That thought brought another wave of tears. Yes, she was utterly alone now. A woman like her needed more than one cat. And the two cats were a comfort, especially right now. Both of them had curled up beside her on the couch, and their contented purrs were the only thing keeping her from flying apart into a million shattered pieces.

The last thing she expected in that moment was for Matt to come knocking at her door. It was barely 10:30 a.m. She'd expected him to remain at the office, hanging out with Arwen. She'd expected him to stay late at work, the way he almost always did.

But instead he was pounding on her door, banging away at her resolve. Dammit.

"Courtney. I know you're in there. Answer the damn door."

"Go away," she finally shouted.

"What the hell is up with you? Why'd you put my stuff in the hallway?" The angry edge in Matt's voice annoyed the crap out of her. Where did he get off being angry anyway? He wasn't the aggrieved party.

Aramis, or was it Porthos—sometimes it was hard to tell these cats apart—looked up at her with a pair of green eyes. Somehow the cat seemed to be judging her. It had to be Porthos. He probably wanted to go home.

She scattered the cats as she got off the couch. She yanked the door open. "I'm not giving Porthos back. You don't deserve him."

He stood there with the patented Lyndon frown riding his forehead and his dark eyes sparking with a fury of his own. "What the hell is wrong with you? Leslie is all upset. She's starting to think maybe she and Sid are rushing things. How could you be so cruel?"

"What? I told Sid I was happy for him."

"Then why did you run away in tears? Honestly, Sid would have come himself, but I told him I'd haul you back down there. Come on. This is a day for—"

"Shut up. Don't. Just don't."

"Don't what? And what's with my stuff in the hallway?"

"You have no clue, do you? You think you've completely fooled me."

"Fooled you. About what?"

"You and Arwen. It all makes perfect sense. You with the late nights, and her wanting someone who could romance her. I should have seen it. I'm such an idiot."

He stood there blinking at her, surprise all over his handsome face, as if it had never occurred to him that she'd figure it out. What was it about Hook-up Artists anyway? Every damn one of them was so sure of himself.

"I can't believe this," he said.

"What about it can't you believe?"

"Everything." He huffed out a breath and leaned into the doorframe. "You know, Courtney, you have a serious trust problem. And even though I understand the reasons for it, I'm not sure I can live with it. I sure as hell don't want to be constantly judged and found wanting. That's bullshit, you know?" His voice had gone low and hard, the anger red-hot.

"Really? You're going to go all Man Baby on me and accuse me of being the problem?"

"Yeah, I am." A muscle pulsed in his jaw as he pushed away from the doorframe. He took one backward step. "You should go back and tell Sid and Leslie that they have your blessing." He turned and gathered his stuff. But before he slipped his key into his front door, he turned and looked over his shoulder. "I want Ghul back."

"Ghul? He's not yours."

"You took Dr. Doom that day you left in the wee hours of the morning. You can keep him. But I want Ghul back."

"In your dreams." She slammed the door in his face.

Chapter Seventeen

Matt dropped his stuff on the floor inside the door and headed back to the office, head down, teeth clenched, and with a strange hollow place in his chest. The morning's happiness had evaporated.

How dare she? After the things he'd done, the things he'd said, the way he'd acted. Didn't she understand? How could Courtney possibly think that he'd hook up with Arwen?

Sure, he had become pretty good at picking up women and showing them a good time. But he wasn't a jerk. He'd never been a jerk. He didn't cheat on the woman of the moment, even if the relationship was understood to be strictly physical and strictly short-term.

He did not mess around with the women he worked with.

And he would never mess around with the best friend of the woman he was sleeping with.

He was truly insulted by her accusations. Insulted and saddened. How could he possibly continue a relationship with a woman who was that insecure? He'd always be looking behind his back. He'd always be trying to prove himself.

And wasn't he tired of doing that? All the time?

He bypassed the protest, which seemed to have gained momentum in the last hour, and returned to his windowless office, where he threw himself into his chair and sank his head in his hands.

Damn. He probably should have defended himself. But what was the use? It totally destroyed him to think that Courtney believed he was capable of that kind of behavior. Maybe he should ask Arwen to set her straight. It seemed like the logical course, but that would require him to tell Arwen how much he truly cared about Courtney. And there was still that small matter of trust.

He was sinking into despair when his desk phone rang. It was Marie Coleman, Dad's assistant, with the summons Matt had been expecting all day.

Well, bring it on. After the fight with Courtney, he didn't care what Dad had to say. He stalked through the hallways of LL&K, a tight knot of hostility twisting his chest.

Dad's office was larger than David's, with an even better view of the protesters marching in front of city hall. The hundred-year-old walnut paneling in Dad's office had been meticulously restored a number of years ago, and the antique furniture added a sense of decorum and power. The office always smelled faintly of lemon oil and beeswax.

Dad stood at the window, his hands behind his back, staring at the protesters. Their chants sounded faintly through the paneled walls and heavy draperies. Matt took several steps across the hand-knotted Persian rug before he realized Dad wasn't alone. Brandon lounged in one of the oxblood leather Queen Anne side chairs, looking relaxed with one leg cocked up over the knee of the other.

What the hell?

"Sit," Dad commanded with a backward wave at the second wing chair.

"Brandon, what brings you out this way?" Matt asked as he crossed the room toward the chairs. He stopped to shake Brandon's hand.

Brandon, one of his oldest friends, gave him only fleeting eye contact. Matt shook off his concern and focused on the remnants of his fury. He took a seat, crossed his legs, and waited.

Dad finally turned away from the window with a long, exasperated sigh. He settled into the gigantic leather chair behind his desk and leaned forward. "Matthew, I have two words for you: Jerry Beyer."

"Who?"

Dad rolled his eyes—an expression Matt had seen all his life. When Dad rolled his eyes like that it always meant that Matt had screwed up something that

Dad regarded as inherently simple. "You're kidding me, right?" Dad said. "What kind of idiot are you?"

Matt clamped his teeth together.

Dad turned toward Brandon. "Explain it to him."

"Jerry Beyer is the CEO of GB Ventures, LLC," Brandon said.

A few puzzle pieces fell into place. "Oh, okay. I get it. I imagine he's not happy. So what?"

"Jerry is one of Heather's biggest contributors," Brandon said slowly, as if Matt were too stupid to understand. Heather was David's sister. She also happened to represent Jefferson County in the United States House of Representatives. Last fall, Brandon had rejected a job here at LL&K to go to work on her Capitol Hill staff.

"Jerry is furious," Brandon added. "He's threatening to withdraw his support this fall unless David calls his mother-in-law off, which David has refused to do."

"Maybe not taking money from GB Ventures's CEO would be a good thing," Matt said, meeting his friend's stare. "Come on, Brandon. You don't want Heather taken down because of the crap that's going on here, do you?"

"Who says there's any *crap* going on? The Jefferson County Chamber of Commerce named Jerry Beyer its man of the year last year precisely because of what he's done to improve things. He's single-handedly responsible for a lot of the growth we've seen the last couple of years."

"Growth that has displaced people who have lived here for generations."

"Come on. We're talking about progress. We're talking about growing the county's tax base. We're talking about jobs."

Matt shook his head. "I'll give you the tax base but not the jobs. The people being displaced are the ones who work for Uncle Jamie harvesting grapes and tending apple orchards. Or the people working for Willow at Eagle Hill Manor. Where are those people going to live when every house in Jefferson County costs half a million dollars? And besides that, it's wrong for the county to help a single developer buy land at less than fair market value. That's a distortion of the market."

Dad slapped his hand down on his desk. "Enough! Matthew, I told you weeks ago that I wanted you to drop this issue. Why didn't you?"

Matt stood up. "Because I cared about my client. The people living in Dogwood Estates have all lost their homes because of Jerry Beyer. And if Heather wants to associate herself with a guy like that, then so be it. But if that's what she's about, she isn't going to get my vote in November."

Dad stood up. "I don't give a damn about your vote. It's your loyalty that I question. I need to know that the people associated with this firm are being honest with me. You and Arwen Jacobs have broken that trust. You've given me no other choice but to fire the both of you.

"Get your stuff and leave the office immediately. Marie will escort you out of the building."

Drinking alone at the Jaybird Café was a pathetic habit—one Courtney would try to break next week, or maybe the week after that, when her broken heart had mended. For now, the Jaybird's exposed-brick walls and scuffed pine floors were like a second home. And the barstools were surprisingly comfortable, even in the afternoon.

She intended to anesthetize herself before Ryan Pierce showed up and gave her a lecture. She had just finished her first Manhattan when Arwen strode through the front door at 3:00 p.m., pale-faced and red-nosed.

Another wave of fury washed over Courtney. How dare Matt make Arwen cry? Courtney hopped down from the barstool and intercepted her friend. "Oh, honey, I told you not to tangle with that guy. He's a total jerk. Come over to the bar, and I'll buy you as many margaritas as you need. I've missed you."

She wrapped Arwen in a big hug, willing to forgive her for kissing Matt because, really, Matt was to blame. How was someone like Arwen going to resist Matthew, especially with all his poetry and romance?

"And I forgive you for everything."

Arwen pulled back. "What are you talking about?"

"Matt is responsible for everything. I—"

Arwen shook her head and turned her back as she

stalked to the bar. "Oh, come on, Courtney. Don't. You've got to stop judging people that way."

"But..." Courtney's voice faded out as she followed Arwen back to the bar.

"Where's Rory?" Arwen asked Steve, the afternoon bartender.

Steve shrugged. "I don't know. His shift doesn't start until five thirty."

Arwen checked her watch. "Damn."

"Can I get you something to drink?" Steve asked Arwen.

Arwen drummed her fingers on the bar top for a long moment before she spoke. "Yeah, I guess. I'll take a margarita, frozen, with salt." Then she turned toward Courtney. "I'm just going to have one, okay? And then I'm going to call him."

"Call who?"

Arwen took a gigantic sigh and let it out. "I'm sorry, Court. I've been keeping something from you. To be honest, I've been keeping it from myself because I'm a wuss and a weenie."

"You are not a wuss. You're my friend...I think."

Arwen's eyes softened. "I'm sorry. I should have called you and had a long talk about this. But I was just so confused. And scared. You know, all I've ever wanted to do was write music and sing. But I hate being on the stage, and nobody ever listens. Except Rory, and you, and Melissa when she comes, which isn't very often. And it's not just the music. I'm so wishy-washy. Look at me. I have no style. My hair is brown and limp. I'm flat-chested. All these years I've just been waiting around, you know, for real life to start."

Steve interrupted Arwen's confused rant. She snatched up the margarita and took a gigantic gulp. Clearly Arwen was trying to anesthetize herself too. How many women could Matt Lyndon slay in one afternoon?

"Honey, you're not wishy-washy. Have you even listened to your own songs?"

Arwen put her glass down with more force than was necessary. "I am wishy-washy. And you know how I know that? A few weeks ago, someone called me on the fact that I've been punting the ball my entire life. Working in a soul-sucking job where no one appreciates me. Walking the straight and narrow in order to avoid rocking any boats. And even though I knew he was right, I didn't have the guts to face the truth. I ran away. Buried myself. And pretended that everything was great. But it's not." Her lower lip trembled, and tears filled her eyes. She picked up her glass and took another gigantic swallow of her drink.

Courtney dug in her purse and offered Arwen a tissue, which she accepted. "Honey, you have a great job. A great relationship with your parents. And a talent for writing killer lyrics. It could be a whole lot worse. Don't let one guy ruin your self-image. Please."

Courtney dabbed mascara from her cheeks and hauled in a huge breath. "He didn't ruin my self-image. He revealed it. And you know what? I couldn't even see it until Matt showed up. I mean, that guy was scared out of his mind the first time we met with Leslie, but he faced that fear like, I don't know, a hero. And then he pushed me to organize a clandestine meeting with a source inside the county government, and I felt like I was in the middle of a murder mystery or something. And then, even when he knew he'd been beat, he still fought. And he did all that knowing it would get him in trouble. I don't think I've ever met a braver man. And I figured, if he can be brave, maybe I can too." She balled up the tissue and hoisted her margarita.

Oh boy, Arwen really had it bad for Matt. And Courtney could certainly understand how that might happen. If you ignored Matt's womanizing, the guy had some pretty terrific qualities. But how could you ignore his womanizing? Her own heart squeezed in her chest, but she refused to give in to the hurt. Arwen needed her to be strong.

"Let's get one thing clear," Courtney said. "Matt's not a hero. Remember he made you feel wishy-washy. Look at how he's crushed your self-esteem. This is precisely what Hook-up Artists do, Arwen."

Arwen choked on her drink.

"It's okay," Courtney said, patting her back. "I don't blame you. Just because he was sleeping with both of us doesn't have to wreck our friendship. I mean, it's on him, not—"

"What?" Arwen's words came out as one-part cough.

"You heard me." Courtney lowered her voice into a whisper. "I failed to follow my own advice. I…well…the thing is…he moved in next door and…"

"Oh my God, you're sleeping with Matthew Lyndon?" Arwen said this in a loud voice. Thank God it was a few minutes past three on a weekday afternoon and the Jaybird was deserted.

"Keep your voice down. I know it's a shock. I mean, I didn't realize he was two-timing us until I saw you with him this morning."

Arwen blinked at Courtney for fifteen awkward seconds before she burst out laughing.

"What?"

"I'm not sleeping with Matt," Arwen managed between belly laughs.

"You're not? But—"

"But what?"

"You kissed him."

"Yeah, on the cheek. Because, well, he's a great guy. He could have punted on those people, Courtney. He could have done what I've been doing for years. He could have accepted the injustice and walked away. But he wouldn't. He kept picking at it. And now he's created a huge shit storm." Her voice wavered.

"What kind of shit storm?" The knot in Courtney's stomach was beginning to loosen, and a strange, almost euphoric sense of relief percolated through her.

"Well, for starters, he's gotten me fired from LL&K." Arwen's voice wobbled.

"What? And you think he's a hero?"

"Yeah. I do. I would never have left LL&K on my own. He did me a huge favor, Courtney. Now I just need to find the courage to follow through."

"Follow through how?"

Arwen pulled her purse from the hook under the bar and dug around in it for a moment before withdrawing a small folded piece of paper. She held it up. "By calling the number on this Post-it note."

"Okay, and whose number is it?"

Arwen blushed a spectacular shade of pink. She leaned in and whispered, "Rory Ahern's."

"Rory?"

She nodded. "He listens to my music."

He was also covered in tattoos, had a bad-boy vibe and a dangerously sexy Irish lilt to the way he spoke. Not the kind of guy Courtney would have chosen for Arwen. But then again, who was she to do the choosing? Wasn't that the lesson she needed to learn here?

A huge wave of remorse and guilt hit her bloodstream. She'd screwed up. Big-time. What an idiot she'd been. About so many things.

"So, ah, you and Rory?" Courtney managed to ask through the ache in her chest.

Arwen shrugged. "I don't know. I've been running from him for a couple of weeks. And really, we only hooked up for a few days."

Courtney refrained from suggesting that running

from Rory might be a good thing. Maybe it was time for her to quit passing judgment. "So you're going to stop running?" she asked instead.

Arwen nodded. "Yeah. I am. And if he breaks my heart, at least I won't have any regrets. Maybe I'll pull up stakes and move to Nashville the way Rory wants me to."

Another shaft to the heart. "I don't want you to leave. Everyone's leaving or getting married or…"

Arwen patted Courtney's back. "I'm not going to hop on his bike and run away. He might have suggested that, but I'm not that crazy. If I moved to Nashville, it would be something I plan. But I'm not ruling it out, okay?"

"Okay. And I'm, uh, sorry about the—"

"Damn," Arwen said. "Tell me you didn't accuse Matt of sleeping with me."

"Uh, yeah, I sort of did."

"Oh my God. You need to go talk to him. He needs you. I wasn't the only one fired today."

"Matt lost his job?"

Arwen nodded. "His own father canned him. He was marched out of the office like he'd committed some kind of high crime or misdemeanor."

Matt sprawled on his couch watching MSNBC without paying much attention. The drone of the commentator helped him to keep his emotions distant, which was fine with him because he didn't want to parse through them. He didn't want to open himself up and try to examine what had just happened.

Besides, dissecting his feelings would do nothing to change them. He'd never wanted to be a country lawyer, so it was no surprise that he'd failed so spectacularly. He'd never wanted to be Don Quixote either.

Tilting at windmills had its downsides. Linda's protests wouldn't change a thing. Not when Jerry Beyer could reach out with his influence and twist the world. People said blood was thicker than water, but that wasn't true in the Lyndon family. Jerry Beyer gave money to Heather, and Heather outranked him because she was smarter and more accomplished.

So he sat alone in his living room, waiting. Always waiting. But for what? The answer came to him when Courtney knocked on his door and said, "I need to apologize."

Yes, she did. But did he want her apology? Somehow the apology meant less than the trust he longed for. The trust she couldn't seem to give. Maybe part of that was his fault. But who knew?

He couldn't let her stand in the hallway, so he dragged himself from the couch and opened the door to find her standing in the hallway with Dr. Doom cuddled in her arms. Everything about her posture screamed regret, from the slope of her shoulders to the glimmer of tears in her eyes.

"I just had a long talk with Arwen," she said in a trembling voice. "I'm so sorry. I shouldn't have jumped to conclusions the way I did, and I understand why I've lost your trust. Here's Dr. Doom." She held the cat out to him. It was one hell of a peace offering since she'd brought over her favorite cat—the cuddly one. And yet some stubborn part of him still wanted more.

"Don't you want him?" Her voice seemed ready to crack open.

His chest tightened with a swirl of emotion he wanted to keep at bay. He couldn't answer her question because he was too confused, angry, lost.

She took a step into the room. "I know you lost your job. I'm so, so sorry about that. And I know my behavior this morning was...I don't know... unacceptable. I probably can't ever get your trust back. And deservedly so. But I do care about you. Can we talk about this?"

He shook his head. "Look, I'm too angry right now. I'm not even sure what happened, not just with you and me but with my father. And—"

"I should never have encouraged you to give all that dirt to Linda Petersen. I mean, I should have realized that getting Linda involved would create huge problems for you. Willow even warned me about it."

"Warned you? How?"

She shrugged. "Just that the Lyndon family is sometimes..." Her voice faded out.

"Yeah, my family." A painful bolt of fury struck him in the chest. His family. His father in particular had done his best over the years to mold him into someone he had never wanted to be.

"I'm sorry." Her voice got thin, and a tear escaped one of her eyes.

He couldn't stand to watch her cry, so he turned his back and took a couple of steps into the room. "You're not responsible for my family. They've always been difficult. And living up to the Lyndon ideal is impossible."

"So don't."

He stopped and turned. Goddammit, she was so beautiful. Despite the pain she'd inflicted this morning, he still admired the way she could cut through the bullshit and speak the unvarnished truth. He didn't have to live up to their expectations. He could be like Amy or Daniel or David, all of whom had rebelled at one time or another.

But was that what he needed? It sure wasn't what he wanted. What he wanted was something else altogether.

"Look, I'm exhausted," he finally said. "And I'm angry and disappointed and kinda lost, if you want to know the truth. I don't need your commentary on my life. I don't need you to dissect me or inspect me or shove me in a pigeonhole. I don't need your advice about how to live or how to be or how to deal with my family. What I want is...you. All of you. Right now." His little speech was so utterly inarticulate. How could he put this feeling into words? All he wanted was a place to rest his head. A place where he didn't have to perform. Where he didn't have to be anything. A place to call home. He bit down on his back molars to keep from saying more. He'd screw it up if he kept talking. And besides, how could Courtney give him what he truly wanted when she couldn't even trust him?

Courtney put Dr. Doom down and moved to stand in front of him. He stifled the urge to reach out to her. The last time he'd truly opened up to a woman, she'd manipulated him in the worst way. And he'd trusted Allison. Courtney, not so much.

Still, when she wrapped her arms around him and pulled him close, he let himself sink into that warmth. Just for tonight, he told himself. Just for this moment, when the world had unraveled. Making love to her wouldn't solve any of his problems. She didn't have the answers he needed to find himself. But it was enough just to be with her, in her arms, forgetting about the father who had never believed in him. About the world he couldn't change. About the woman he couldn't trust and who clearly didn't trust him.

Their lovemaking was excruciatingly tender, as if they had reached a deeper connection somehow. And when he left her breathless and spent, she almost said the words she'd been holding back.

Thank goodness her instincts for survival kicked in before she opened herself up completely. Because the minute they were done, he rolled away, presenting his back to her and driving home the point. He didn't love her.

And she didn't blame him.

She'd learned her lesson. Maybe there was value in pinning labels on people if all you wanted was an excuse not to care, not to love, not to get too involved. But she'd crossed that line a while ago with Matt. She'd been hoping that he wasn't like the stereotypes on her list, but she'd gone right ahead and pigeonholed him anyway.

Stupid woman. If she couldn't trust him, she couldn't love him. And vice versa. His solid back said it all. In one foolish act of jealousy, she'd destroyed whatever trust they'd been building together over the last couple of weeks.

For the first time in her life, she had no one to blame but herself. And it mortified her to think that she'd hurt him so badly that he hadn't even been able to accept her apology. The sex had been about comfort, not love and not hate. It had been sweet and kind, but it was the last time. She knew that now.

She lay in his bed for a long time fighting her tears. She had no right to cry in his presence. When his breathing evened out in sleep, she gathered her clothes, dressed in the darkness, and left him.

Chapter Eighteen ——————

Arwen drank two margaritas and ate a whole plate of loaded potato skins while she waited for Rory to show up for his shift. She probably should have gone directly to his apartment, but who knows what she might have said or done? She didn't trust herself around him, especially not in his bedroom. And she wasn't about to capitulate. If he wanted something lasting, there had to be movement on both sides.

Her determination to control their meeting evaporated the moment Rory strolled through the door, wearing faded jeans that hugged his hips and the black T-shirt that displayed his beautiful tattoos. He took several steps into the café before he spied her at the bar.

He stopped, and the expression on his face softened

somehow. The folds above his eyebrows evened out, the corners of his eyes turned up, and his stubborn mouth relaxed. In that moment, the bad boy morphed into something else. Something both dark but also romantic. No, he wasn't the kind of man who would take her to a fancy restaurant, but he was the kind of man who listened to her songs and believed in her.

Arwen's core exploded. She'd missed him. She'd missed the sex, but more than that, she'd missed the way he looked at her, as if she were something grand and special.

He continued toward her, stopping when he'd thoroughly invaded her space. "You're here," he said. "I was after missing you, love. Every day this last week or two. Are you back to stay?"

"Um, you got a minute, out in the alley?"

He nodded, and she followed him through the ready room and out into the alleyway, which was far less romantic in the afternoon light than it was in the dark.

"So," she said once the door shut behind them, "are you going to move away?"

His shoulder hitched, and he broke eye contact. "Linda offered to rent her upstairs bedroom to me if I couldn't find a better flat somewhere close. And Juni gave me a raise. Said she couldn't manage the place without me."

A wave of relief washed through Arwen. "Thank God. I was afraid you were going to take off for parts unknown."

He looked back at her, his blue eyes filled with

emotion. "How could I do that, love? When I understood that you needed to stay?" He took a step toward her. "Look, maybe I didn't make myself plain. I want you, Arwen. I care about you. And I want to see you succeed."

Arwen's heart cracked open a little. "I'm sorry I didn't understand that at first. And I'm... I'm blown away that you believe in me. I mean the part of me that I don't believe in myself."

He nodded. "I know."

"But here's the thing. I can't change everything about me. I mean, I'm uptight. I want to be more relaxed, but I'm never going to be a rebel. And I'm never going to be happy with you unless you change. And I would never ask you to change. It's got to be something you want for yourself."

"I know," he repeated. "I've never had a reason to change or to stay anywhere for very long. I've been a rolling stone for a long time. But..." He stopped for a moment, taking a breath and stepping closer. "I never had anyone who cared either. There's nothing for me back in Ireland. In a lot of ways, I found a home here at the Jaybird. And you're the most important part of that home."

He reached out and tucked a strand of hair behind her ear. "I'm going to stay, and I'd like to be your man for a while. I've got some money stashed away, and I was thinking about setting up a recording studio. I can't write or sing, but I think I'm a good listener. At the very least, let me help you."

Arwen stepped into his embrace. "I think I need help," she murmured against the fabric of his T-shirt, which smelled like smoke and laundry detergent. "'Cause I lost my job today."

He pushed her back a little and looked her in the eye. His face was a picture of concern, and Arwen's heart opened up completely. She could love this man.

"How did that happen?" he asked.

She cuddled up against him again. "It's a long story. How about you make me another margarita and I'll tell you all the details?"

"Sounds like a good first step. I promise to listen diligently."

Courtney's face looked tear-swollen in the mirror, and no amount of concealer was going to hide the fact that she'd cried herself to sleep. She considered her options.

Tuesday was her day off. She could crawl back into bed, where she would probably end up crying some more. Or she could pull herself up and get on with her life. She'd fallen for Matt Lyndon, and it hadn't worked out. This was a surprise? She stared at herself. "You knew the risks when you crossed the hall and knocked on his door," she said to herself in a watery voice.

Shit. It was going to take a long time to get over him. But loafing around the apartment having crying jags wouldn't roll back time or change her stupidity.

She should get up and get out. Take care of her

errands. But before she hit the grocery store and the dry cleaner, she needed to apologize to Leslie and Sid.

So she took a long shower and tried to wash away Matt Lyndon. It didn't work, but at least it woke her up.

An hour later, she pulled into the Dogwood Estates parking lot determined to make it through her day with calm and grace. But the sight before her was so depressing. Dogwood Estates looked almost abandoned. The windows on half of the units had been boarded up, the weeds hadn't been mowed in weeks, and a group of young men were loading boxes into a U-Haul trailer parked way on the other side of where Sid and Leslie lived. People were moving out.

A ten-pound weight dropped onto her chest. In a few days, it would be Leslie and Sid packing up a U-Haul and moving away, maybe as far away as Arizona. Courtney would probably never see them again. She wiped an errant tear that dribbled down her cheek. She needed to stop crying. Now. Leslie and Sid didn't need her tears.

She held this thought in her mind as she knocked on Sid's door. Leslie answered, looking like an aging Rosie the Riveter in a chambray shirt knotted on one side and a cute red bandanna around her head.

"Hi," Courtney said, trying in vain to keep her lips from trembling.

"Oh, honey, what's the matter? What's happened?" Leslie grabbed her by the shoulders and pulled her into a motherly hug that smelled exactly like Estée Lauder. All of Courtney's resolutions melted like a lump of sugar in a cup of hot tea.

"I'm so sorry," she sobbed against Leslie's shoulder.

"About what?" Leslie dragged her across the threshold and shut the door.

"About making you think I was angry, you know...about...about you and Sid. I'm not angry. I'm just...sad...sad...'cause you're moving away," she wailed.

"Hush, now." Leslie patted her back and made soft cooing sounds as Courtney fell apart for the second or third time in many days. What the hell was wrong with her? She couldn't seem to stop crying.

"What's the matter?" Sid asked.

Courtney finally raised her head to find Sid standing at the end of the short entrance foyer looking confused and adorable in his madras shorts and Rolling Stones tongue-and-lips logo T-shirt.

"I came to apologize." Courtney sniffed. "About yesterday. I didn't leave the protest because I was angry with you guys."

Sid dug into the pocket of his shorts and handed her a handkerchief. "Here, honey. Dry your eyes. We didn't think you were angry with us."

"But we were worried about you," Leslie said. "That's why we sent Matt to find you."

"But he said—"

"Well..." Sid drew out the word. "We might have led him to think that."

"Why?"

"Can I get you some ice tea? A piece of pound cake?" Leslie asked like the perfect hostess.

Courtney shook her head. "What are you two up to?"

Sid turned away and sank into his recliner. "Sit down, sweetie."

Courtney sat down on the couch, and Leslie sat beside her, reaching out to snag her hand. "When Matt kissed Arwen yesterday, Sid and I both saw how you reacted, and it—"

"Oh, for crissake," Sid interrupted. "Arwen's been shacking up with that Rory character over in apartment 5B. I can't imagine what she sees in that guy. He's—"

"Rory Ahearn lives here?"

Leslie and Sid nodded.

"So you see, dear," Leslie said, "we knew Arwen and Matt were just work colleagues. That kiss was as innocent as can be. But you reacted like a woman in love."

Courtney's emotions took another wild flight, and she pressed Sid's handkerchief to her eyes. "I'm such an idiot."

Leslie put her arm around Courtney's shoulder and hugged her close. It felt so nice to have someone care. Suddenly she understood why Sid had fallen for Leslie. She had a big heart, and she needed to take care of people. Now that Courtney had found her, she didn't want Leslie to move away. Leslie had the capacity to become a stand-in for the mother Courtney had missed all her life.

"You two had an argument, didn't you?" Leslie asked.

Courtney nodded. "And I apologized when I found out the truth, but..." Her throat knotted up. Dammit, what was wrong with her? She took a deep breath. "He's made it clear that he can't accept my apology. And I really don't blame him."

"Oh, honey, give him time."

She shook her head. "No. I messed up this time. And besides, he's like you and Sid, and probably Arwen. He's going to be leaving. Soon."

"What makes you say that?"

Courtney dabbed at her eyes and pulled herself together enough to tell Leslie and Sid the entire story, sparing nothing. When she had finished, Leslie looked at Sid. "That's ridiculous. How could Matt's own father fire him that way? And poor Arwen. She's been our advocate for months and months."

"And where the hell were Andrew and David?" Sid asked. "If you ask me, the only one who really cared about us was Matt."

"I told you that boy had a heart of gold. Are you willing to admit that I was right and you were wrong?" Leslie asked.

Sid nodded. "Yeah, I am. I had that guy read all wrong. Look, we need to go over to LL&K right now and give Charles Lyndon a piece of our minds. I mean, we're the client, aren't we?" Sid stood up.

"You're right, dear, we are," Leslie said in a mild tone. "But before we go charging into LL&K with our guns flashing, we need to plan a strategy." She stood up. "I think we need to consult with Linda."

"Look, guys," Courtney said, "no amount of protesting is going to change things. I mean, you guys are going to Arizona, and who knows where Rory's going to go. He'll probably take Arwen to Nashville or something. And Matt will move back to the city because he's not cut out to be a small-town lawyer. And..."

Her voice wavered again, and she had to swallow back a lump. "I don't want you guys to pick a fight with Charles Lyndon," she finally managed to say. "I want to find a way for you guys to stay here."

"But aren't you furious with him?"

Courtney parsed through her emotions and shook her head. "I'm sad, Sid. I'm so very sad. I feel like everyone I care about is leaving and I'm going to be left here all alone."

"Oh, honey, don't." Sid crossed the living room and sat down beside Courtney on the couch. "I had no idea you felt that way."

"You're my last link to Dad," she said, tears falling down her cheeks. "You're like family. Please don't go."

"I don't want to go, sweetie. But Leslie and I have

been all over the county looking at apartments. There aren't any here that we can afford."

"Well," Leslie said with a firm nod, "that's not entirely true."

"What?"

"These apartments still exist. If we could find some way to stop GB Ventures from tearing them down."

"How are you going to do that?" Sid asked.

"Oh my God, I just had an incredible idea," Courtney said.

"What?" Leslie and Matt asked simultaneously.

"There's one man in Jefferson County who has the money to do it. And he happens not to give a rat's behind about what the Lyndon family wants or needs."

"Who is that?"

"Jefferson Talbert."

Chapter Nineteen

Matt would have boycotted the Lyndon family's Fourth of July barbecue if left to his own devices. Showing up and having to face his father sounded like a recipe for the kind of family drama he'd always hated. He wasn't like his older brother, Daniel, who thrived on rebellion. No, Matthew was the middle child, sandwiched between Daniel the rebel and Jason the brainiac. Matthew had always tried to toe the line. Always. Not that it had ever gotten him much approval.

Dad wasn't his only problem. Mom would be all over him, and he'd have to rain on her parade by telling her she needed to stop her clandestine planning for his apartment. If he didn't have a job here in Shenandoah Falls, then he wouldn't be living here for much longer.

So all in all, avoiding his parents sounded like a good plan of action.

But at 8:30 a.m. on Independence Day morning, someone knocked at his front door and roused him from the couch where he'd fallen asleep the night before. He sat up, his mouth dry and his head pounding, payback for the bourbon he'd consumed last night.

He didn't want to answer the door for fear it might be Courtney. What would he say to her? He'd been pretty crappy to her on Monday night—asking for her kindness and repaying it with his anger.

He should have accepted her apology.

Dr. Doom jumped up on the coffee table and meowed just as Matt's unwanted guest knocked again. "Guess I'm done hiding out, huh?" he said to the cat.

Dr. Doom meowed again. The sun was up, and he was hungry.

Matt pushed up from the couch and answered the door, finding his cousin Jeff, dressed in a pair of skinny jeans and a white T-shirt bearing the words "We hold these truths to be self-evident, that all men are created equal" leaning against the doorframe. Jeff took one look at Matt and said, "Tied one on last night, huh?"

Matt nodded and opened the door a little wider. Jeff was the last person on earth he expected to see at his front door.

The Lyndons were a clannish lot, and Matt had grown up with cousins to the right and left. In fact, the children of Mark, Jamie, and Charles Lyndon were almost like siblings. All of them had grown up in Shenandoah Falls. All of them had gone to the Episcopal High School. All the boys, except Daniel, had gone to law school at the University of Virginia.

Jeff had missed all that. His father, Thomas, had moved away from Shenandoah Falls and married Nina Talbert, heiress to the Talbert billions. Jeff had been raised in New York City and had visited Shenandoah Falls only once as a child. A few years back, Jeff had come for an extended stay in his father's fishing cabin and met Melissa Portman, the owner of the used book store on Liberty Avenue. They'd fallen in love and had gotten married, but even though Jeff now lived in Shenandoah Falls, his relationship with the family remained strained.

He refused to use his father's last name, and he tended to avoid family gatherings at Charlotte's Grove.

"Why are you here?" Matt asked.

"Invite me in and I'll explain."

Matt nodded and stepped away from the door. "The place is a mess, but..."

Jeff gave the apartment a quick inspection. "Not really. You should try living with Melissa for a while. Then you'll know what a real mess is all about." Just then, the kitten came bouncing in Jeff's direction. "Hey, Porthos, wazzup?" Jeff scooped the cat into his arms, where Dr. Doom made an idiot of himself. A frisson of guilt worked its way down Matt's back. Doom ought to be living across the hall with Courtney. He needed the cuddles and lap time more than Ghul did.

The thought of Courtney's lap simultaneously aroused and depressed him.

"Can I get you something? I've got Cokes, water, beer," Matt asked.

"Nothing, thanks." Jeff sat down on the couch, and Matt sank into one of the side chairs. The moment his ass hit the leather, he wished he'd gotten himself a glass of water. "So?" he asked.

The cat had already curled up in Jeff's lap. "Yesterday I made a cash offer to buy Dogwood Estates from GB Ventures. Considering the negative press in the *Daily*, the company agreed. Of course, I offered them twice what the property was worth. I thought you'd want to know."

"You what?"

He shrugged. "My wife wanted this to happen. And I have a blind spot when it comes to her. Dogwood Estates is going to be a huge money loser. But hey, a guy needs tax deductions, right?"

"Right." Matt frowned. "What the hell is going on?"

"A couple of things. First, Courtney is Melissa's best friend. Second, Courtney had a couple of good reasons for wanting this to happen." He ticked his reasons off on his fingers. "She didn't want Sid and Leslie to move away. She didn't want Rory Ahern to leave the county and take Arwen with him, especially since she's not sure Rory and Arwen are a match made in heaven. And finally, she wanted to get you off the hook with Uncle Charles and Heather."

"What?"

"I tried to explain to her how things work in the family, but she was adamant on that point in particular. It really didn't matter to me because I'd already read the stuff in the paper. Nice job, Matt. Have you ever thought about becoming an investigative reporter?"

"No."

"A candidate for office, maybe?"

"No. Absolutely not. Who would vote for me?"

Jeff settled back on the couch. "Uncle Mark has been pestering me for the last six months about running for the County Council. He thinks someone needs to challenge Bill Cummins this fall. The only problem is that the party doesn't have anyone willing to run. Mark thinks this is great because I wouldn't have to mess with a primary or anything. But the thing is, I have no desire to enter politics. Do you? I think you'd be good at it. Of course, it would mean staying here in Shenandoah Falls."

"I wouldn't know the first thing about—"

"We're talking the County Council, Matt. And your name is Lyndon. Plus, you've single-handedly exposed some pretty rampant corruption—enough for someone to wonder if Cummins was getting kickbacks from GB Ventures. I don't think you'd have any problems raising money."

"I didn't expose GB Ventures on my own. I had some help from inside the county government and from Arwen Jacobs."

"Okay, so you've already assembled a team. That seems like a good start."

Matt shook his head. "A team? What are you talking about? I mean, Heather took money from Jerry Beyer, the CEO of GB Ventures and—"

"Who hasn't taken money from Jerry? He spreads his money around like manure, currying favor wherever he can. Heather's an idiot if she continues to take his money now that your exposé has appeared in the paper. To tell you the truth, I'm surprised Brandon tried to intimidate you and Uncle Charles. I can't imagine Heather knew he was doing that."

"You think she's going to be okay?"

"Of course she is. She didn't do anything unlawful. And neither did Jerry Beyer, unless he made under-the-table payments to Bill Cummins. In which case, they are both going to jail." He smiled.

"And who's going to pursue that angle in this county?" Matt asked.

"You. If you ran against him, you'd have a lot of opportunity to raise questions. And those questions would interest any number of hungry journalists. If you want to finish the job, you need to run. And you'd be doing me a favor. It would get Uncle

Mark off my back. He really wants a Lyndon on the council."

"But would he be happy with me? I mean, I'm—"

"The guy who exposed Bill Cummins for the crook he probably is? Yeah, I think Uncle Mark would be delighted to have you. And so would Uncle Jamie. You do realize that several of his farmhands had to quit because they couldn't find housing in the county. So get your ass in gear. Go take a shower and a couple of aspirins and make yourself presentable. We're going to Charlotte's Grove for the barbecue and a long conversation with Uncle Mark and Uncle Jamie."

Courtney sat on the folded seat of the commode in her bathroom staring at the little plus sign on the early pregnancy test. Really? This was like some epically cosmic joke or something. How could she be pregnant?

Easy answer: They hadn't used a condom that very first time. They'd lost control and . . .

Damn. Now what? A week had passed since her argument with Matt—a whirlwind week in which so many things had changed for the better, thanks to Jefferson Talbert's incredibly big heart.

Courtney would be forever indebted to Jeff for rescuing the tenants of Dogwood Estates. Although it would take more than a year to fully renovate every one of the apartment units, Jeff had already sent in a group of landscapers to hack back the weeds and resurface the parking lot. Roof repairs were also underway, and the trash containers had been secured against wildlife.

The renovations would be staged so that any of the remaining residents could stay in their units until newly refurbished apartments were ready for them. Best of all, Jeff had frozen the rent for the next three years for all remaining tenants. Leslie and Sid had decided to move in together, and yesterday they'd asked Courtney if she would plan a small wedding for them.

Matt's life had changed too, although she hadn't spoken one word to him. His mother and aunt had been swarming over his apartment for the last week, redoing everything. Courtney had run into them only once, thank goodness. She didn't know what she would do now. Julia was going to be her baby's grandmother.

She was curious to see what they were doing to his place. Anything would be an improvement over the stuff he'd bought at IKEA. And if he was running for office, he needed a little more class.

Courtney hadn't expected Jeff to talk Matt into running for the County Council. But last Friday, Matt had stunned the county politicos by announcing his candidacy for Bill Cummins's seat. Matt had the right political breeding, not to mention the full endorsement of Senator Mark Lyndon himself. The party, which had all but abdicated the seat, had been overjoyed to suddenly find a candidate with ready-made fundraising clout. Although it was early for editorial endorsements, the *Winchester Daily* had launched its own investigation into Bill Cummins and his relationship with Jerry Beyer. Sally Hawkes hadn't yet discovered any kickbacks, but every day the newspaper published some new, damaging revelation of a very close, and potentially corrupt, connection between the two of them.

Arwen's life had also changed. She'd moved in with Rory in order to save money, and she was helping him set up a recording studio right in downtown Shenandoah Falls. She planned to be the first artist to record there, and she had big plans to send her songs off to several recording artists in Nashville.

And now Courtney's life was about to change more than anyone else's. With stunning irony, her tasteless joke about the sperm bank had come back to bite her in the butt. The timing for this was spectacularly bad, what with Matt running for the County Council. Courtney had no illusions about her situation. Matt didn't love her. He didn't want to make a life together.

And the last thing he needed was an out-of-wedlock child.

But he would have one. And he'd probably hate her for it, although the only emotion Courtney felt when it came to Matt was love. And she truly hoped he'd love their child.

She got up from the bathroom and phoned Dr. Lawrence's office, making an appointment for next week. Once that was done, she sat in her living room awash in a strange mixture of feelings: elation, fear, sadness, joy, all mixed together. She would be having this child one way or another. And that meant Matt would have to know about it. She decided not to wait to tell him the news. She had no desire to surprise or manipulate him.

So she stayed home and waited for him.

It was almost 10:00 p.m. when Matt finally came home. Courtney had spent the evening on her balcony keeping a lookout and had just about given up for the night when he came strolling down the street with his suit jacket over his shoulder and his shirtsleeves rolled up, like a campaign-poster portrait of a young politician.

He looked good enough to eat. Or to hug. Or to love for the rest of her life.

He paused a moment on the sidewalk, and Courtney's heart soared. *Please give me a poem.*

It didn't happen. It wasn't ever going to happen again. Instead of poetry, Matt made a point of glancing away before turning toward the door.

This confrontation wasn't going to be easy, but he needed to know the truth. So she opened her door and met him in the hallway, her stomach tied into knots and her pulse hammering in her head.

"I need to talk to you," she said as he came up the stairs.

When he reached the landing, he turned those incredible brown eyes in her direction. "Look," he said,

"I probably should have come over a couple of days ago to tell you how much I appreciate the fact that you talked to Melissa and Jeff about Dogwood Estates. Honestly, if you hadn't gone to Jeff, I don't know where those tenants would be. Hell, I don't know where I'd be. So, I owe you one. But I can't—"

"Matt, I need to talk to you," she interrupted. Courtney's voice remained firm, which was nothing short of a miracle. His words of thanks were totally unexpected and knifed into her heart so much more effectively than his anger might have. "I have something really important that I need to tell you." She opened her apartment's door. "Please."

He nodded. "Okay."

A moment later, he stood in her living room, his presence making her apartment seem small. How would she manage without him? Hell, how would she manage if he wanted a relationship with their child? Would she be stuck loving him forever while he kept her out of his heart?

Her runaway thoughts settled in her throat. "Can I get you something? A beer, a Coke?" she said around the lump.

He shook his head. "What is it, Courtney?"

She pointed at the couch. "Sit down."

Something in her tone must have warned him that she meant business because he dropped onto the couch and cocked one foot over his knee. "Okay. I'm here. I'm listening."

"This is very awkward. I want you to know that I'm as surprised as you are."

"Surprised about what?"

"I'm pregnant," she blurted.

The news had the expected effect. Matt's face paled, his eyes narrowed, and his mouth dropped open. "But we used—"

"No. Not every time. Not the first time. The first time we forgot all about contraception."

His brow came down into the signature Lyndon frown, and every muscle in his body tensed. Something hard and ugly burned behind his gaze. "I can't believe it. Dammit. I'm an idiot."

"No. We were both idiots. And I just want you to know—"

"If you think you can trap me into something, you are out of your mind. What was it? My name? My trust fund? What?" He jumped to his feet and pointed a finger at her. "I should have taken that joke about the sperm bank seriously."

"Matt, come on. This is me you're talking to. Not Allison Chapman. I didn't set out to trap you into anything. I set out to take you down a peg or two, but instead..." Her throat knotted up again, and it became impossible to say anything else. Matt didn't trust her, and she had only herself to blame.

"What do you know about Allison Chapman?"

"I know she's a bitch. I have a feeling she took you for a ride."

"How do you know that? I never told you."

"You didn't need to tell me. Allison did."

"She what? I don't believe you."

"You can believe me or not. But Allison implied that she tried to trap you into a marriage. And to be honest, she suggested that I do the same. In my book, that made her a—"

"I can't believe this." Matt's voice swelled with anger, and Courtney took a step back, her stomach suddenly roiling. "Here's the truth: Allison befriended me back when I was an idiot about women. And the only reason she ever paid any attention to me was because she wanted to screw my brother. But when Daniel told her to get lost, she decided she'd settle for me. She seduced me. I know it's hard to believe, but I fell for her BS hook, line, and sinker, especially when she played the 'I'm pregnant' card. But I'm sadder and wiser now, so—"

"Matt, please, I'm—"

"What was it? Did you two get together just to yank my chain? How many times do I have to apologize for taking Brandon's bet?"

"Brandon's bet? I don't—"

"Don't pull that wide-eyed innocent look on me, Courtney. I may have fallen for it once. But not now. This has all been about Brandon's stupid bet, hasn't it? You decided you'd take me down just to prove a point. Well, get this. I'm still standing."

Matt's fury knew no bounds. He ran from Court-

ney's apartment and slammed his apartment door
before he exploded with a stream of profanity, scar-
ing Dr. Doom, who'd been waiting for him to come
home.

The cat slunk down the hall to the bedroom, and
Matt felt a small inkling of regret. But not enough to
counter the rage running through him.

Allison Chapman had played him like a fine violin. He'd fallen head over heels in love with her,
and he'd convinced himself that she loved him back.
When she'd announced her pregnancy, he'd been
overjoyed. He got right down on one knee and asked
her to be his bride. He might even have quoted Elizabeth Barrett Browning. He'd been all of twenty years
old.

She'd wanted to elope, of course. She'd given him
some mumbo jumbo about her parents pressuring her
into an abortion, about how they would be opposed
to a shotgun wedding.

But he hadn't wanted to run away. He'd wanted
to be honest with his parents and his large family.
And fool that he'd been, he'd wanted to celebrate
his love and the arrival of a child. Besides, Grandma
would have disapproved of a secret Vegas wedding.
Grandma had passed away the year before his spectacular miscalculation over Allison.

So he'd gone to his parents with the news.
They hadn't reacted with joy. In fact, Dad had immediately interceded, calling Judge Chapman for
a father-to-father chat. Twenty-four hours later,

Allison Chapman confessed that she was not pregnant. And four years later, either Allison or her father had exacted a small revenge by sabotaging his chair during moot court competition. Such an immature thing for them to do. But then, Dad had humiliated both of them.

No, wait, it hadn't been Dad. All of it, from beginning to end, had been Matt's fault. For being so stupid and so gullible. He'd promised himself never to be played again.

He roared and punched the newly painted wall in his living room. The Sheetrock dented, and pain knifed through his hand and up his arm. Damn. Damn. Damn. How could he make the same mistake twice?

He cradled his bruised hand and paced. Bill Cummins would use this against him. He could see the headlines. Suddenly the crusader would turn into the womanizer. It was practically inevitable. And when he lost the election, he could imagine the disappointment.

Damn. He needed to head this off at the pass. But how? He certainly wasn't going to Dad with this. Dad would call him an idiot, the way he always did. Matt was an idiot, but he didn't need Dad to rub his nose in it. Why couldn't he fall in love with an ordinary woman?

He threw himself onto the new leather and chrome couch in his living room and rested his head in his hands. He'd been fighting his emotions for a solid week. How many times had he stopped himself from making that journey across the hallway?

Dozens. More. Courtney had changed his life. If she hadn't encouraged him to take his research to Linda and the press, Bill Cummins would continue to rip people off. If she hadn't talked to Jeff, he'd be without a job or purpose in life, and the tenants at Dogwood Estates would be scrambling to find new homes. For a week, he'd been trying to convince himself that he could still trust her, and all the while she'd been sitting across the way plotting her next move in her cat-and-mouse game.

Like Allison, she'd trotted out the pregnancy card the moment he backed away.

He would have to tell someone, but the idea of dumping this news on Uncle Mark or Jeff made his stomach churn. They had trusted him. They had believed in him. And he would fail them all. Again.

Courtney dragged herself to work early on Wednesday morning. After spending most of Tuesday night sequestered in her bathroom alternately crying and hurling, she didn't look her best, but she was happy to get out of her apartment.

Funny how easily Matt had lost trust in her once she'd lost trust in him. Maybe neither of them had ever trusted. It didn't matter. It was over.

At least she'd told him the truth, and sooner or later, he would come to realize that she hadn't been lying about the baby, and she hadn't been trying to

trap him into something either. She had every faith
that Matt would want to be part of his child's life. It
would be okay. They lived across the hall from each
other. Maybe they could share the baby sort of like
they'd been sharing the cats.

She headed straight to the Eagle Hill Manor
kitchen on Wednesday morning, where Antonin always kept hot water for tea, even in July. She made
herself a cup of chamomile tea, and when Antonin
asked if she was ill, she requested a couple of pieces
of dry toast.

She took her breakfast, such as it was, up to her
office, where she tried to focus on the weekend's
upcoming events. The chamomile almost settled her
stomach, but it didn't settle her head or her heart.

Amy arrived—with that pregnant-lady glow in her
cheeks that Courtney had yet to achieve—took one
look at her, and said, "Wow. Antonin's right. You do
look a little *gueule de bois*." Amy, spoiled rich girl
that she was, never tired of using her French.

Courtney rolled her eyes. "And that means...?"

"It's French for hungover."

"So glad you got to practice your French on my
account."

"Not on your account. I like speaking French with
Antonin." Amy crossed the room and sank into her
chair. "So, where are we on the Boysco-Lopez wedding? Did the bride ever decide on the table linens? I
have to put in an order for them today."

Courtney pawed through the papers on her desk,

trying to find the notes she'd taken on Friday. She couldn't find them, and for some reason, that seemed like the end of the world. Her throat thickened, and a sense of doom settled over her. "I know I have my notes somewhere," she muttered. She hated feeling disorganized.

"Are you okay?"

Courtney stopped looking for her notes and dropped her hands into her lap. She shook her head, and the tears started again. It was like God was punishing her or something, paying her back for all those dry-eyed years when she'd always kept it together. It was almost as if she'd banked her tears for a rainy day and the rainy day had suddenly arrived.

"Oh my God, what's the matter?" Amy got out of her chair and crossed the short distance between their desks. "Tell me. Don't be stoic." Amy parked her behind on the edge of Courtney's desk and gave her a knowing look. "Stoicism is highly overrated."

Courtney dug in her desk drawer for a box of tissues just as Willow, also with that pregnant-lady glow, came through the door looking very concerned. "Antonin said you looked like hell, and Mom says you haven't returned a single one of her phone calls. What's going on?" She stopped in front of Courtney's desk, crossing her arms.

Courtney may not have sought this intervention, but she welcomed it. Over the last week, she hadn't spoken with Arwen about her heartbreak, and she didn't want to go back to Melissa after all Jeff had done for Matt and the tenants of Dogwood Estates. She hadn't wanted to burden Amy or Willow either.

But she didn't want to do this alone anymore. And it broke her heart to think that Matt didn't want anything to do with his own child. Of course she wanted him to want the baby. Hell, she wanted him to love and trust her. But that was like wishing for the moon.

The two of them had been so scarred by the past that they would probably never find a way toward the deeper trust necessary for a real relationship.

She looked up at Amy and Willow. She didn't want to bare it all to them, but someone needed to inform the Lyndon family that it was about to get a little larger. And what better messengers could she possibly have? Amy and Willow would be her child's cousins. And their babies and hers would all be part of the same family.

So she dabbed her eyes and said, "Pull up a chair. This is going to take a while."

Matt spent the rest of the week living on the edge, waiting for Courtney's next move. But when no negative stories appeared in the *Winchester Daily*, he allowed himself to breathe easier. Maybe he'd discouraged her.

Or maybe she was just waiting for the right moment, the way she'd waited to exact revenge on Brandon before she'd gone after his Camaro.

Or maybe she'd told the truth. That thought deeply disturbed him.

But he kept his mouth shut and focused on hiring a campaign staff. Heather, who had apologized for Brandon's aggressive behavior on the whole Jerry Beyer front, had connected him with Hale Chandler, a political consultant familiar with Jefferson County politics. Hale had been brought on as his campaign chairman and had started vetting people for various positions. They were late getting into the game, and they had a lot of ground to cover in a short time.

The work kept his mind off Courtney, although it didn't stop him from thinking about her every night when he returned home. The idea that she might be telling the truth always seemed to hit him around midnight.

It never failed to disturb his sleep. And the unrepentant romantic that still lived deep within him wanted to believe that Courtney loved him despite the way he'd treated her. He wanted to believe she was telling the truth, but he just couldn't manage it. So he tossed and turned, night after night.

The lack of sleep left him wooly-eyed and cotton-headed on Sunday morning when he showed up for the standing brunch at Charlotte's Grove. If ever he was going to confide in someone, today would be the day.

He needed advice. He couldn't go on like this, waiting for the worst to happen and yet still hoping he was wrong about Courtney. But he couldn't talk to Dad. After the Allison debacle, he'd lost faith in his father. The feeling was mutual.

Should he bring this to David? Maybe. Although his own insecurities made that difficult. He'd spent his life being told that he should be like David. David would never have gotten himself into a situation like this one.

He couldn't talk to Uncle Mark either. Mark had believed in him when no one else had. He didn't want to wreck that new beginning. So he entered Charlotte's Grove unsure of himself, which was nothing new.

The July heat and humidity had descended upon the Shenandoah Valley with a vengeance that week, so Aunt Pam had laid out the buffet in the dining room. The family gathered in the adjacent den, which was already crowded when Matt arrived.

The moment Matt entered the room, Uncle Mark lifted his Bloody Mary and said, "The man of the hour has arrived."

Matt stopped in his tracks, blinded by the sight of the family lifting their glasses in his direction. The insane urge to turn tail and run overwhelmed him. He suddenly needed to confess, in excruciating detail, why he could never be anyone's man of the hour. How utterly ironic that the moment he'd waited for all his life didn't ease his worry.

Nor did it erase the deep-seated ache in his heart.

But coward that he was, he didn't say a word. Instead he snagged his own Bloody Mary and headed across the den in Uncle Mark's direction.

But he didn't get far before Uncle Jamie intercepted him. "You got a minute?"

The sober look in his uncle's eyes put Matt on guard. Uncle Mark might be the oldest sibling and the one with the political connections, but Uncle Jamie was probably the most powerful man in Jefferson County.

If Matt were to become a member of the County Council, he'd have to worry about Uncle Jamie all the time. It occurred to him that the close family bonds might be a problem in the future. But for now he didn't want to rock any boats.

"Sure. What's up?" Matt said.

"Not here. Let's step out onto the terrace."

What the hell? It was ninety-six degrees out on the terrace. But Uncle Jamie snagged him by the arm and gently tugged him out through the French doors. No one, except David, seemed to notice. David, on the other hand, followed them with his dark, sober stare.

"Let's sit in the shade," Jamie said as he crossed the terrace and sat down under one of the umbrellas. Even in the shade it was muggy. Sweat began to dampen Matt's skin. He took a long sip of his drink and then asked, "What's up?"

"What's up is that I'm deeply disappointed in you."

Damn. Story of his life. He sat straighter in his chair. "About what?" He did a poor job of disguising his annoyance.

Jamie shook his head. "Don't take that tone with me. I think you know what I'm upset about."

Damn. This made no sense. Courtney wouldn't have gone to Uncle Jamie. If she had wanted to mess up his life, she would have gone to Bill Cummins or the press. She could have made him pay. But she didn't. All she'd ever done was help him and his clients.

"I'm confused." He collapsed back in the chair and closed his eyes, the heat melting him.

Jamie chuckled. "I'm not surprised by that."

Matt opened his eyes. "Wait. I really am confused. You're disappointed and you're not surprised. Oh yeah, I guess the story of my life."

Jamie leaned forward and gave his knee an avuncular pat. "Son, Courtney Wallace apparently had a crying jag at work on Wednesday morning. And as you know, your cousin Amy, who is not here today because she works on Sundays, happened to mention it to me yesterday when she came by the vineyard to pick up some reserve wine for a reception."

"Courtney had a crying jag? That doesn't sound like her."

"No, it doesn't. And apparently she's drinking a lot of chamomile tea these days."

"Chamomile tea?" A very bad feeling was beginning to settle into Matt's gut.

"That's the foul-tasting tea women drink when they're pregnant. Debra swore by it." Jamie's stare was both direct and compassionate.

"Are you telling me that Courtney really is pregnant?"

"Courtney is not Allison."

"You know about Allison?"

"Everyone knows about Allison and what she tried to do to you. Thank God for your aunt Pam, who can be a royal pain in the ass much of the time. But in the case of Allison Chapman, she saw that girl coming from a mile away."

"Aunt Pam?"

"Are you telling me that your father never told you how Aunt Pam cornered that girl and cut right through her lies?"

Matt shook his head. "No. I thought he went to Judge Chapman or something."

"Why would your father do that? He regularly argues cases before Judge Chapman. And believe me, there was some fallout, even though Pam did the dirty work." Jamie let go of a long sigh. "Look, son, I know you were heartbroken over Allison. Everyone in the family knows that. But Courtney is not Allison. I understand if you don't want to marry her. But you're a fool if you walk away from a child."

Uncle Jamie's voice got hard and a little emotional. The look on his face pierced Matt's armor. If he didn't know better, he might think Uncle Jamie had a child somewhere no one knew anything about.

"Are you saying that—"

Jamie put up a hand, palm outward. "We're not

talking about me. Or my regrets, of which there are many. I've been an asshole on any number of occasions. And in this case, it takes one to know one."

Matt braced his elbows on his knees and sank his head into his hands. Sweat rolled off his back. It was hotter than hell, even under the umbrella. "I guess if the shoe fits…"

"But here's the thing. Redemption is possible. I have discovered this. There was a moment, not long ago, when I had lost Amy's trust. But look at us now. I even like her husband. But don't tell Dusty that. He might get a swelled head."

Matt chuckled but said nothing.

"Do you love her?"

Wow, that question jolted him right out of his complacency. He raised his head. "Yeah." He spoke the word on a long sigh. "But I screwed it up. I got all bent out of shape when she accused me of cheating on her when I didn't."

"And you paid her back by not believing her when she came to you with her life-altering news, is that it?"

He nodded and then shook his head. "I guess trust goes both ways, huh?"

"If you're interested in a real relationship it does. Take it from me, the guy who strayed and ended up without his wife's trust."

Damn. That was news. Uncle Jamie had lost his wife a number of years ago to cancer, but Matt had never dreamed that Jamie had cheated on Debra.

Uncle Jamie must have read the surprise on his face because he said, "Look, I get the allure of playing the field. It's fun. But love is something else again. It'll mess with your head and make you feel like you're gonna die. But it's worth it. And if you want to know my biggest regret? It's that I didn't let myself love.

"So, I'm not advising you to marry Courtney Wallace if it's only because you're running for office or you're afraid of a scandal. These days, nobody cares if you have a baby out of wedlock. Everyone is doing it. But if you love her, then don't be an asshole. You get up right this minute and you go find her and you tell her how you feel. Have you told her how you feel?"

He shook his head.

"Why not?"

He shrugged. "Fear, mostly. I don't know. Stupidity?"

Jamie nodded. "I am familiar with these feelings." The older man stood up. "And just remember this, even if you decide that it's not going to work out between the two of you, you only get to be a father to that baby once. Don't blow it."

Jamie strolled back toward the French doors. He stopped halfway and turned to look over his shoulder. "And one other thing I've learned from my many mistakes. Giving love, especially to a child, won't diminish you. You don't run out of love. It's funny that way."

He turned and continued his journey into the air-conditioned den.

Matt stayed behind, enduring the July heat in his own private hell, thinking deeply about his next move.

Courtney dragged herself home on Sunday evening. It had been an easy day at work with only one small event—a thirtieth-anniversary luncheon and vow-renewal ceremony—and yet she was exhausted. As she climbed her apartment's steps, her only thoughts were about a glass of tea and a tepid bath. The weatherman said the heat index had reached one hundred and six. She believed it.

Her bones were limp, her skin sticky, and her stomach unsettled, as if a body snatcher had taken possession of it. That brought a little smile. In a way, she had been invaded, and the little stinker was changing her body chemistry—even though she was only about four weeks into this unexpected adventure. Her appointment with Dr. Lawrence wasn't for another couple of days, but she didn't need a doctor to fully confirm the pregnancy. Her nipples were already turning a dark rosy color.

She gave Aramis a can of food and then headed to her bedroom, where she peeled off the slightly damp little black dress she'd worn to work. She had several little black dresses, which served as a kind of uniform when she had to manage receptions and weddings. Black was a fine color for the fall, winter, and spring. Summer, not so much.

She'd just changed into her terry-cloth robe when something rattled the French doors in her bedroom. It almost sounded like someone was throwing pebbles against the glass.

It was probably Ethan Riley from downstairs. The kid needed a little discipline. She tore open the doors. "Ethan, I swear, if you break my window, I'm going to make you scoop cat poop for a solid month." She stepped onto the small Juliet balcony and leaned on the iron railing.

"I'd be totally willing to scoop poop for you," Matt said. "In fact, I was just reading in this book that it's probably not a good idea for you to be doing any poop scooping at all." He waved a paperback book that looked suspiciously like a copy of *What to Expect When You're Expecting*.

Her body flushed hot, and not from the evening sun that baked the front of the apartment building. This wasn't happening, was it? This was a fever dream.

Matthew Lyndon, wearing a Ralph Lauren polo shirt and khakis, with his longish hair curling in the July heat into a slightly sweaty tangle over his forehead, was standing below her balcony.

Like Romeo.

Stupid romantic heart. It should have given up a long time ago. But she had to hand it to him. He was standing out there in the hundred-degree weather when he could have just as easily knocked on her front door.

"You should get out of the sun before you give yourself heatstroke."

He tucked the book under his arm and folded two hands over his chest. "I'm proving my adoration down here by enduring the elements."

"Oh, is that what it is?"

"Yes. Now be quiet. I have something to say." He paused a moment. "Um, but before I say it, you might want to tighten the belt on that beautiful robe because, uh..."

She looked down. Her boobs were about to make an appearance. She tucked them back in place and tightened the belt. "Okay, I'm ready. Now what?"

He cleared his throat again. And then he started talking in that voice he used whenever he recited poetry.

"Let me not to the marriage of true minds
Admit impediments. Love is not love
Which alters when it alteration finds,
Or bends with the remover to remove.
O no! it is an ever-fixed mark
That looks on tempests and is never shaken;"

She recognized the Shakespeare sonnet immediately. No truer words were ever written about the power of true love. And as those words floated up on the hot summer air, a knot swelled in her throat, and her eyes got all misty, and tears started flowing like water. The book and the poem and the pebble against her window. Who said romance was dead in the twenty-first century?

"Don't cry, please," he said when he'd finished reciting the poem. "I know you can never forgive me for what I accused you of, but I'm hoping against hope that you will forgive me. Because I don't want to abandon a child, Courtney. And the truth is, I don't want to abandon you either.

"We may have started out trying to one-up each other, but that changed somewhere along the line. The truth is, you've done nothing to hurt me. In fact, I owe you for just about everything. There are people who regard me as some kind of hero because I gave my research to Linda Petersen, who is probably a much bigger hero than I am. And I would never have taken even that small step without you.

"And most of the tenants of Dogwood Estates seem to think I was the one who went to Jeff and convinced him to save those apartments. You did that too.

"Everything I've become over the last few weeks is all because of you. And your kindness to the tenants should have told me right from the start that you weren't like Allison.

"So I know you can't forgive me, but I'm hoping. On bended knee." He got down on his knees and looked up at her out of those big, dark, sad puppy-dog eyes.

"Oh, for God's sake, get up, you silly man. And get out of the heat."

He grinned. "Okay. I'm coming up."

She met him at the door. "So will you forgive me?" he asked.

She nodded, tears streaming down her face. "Will you forgive me?"

He cocked his head. "I'm sorry about that too."

She shook her head. "No. That was my fault. All my fault. How on earth can I expect you to trust me when I didn't trust you?"

He cupped her face and swiped her tears away with his thumbs. "We both got played, Courtney. A long time ago. And I guess it's not easy to come back from that. It's not always easy to trust when you've been hurt before."

She nodded. "I only cared because I love you. I never would have called you on it otherwise. I truly believed that you were a player, Matt, but you're not. You don't fit the boxes I've labeled. You never have."

"So, are we going to do this? The last time a woman told me she was pregnant I immediately got down on one knee."

"What?" She blinked. "Really?"

He cocked his head. "I thought you knew about Allison."

"I know she played you, but—"

He took a step forward into the apartment and closed the door behind him. "One day I'll tell you the whole story. I only just learned all the details this morning. But suffice it to say that I would have been trapped by that woman were it not for Aunt Pam's quick thinking. Who, by the way, has a surprising amount of respect for you. Something about the way you stood up to Daniel's ex-fiancé when she wanted to turn her wedding into a three-ring circus."

"Really? Pam likes me? To tell you the truth, she intimidates the crap out of me."

He nodded. "Well, that too. Pam also thinks we should name the baby George after my grandfather, which is not a suggestion so much as it's a command."

"Let's hope it's a girl, then."

He pulled her into a kiss so sweet and so hot it buckled her knees. He pulled back a little. "Will you marry me?" he asked.

She'd waited all her life for someone to ask that question. But for some reason she hesitated in her answer.

He nodded. "I'm not worried about my campaign, and I'm not asking because of the baby. And I'm not even worried about your eventual answer. I want you to know the truth about how I feel. I'm tired of waiting for my real life to start. And the truth is, in the last few weeks, I found myself. That would never have happened without you. And it's so clear to me now. My real life is right here, right this minute, with you. So if you want to wait, that—"

"No." She shook her head. "I'm tired of waiting too. Let's elope."

He laughed. "No way that's happening. But we'll

let Amy and Willow plan the shotgun wedding, okay?"

And then, just like Mr. Right, he pulled her close for another long, erotic kiss before he hoisted her into his arms and carried her to the bedroom, where he made slow, beautiful, soulful love to her.

Epilogue ————————————

Courtney had planned hundreds of weddings for other people, but when it came to hers, she let Amy and Willow handle every single detail. Her friends worked overtime, and the wedding took a mere four weeks to plan.

On the day before Labor Day, she stood in the small room off the vestibule at the Laurel Chapel staring at herself in the mirror.

"I remember your mother in that dress," Sid said as he gave her shoulders a squeeze.

"I have a picture of her wearing it," Courtney said in a hushed voice. She wished she could remember her mother better. But Mom had been gone for such a long time—so long, in fact, that Courtney had considered getting rid of the box containing Mom's wedding dress dozens of times over the years. For some reason, she'd never been able to let it go.

Now she was glad she'd hung on to that silly memory.

Courtney looked up at Sid's reflection in the mirror. He had recovered from his heart surgery and seemed bigger and more full of life than ever. "Thanks for giving me away."

He chuckled. "Honey, you don't need giving away. But I'm honored to stand in for your dad."

Just then, Amy, Melissa, and Arwen came through the door. They wore short rose-pink dresses with high waistlines to accommodate Amy and Melissa's baby bumps. Courtney's bump wasn't all that visible yet.

"It's time," Amy said, handing Courtney a beautiful bouquet with a vintage look that blended perfectly with the dress's ivory satin. The peonies and dusky roses were gorgeous, and all the more precious because Amy had made the bouquets herself. And Amy had become such a good friend.

But today, Courtney and Amy would become more than mere friends. This wedding would bind Courtney to Willow, Amy, and Melissa as family. It had been such a long time since she'd had any family to speak of.

Arwen, her maid of honor, was the odd woman out. She'd threatened to write a song about a wedding where all the bridesmaids were married and pregnant except herself. But she'd also made it clear that she was very happy not to be joining the Lyndon family. She had Rory, and he was enough to keep her busy.

They took their places in the vestibule. The music swelled, and the processional began.

When it was Courtney's turn, at last, to walk down the aisle, she hung on to Sid's arm like a lifeline. She'd dreamed this dream a million times, but somewhere along the line, she'd lost faith.

And now, like some fairy tale, here she was, looking at her imperfect prince with his curly hair and espresso eyes, which were trained on her as if she hung the moon for him or something.

Matthew was so much more than he appeared. Thank God she'd had a chance to get beyond the surface. Because underneath, he was kind and sweet and incredibly good to her and for her. Plus, his store of romantic poetry was nothing short of amazing.

He grinned at her. And she smiled back.

I love you, he mouthed as she came to stand beside him.

"I love you back," she said, and meant it with all her heart.

For Professor Laurie Wilson, planning her wedding to longtime boyfriend Brandon Kopp has been a whirlwind. But somehow, between all the cake tastings and dress fittings, she never imagined being left at the altar.

Please turn the page for an excerpt from *Here Comes the Bride*.

Available now.

Chapter One————————

If Laurie Wilson could have controlled the weather for her wedding, she would have. She had controlled, planned, organized, and directed every other aspect of her special day. So when it rained for a solid seven days before the ceremony, Laurie exhausted herself with worry.

She could have saved herself the angst because August twenty-sixth arrived with an endlessly azure sky more like September than late summer. And in true silver-lining fashion, the rain had broken the deep August drought leaving the asters, woodbine, and rudbeckia that grew in the meadow beside Laurel Chapel in full, glorious bloom.

The day was as perfect as her dream.

So was her wedding dress.

The full-length mirror in the church's waiting room provided a stunning reflection of the woman who was about to become Mrs. Brandon Kopp. Alençon lace dripped from her gown's bodice while the Swarovski crystals along the sweetheart neckline sent colorful sparks of light along the walls and ceilings. Laurie pressed her hands down into the yards of netting in the skirt, feeling giddy.

"You look gorgeous, princess," Dad said from behind her, a tremor in his voice.

For the first time in her life, Dad's pet name actually fit. The A-line ball gown was princess-worthy, and her thick, unruly tresses had been braided into a crown that now bristled with baby's breath like a living tiara.

She turned around to find Dad, his hands jammed in the pockets of his dark gray suit, his dahlia boutonniere slightly askew. She stepped up to him and fixed the flower. "There," she said, with butterflies flitting around in her core.

He captured her hand and gave it a little kiss. "I can't believe my little princess is getting married," he said, a sheen in his eyes. "But I heartily approve of your groom."

"I do too," she said with a grin. "And I'm happy the planning is finally over. I thought Mom and I would come to blows a few times over the last few months."

The door opened, and Laurie's bridesmaids invaded in a swirl of burgundy chiffon and laughter.

Madison Atwood, Emma Raynerson, and Jessica Westbrook were dear friends from college, and Brandon's sister, Roxanne, was the maid of honor.

"We've been sent to let you know that Brandon and the groomsmen are about to take their positions. It's only a few more minutes," Roxy said. "And I just wanted to tell you before the wedding toasts start that I'm so happy you're going to be my sister-in-law. Brandon couldn't have chosen any better."

A wave of joy percolated through Laurie. "Thank you so much." She gave Roxy a fierce hug. "Not just for saying that, but for holding my hand the last few months. All of you have been terrific, really. I know I can get a little OCD about things, and you all have been so supportive, especially when Mom started throwing her weight around."

A tearful and slightly giggly group hug followed, but it didn't last long because Courtney Wallace, the events coordinator for Eagle Hill Manor, opened the door and said, "It's show time, ladies...and gent." The strains of the Air from Bach's *Suite No. 3 in D*—arranged for organ and violin—floated in from the sanctuary. A little flutter of excitement gnawed at Laurie's insides as her friends left the room, lined up in the chapel's small vestibule, and one by one, made their way down the aisle.

She took Dad's arm and looked up at him. He smiled and winked. "I love you, princess," he said.

"I love you too," she murmured as the music changed from the Bach to Pachelbel's Canon in D.

She'd had a huge argument with Mom about this music choice. Mom wanted the traditional "Bridal Chorus" from Wagner's opera *Lohengrin*. But Laurie was a bit of an opera buff, and in her estimation, the wedding in *Lohengrin* wasn't one she wanted to emulate since the bride ends up dead at the end of the opera. So no "Bridal Chorus" for her. She regarded it as bad luck.

Without the opening fanfare of "Here Comes the Bride" to signal her arrival, the wedding guests didn't rise to their feet very quickly. But they did eventually get the message. She gripped Dad's arm and looked ahead to where Brandon waited, dressed in a dark gray suit with his curly, almost-black hair falling over his forehead. He aimed his big blue eyes at her, and her heart beat a little faster.

They'd known each other for ten years, since freshman year at George Washington University. They had hooked up a time or two in college but not seriously until five years ago. Brandon was the love of a lifetime. The only man she'd ever slept with. Her heart swelled in her chest as she arrived at the altar without tripping on the train of her dress. Thank God. She could check that worry off her list of possible disasters.

She looked up into Brandon's eyes. She'd imagined this moment thousands of times. His eyes would sparkle, maybe with unshed tears of joy. His mouth would curl at the corner and expose his adorable dimple. He'd wink...

Wait. She'd never imagined him frowning at her. What? Did he hate her dress? Was it too princessy? She knew it; she should have gone with the mermaid dress even though Mom hated it. Crap. The moment was spoiled forever.

The minister interrupted her inner rant. "*Dearly beloved. We have come together in the presence of God to witness and bless the joining together of* —"

"Wait," Brandon said.

"What?" The minister laid his finger down to mark his place in the *Book of Common Prayer*. Then he looked up at Brandon over the rims of his half-glasses.

The bodice of Laurie's dress chose that moment to become a tourniquet, shutting off her air supply.

"What on earth are you doing?" In the front pew, Brandon's father stood up with a thunderous look on his face.

Brandon ignored his dad. He kept staring at Laurie with panic in his eyes. "Uh, Laurie, um…"

"How dare you!" This came from Mom in the pew on the opposite side. Like Brandon, Laurie tried to ignore her mother while simultaneously trying to breathe.

"I can't," Brandon said.

"You can't or you don't want to?" Roxy asked. "Because, baby bro, there is a big difference."

"I…Well, both of those, actually."

"What?" Laurie finally managed to push out the word and suck in a gulp of air.

Brandon took her by the hand, and the touch sent ice up her arm. She wanted to pull away from him but she was frozen in place. "Look, Laurie, you're more or less the only girl I ever dated."

"So?" someone asked. Laurie wasn't sure but it sounded like Andrew Lyndon, the best man.

"I just don't think either of us is ready for this. I mean, we don't have enough experience."

"What?" That was definitely Mom's voice. "You're twenty-eight years old, for goodness' sake. You're not a couple of teenagers."

"Is there someone else?" Laurie could only whisper the words as the foundation of her world crumbled beneath her.

Brandon's eyes widened. "No, never. I swear, Laurie, I have never cheated on you. But I think we got on the wedding carousel and..." He stabbed a hand through his hair. "Shit," he said under his breath as he turned away.

"If there's no one else, then—"

"I just want a break, okay? Like six months. You know, like a trial separation."

"For crap's sake, how can you have a separation if you're not even married?" Dad asked in a tense voice.

Laurie glanced at Dad, still standing there waiting to give her away. His face had gone pale and grave. He turned toward Brandon. "What is it you want, son?"

"I just need time. You know, to make sure this

isn't a mistake." And then he gave Laurie a sweet, sad smile and said, "And you need time too, Laurie. I think it would be good if we saw other people. Really. And then we can decide."

"Are you crazy? I love you. I don't want to see other people."

He shook his head. "I'm really sorry. I know you spent a lot of time and money planning all this." He turned and strode down the aisle and out of the chapel. His father climbed over a couple of wedding guests and hit the aisle at a dead run. Laurie hoped the old guy didn't give himself a heart attack chasing after his son.

Roxy must have had the same thought because she dropped her bouquet and tore after Mr. Kopp, saying, "Daddy, don't kill yourself."

Dad glanced at Mom and snarled something obscene while the wedding guests went ominously silent, except for Mom, who collapsed in the front pew, openly weeping and maybe even wailing a little.

Someone grabbed Laurie by the hand. "Come on, let's get you out of here."

She looked up. Andrew Lyndon, the best man. Funny how he'd stayed and Roxy had gone. He tugged her forward, and she followed him down the aisle like a confused puppy. Behind her, the bridesmaids and the groomsmen followed in a disorderly retreat, and all Laurie could think about was that the musicians were supposed to play Mendelssohn's "Wedding March" during the recessional.

Andrew marched out of the chapel and down the path to the inn, his little sister, Amy, running ahead of him clearing the way. Behind him, the remaining bridesmaids and groomsmen, including his brother, Edward, and cousins Matt and Jason, followed like a formally clad flash mob.

They hurried across the lawn, into the inn, up the sweeping staircase, and arrived at the Churchill Suite—Eagle Hill Manor's signature guest room on the second floor. Amy, who was also an assistant wedding planner at the inn, opened the door with her passkey.

"C'mon, boys, let's go get wine," Amy said, snagging Andrew's brother and cousins. She looked up at Andrew. "We'll be back. In the meantime, you hold down the fort. I can't think of anyone better. You are the most levelheaded member of the Lyndon family." She winked and gave him a sisterly smile.

Wow, Amy had really grown up in the last year. Instead of a spoiled brat without ambition or focus, she had grown up to become a clever and competent woman. She'd married Dusty McNeil earlier in the summer over everyone's objections, including his own. But as it turned out, everyone was wrong. Amy and Dusty were wildly happy, and Dusty had been exactly the medicine Amy had needed to heal the broken places in her once-aimless life.

Amy took charge of Andrew's younger brother and cousins like a mother hen and ushered them down the hall, leaving Andrew to deal with the distraught bride. He guided Laurie into the room, which was cluttered with suitcases packed and ready for a five-day honeymoon in Bermuda.

He came to a stop on the Persian rug just inside the door. Now what?

In his professional life, he'd mediated plenty of disputes, from simple divorce cases to complicated disagreements between litigants. This situation had Humpty Dumpty written all over it. No one was going to put this back together.

He turned and allowed himself to look Laurie in the face. Her big hazel eyes stared back, oddly vacant. She might have been a wax statue, the way she stood stiff and unmoving without real expression. A beautiful wax statue, with her golden hair braided with flowers.

What kind of idiot walks away from a woman like this?

Before he could act, Madison, Emma, and Jessica closed ranks around Laurie and guided her to one of the wing chairs in the sitting room. She sank down into it, her big skirt billowing up around her, making her look like a frothy white cupcake.

"I think we should find Brandon's Camaro and mess it up," Emma said.

"Screw that, I want to kill him, not his car," said Jessica.

"Can I castrate him first?" Madison asked.

"But I love him," Laurie said in a watery voice as the first tear escaped the corner of her right eye.

"Oh, baby, don't cry for that SOB," Madison said and then hurried into the bathroom, returning a moment later with a big wad of tissues, which she pressed into Laurie's hand. Laurie accepted the tissues but did nothing to stanch the slow drip of tears. That controlled release of emotion wrenched Andrew's heart more than sobs could have. She ought to be disconsolate. She ought to be angry.

Fury boiled down in the pit of his stomach. He hadn't felt rage like this since last spring, when he'd gone after Amy's boyfriend in the mistaken belief that Dusty was taking advantage of his sister. Dusty, who knew how to settle disputes with his fists, had put a serious hurt on him.

So much so that he'd enrolled in a weekly aikido class, where he'd learned something he'd always known. That the only way to defuse a fight was not to fight at all, but to find a way to make peace. And yet, despite all the training in the dojo, Andrew still wanted to strangle Brandon. How could his best friend do something so outrageously hurtful? Andrew knew what being dumped felt like. Val had walked out on him two years ago without any kind of warning. He'd almost moved on, but he would never forget that feeling of lost trust.

The door banged open and in walked Andrew's younger cousins, Matt and Jason, with several bottles of champagne and a big bucket of ice. Amy trailed behind with a tray filled with champagne flutes.

"We nabbed some of the champagne reserved for the wedding toast. We figured since it was already paid for, we—"

"Shut up, Matt," Andrew said, rolling his eyes toward Laurie. "And what happened to Edward?"

"Our dear darling brother decided to find Brandon and talk to him," Amy said, her voice unusually grave.

Damn. That should have been Andrew's job. Not only was he the best man, but he and Brandon were almost like brothers. They'd been in nursery school together, and their parents were old and dear friends. Maybe he could defuse the situation. Although if he were honest with himself, the only things he wanted to say to Brandon at the moment would probably not calm the situation down.

So instead of leaving the bride to talk to the groom, he nabbed a bottle of champagne and started pouring. When everyone had received a glass, Jessica raised hers and said, "Here's to castrating and then murdering Brandon Kopp, but only after we destroy his car."

The bridesmaids chorused, "Hear, hear."

Jason and Matt looked uncomfortable. Laurie just sat there holding her wineglass without drinking.

"Uh, I don't really feel like killing or castrating Brandon, and if you mess up his Camaro, he's going to be really pissed," Matt said, ever the socially insensitive one.

Everyone looked at him as if he'd just farted in church. But Matt held his ground. "Look, you guys, Brandon is a friend. He's more than a friend, really, since we all grew up with him and Roxy. I'm just saying that he should be praised for walking away if he wasn't three hundred percent sure about getting married."

"Get the hell out of here." Jessica got right up into Matt's face and almost pushed him out of the room. Good for her. It saved Andrew from doing the same thing.

"I think I'll go too," Jason said, leaving his untouched champagne glass on a side table.

"Uh-oh," Amy said, once Jason was gone. "This is going to get messy, isn't it? Like a divorce. Edward was pretty blunt with us. He said Laurie had enough support and someone should be thinking about Brandon."

"Yeah," Jessica said, "in order to torture him, slowly."

Amy touched his arm, and Andrew looked down into his sister's dark eyes. "You really need to do something before everyone gets angry with everyone else," she said. "I hate it when the family's in turmoil. And the Kopps are like members of the family." There were tears in Amy's eyes.

Why me? Andrew wondered. But he already knew the answer. He often played referee. But this time, keeping the peace might be impossible. Brandon breaking up with Laurie would shatter the dynamic of their tight-knit circle of friends and family.

Negotiating those fissures and cracks would be doubly difficult because Laurie's father, Noah Wilson, was Andrew's boss at Wilson Kavanaugh, a law firm with a nationally respected mediation practice. For the last five years, Andrew had been busting his butt trying to make partner. This breakup would put him in an awkward position to say the least.

He downed his champagne and stepped across the room, sinking into the ottoman beside Laurie's chair. "Laurie," he said gently.

She looked up at him, her face marred by tear tracks. He wanted to pull her into his arms and tell her to weep and sob and yell, even though he knew from experience that none of those things would change the situation. Still, there was something to be said for the cathartic property of throwing things. He'd broken an entire set of dishes the day Val walked out on him.

No one knew he'd done that, of course. Andrew kept his emotions tightly reined when he was in public. Laurie was like that too. It was something he admired about her.

"What would fix this situation for you?" he asked.

"I love him," she whispered, her voice so tight, it sounded brittle.

"So you'd be okay if he changed his mind and we started over? You still want to marry him?"

She nodded, biting her lower lip. "I certainly don't want to kill or maim him." She glanced at Madison. "Or mess up his car."

"Let me go talk to him, okay?" Andrew said gently.

"You can't be serious." Emma downed the last drop of her champagne and glared at him. "That asshole left her at the altar. That's like the worst humiliation a woman can suffer. It's like he—"

"Shut up," Laurie said, her voice surprisingly strong. "I'd take him back," she said.

"Okay, let me see what I can do." Andrew got up and headed toward the door, but Emma followed him.

"You aren't seriously thinking about talking Brandon into going forward with the ceremony, are you?"

"Why not?"

She rolled her eyes. "Because he's a dickwad, and Laurie deserves better."

"He wasn't a dickwad two hours ago, was he? Maybe he just had a moment of—"

"Doesn't matter who he was two hours ago. He walked away from her on her wedding day. And it's not her place to grovel and ask him to come back."

"I wouldn't ask her to grovel, Emma. But if she's willing to take him back, don't you think it's worth trying to see if that's possible? The object is to find a win-win situation for both of them."

"You're unbelievable. Laurie is not capable of judging what she wants right now." Emma's fists landed on her hips.

"And you are?" he asked, suddenly annoyed at Laurie's best friend.

Emma shook her head. "No. But I think Laurie loves the idea of Brandon. I think she's been overlooking a lot of problems with the real Brandon."

Andrew let out a long breath. "Look, she asked me to talk to him, okay? I'm the best man—reasoning with the groom comes with the territory. And besides, I'm a mediator so talking to people in crisis is sort of my thing."

Emma folded her arms across her chest. "Knock yourself out. But you aren't going to change Brandon's mind. My guess is that he's been cheating on Laurie." She turned and ducked back into the Churchill Suite.

Was there someone else? Andrew didn't think so. But he'd certainly been surprised that day when he'd come home from work and found Val all packed and ready to run off to her lover.

Laurie looked down at the champagne flute, studying the way the late afternoon sun sparkled on the bubbles and her two-carat pavé-set Tiffany engagement ring. She remembered the day Brandon had put that ring on her finger. It was at her birthday party, two years ago. She hadn't thought too much about the fact that members of their close group of friends each brought a balloon to the party with a single letter on it. But it all became clear when Brandon suggested a group picture with the balloons, which, when lined up in the right order, spelled out: LAURIE, WILL YOU MARRY ME?

Brandon had gotten down on his knee and presented the ring in its beautiful robin's-egg-blue Tiffany box. She'd loved the ring from the first moment she'd laid eyes on it. It was classic and maybe a tiny bit old-fashioned.

And now she would have to give it back.

Something broke inside her heart, and the tears she'd been trying not to shed welled up like a fountain. How could such a romantic man walk away from their wedding?

She slipped the ring from her finger. "Someone needs to give this back," she managed to choke out.

"Aw, honey," Jessica said, "you are not giving that back. You're going to sell it on eBay and pocket the ten grand. You'll need the money to fix up that house Brandon talked you into buying. Now drink your champagne. It'll take the edge off."

She did as she was told, and just as soon as she'd drained the flute, Madison refilled it. "I just don't get it," Laurie said through her tears.

"Neither do we," Emma said. "But the important thing is that a man who leaves his bride at the altar is a jerk."

Laurie shook her head. No. Brandon was a great guy. The problem wasn't Brandon. It was her.

She sniffled back her tears and downed another glass of champagne. Yes, definitely. She was the problem. She'd been a fool to think that they had a special relationship that could weather her problems in the bedroom. She needed to accept the fact that she was a dud when it came to sex. She was uptight and OCD and had trouble turning her brain off. Who wanted to be chained to a wife like that?

She downed another glass of champagne.

"So, girls, you know we really can't kill him or castrate him. But the Camaro... we could really mess it up," Emma said in a solemn tone.

"Maybe we could find a bottle of spray paint and write the words 'Left the Bride at the Altar' across his back window," Madison said.

"You're an amateur," Jessica said. "I vote that we go to Lowes and buy a pickax and turn the Camaro into Swiss cheese."

"That would be too obvious," Emma said. "We should just put sugar in the gas tank."

The girls continued to discuss ways of destroying Brandon's beloved car while they sipped several more glasses of champagne.

Meanwhile Laurie obsessed over all the things she'd done wrong. It was amazing that Brandon hadn't found someone else. Assuming he'd told her the truth. But it didn't matter because he'd lose interest in her as soon as he started playing the field. She bored him in the bedroom, and that's why he wanted her to date other guys. Maybe he thought she needed the experience. Like the opposite of slut-shaming or something. But sleeping around would be like cheating on him.

Except it wouldn't be cheating. Not now.

The truth exploded on her like a stinger missile,

and suddenly all the champagne she'd been sipping didn't want to stay down. She didn't make it all the way to the bathroom before she hurled it up.

Well, that was it. Her beautiful $7,000 wedding dress was utterly ruined. Even if Andrew could talk Brandon into marrying her, Laurie now had nothing to wear to the wedding.

About the Author

Hope Ramsay is a *USA Today* bestselling author of heartwarming contemporary romances. Her books have won critical acclaim and publishing awards. She is married to a good ol' Georgia boy who resembles every single one of her Southern heroes. She has two grown children and a couple of demanding lap cats. She lives in Virginia, where, when she's not writing, she's knitting or playing her forty-year-old Martin guitar.

You can learn more at:

HopeRamsay.com

Twitter, @HopeRamsay

Facebook.com/Hope.Ramsay

Fall in Love with Forever Romance

USA TODAY BESTSELLING AUTHOR

HOPE RAMSAY

The Bride Next Door

"Every story by Hope Ramsay will touch a reader's heart."
—BRENDA NOVAK, *New York Times* bestselling author

THE BRIDE NEXT DOOR
By Hope Ramsay

Courtney Wallace has almost given up on finding her happily-ever-after. And she certainly doesn't expect to find it with Matthew Lyndon, the hotshot lawyer she overhears taking a bet to seduce her. Matt never intended to take the bet seriously. And moving next door wasn't part of his strategy to win, but the more he gets to know Courtney, the more intrigued he becomes. When fun and games turn into something real, will these two decide they're in it to win it?

Fall in Love with Forever Romance

TOTAL BRAVERY
By Piper J. Drake

Raul's lucky to have the best partner a man could ask for: a highly trained, fiercely loyal German Shepherd Dog named Taz. But their first mission in Hawaii puts them to the test when a kidnapping ring sets its sights on the bravest woman Raul's ever met...Mali knows she's in trouble. Yet sharing close quarters with smoldering, muscle-for-hire Raul makes her feel safe. But when the kidnappers make their move, Raul's got to find a way to save the life of the woman he loves.

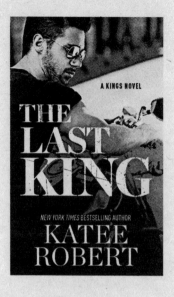

THE LAST KING
By Katee Robert

The King family has always been like royalty in Texas. And sitting right at the top is Beckett, who just inherited his father's fortune, his company—and all his enemies. But Beckett's always played by his own rules, so when he needs help, he goes to the last person anyone would ever expect: his biggest rival. Samara Mallick is reluctant to risk her career—despite her red-hot attraction—but it soon becomes clear there are King family secrets darker than she ever imagined and dangerous enough to get them killed.

Fall in Love with Forever Romance

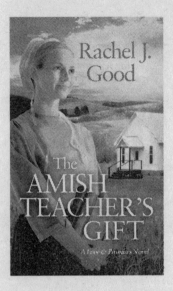

THE AMISH TEACHER'S GIFT
By Rachel J. Good

Widower Josiah Yoder wants to be a good father. But it's not easy with a deaf young son who doesn't understand why his mamm isn't coming home. At a loss, Josiah enrolls Nathan in a special-needs school and is relieved to see his son comforted by Ada Rupp, the teacher whose sweet charm and gentle smile just might be the balm they *both* need.